SPOONFED

My Life with The Spoons

Gord Deppe

SPOONFED

Library and Archives Canada Cataloguing in Publication

Deppe, Gordon, author
        Spoonfed : my life with the Spoons / Gordon Deppe.

ISBN 978-1-897453-43-8

    1. Deppe, Gordon. 2. Musicians--Canada--Biography.
3. Spoons (Musical group). I. Title. II. Title: My life with
the Spoons.

ML420.D423A3 2014   782.42164092   C2014-906505-1

Our thanks to the late Andrew MacNaughtan for cover photos.

Front cover design/ photo processing by Jeff Carter, Sky
Productions, 519-242-6863, jeff.george.carter@gmail.com

Back cover design/realization Donovan Davie: 519-501-2375

For more on the Spoons visit: www.spoonsmusic.com

Printed and bound in Canada
First Edition. 240 pages. All rights reserved.
Published October 15, 2014
Manor House Publishing Inc.
www.manor-house.biz (905) 648-2193

We acknowledge the financial support of the Government of
Canada through the Canada Book Fund (CBF) for this project.

SPOONFED

Foreword

With a string of smash hits – *Nova Heart, Tell No Lies, Old Emotions, Romantic Traffic* – the Spoons redefined the musical landscape and captured the hearts of fans everywhere.

The Spoons toured extensively, playing sold-out shows with an array of fellow icons including Talking Heads, Police, Culture Club, Simple Minds and many more, during a decades-long journey-adventure that continues to this day.

The Spoons gold album *Arias & Symphonies* was named one of the 20 Most Influential Albums of The '80s by The Chart Magazine and *Nova Heart* was recently included in Bob Mersereau's book *The Top 100 Canadian Singles*.

SpoonFed is the compelling life story of Gord Deppe, the Spoons' driving creative force, principal songwriter, lead singer and lead guitarist, whose creative vision defined one of the most influential and original bands of the '80s and beyond.

From a childhood spent moving back and forth between two worlds – Canada and Germany – Deppe became an early outsider-observer, a persona that first crystalized on entering the Canadian school system unable to speak a word of English.

Further culture shock ensued from the endless suburbia of his Burlington, Ontario, neighbourhood. The shy young outcast turned inward, spending nights writing alone in his room.

Then, he discovered a natural talent for music – and his world suddenly opened up with truly endless horizons and seemingly limitless possibilities. A succession of teenage bands ensued, leading to the Spoons, huge concerts, gold records, world travel and a life of adventure across North America Europe, even the Canadian Arctic. This is the story of Gord Deppe and the Spoons – turn the page and enjoy the ride.

- **Michael B. Davie**, CEO, Rockport Records International

SPOONFED

Contents

SPOONFED

Prologue: A Matter Of Time

There's a theory about time; that it isn't linear, that it doesn't move from one moment to the next in a straight line, but rather in a spiral that overlaps as it comes around again and again, bringing previous twists and turns within reaching distance. I suppose this could somehow explain time travel or, at the very least, the feeling of déjà vu we sometimes get. I don't wholly understand the theory, but it amazes me how many times things from the past lined up with what I was writing about in this book at any given moment.

Out of the blue, someone would mention something I just happened to be putting into words that day. Sometimes something would happen directly related to events from the past that I'd just been writing about. Sometimes the synchronicity was so strong it scared the hell out of me! If nothing else, it amplified my belief in some kind of shared awareness between us all. Either that or we're all mind readers and we just don't know it.

Here is the story of my life and the Spoons and how the two interconnected. How they still interconnect today. I don't remember everything, but I figure that what I do remember must be the stuff worth writing down. They're like pictures in a mental scrapbook that have left a permanent mark on me and, as a collection, have made me who I am. And whenever the spiral of time caught up with my story, I decided it must be something important, something I shouldn't question. So I gave in to it and followed its lead. That way, the words would almost write themselves.

But that, in itself, could be a whole other story on its own.

Dedicated to everyone who helped us on our journey
and Spoons fans everywhere…

Early Spoons, circa 1980: Sandy, Rob, me and Derrick.

SPOONFED

1 A Rocky Start

We had no idea that the night that lay before us would change everything. Then again we were so new there wasn't much to change yet. We were young and naive; our faces innocent enough to twist our principal's arm into letting our band perform at the final school dance of our last year at Aldershot High School. Enough to coerce someone who was as anti rock, or loud music of any kind that provoked unholy behaviour, as a southern preacher might be. His face swelled, it turned red, it never smiled. But somehow, as we sat in his office pleading our case and promising a nice, calm evening somewhere in the ballpark of a Donny Osmond concert, he gave in. Just like that. It would be something he'd regret for a very long time. Little did we know, as we left his office all proud of ourselves, we'd soon be banned from playing any other high school in Southern Ontario – in all of Canada, if our principal could help it.

It was June of 1979, the end of Grade 13, and the whole world lay before us. Burlington really was Stick Figure Neighbourhood to us then. It was miles and miles of suburbia in the pre-kilometer age, with a glimmer of civilization shimmering on the distant horizon. About forty-five minutes from Toronto, a Toronto where the tallest structures were the TD buildings and there was no CN Tower yet to look down from (or do album photo shoots in, for that matter), Burlington was Toronto's squeaky clean, Brady Bunch-esque younger sibling. It was a picture postcard stop on Lake Ontario between Toronto and Niagara Falls that my father stumbled on during one of his early visits to Canada. Over a sandwich at a picnic bench in what is now Spencer Smith Park, he decided this was the perfect place to raise a young family. We've played some huge festivals in that park over the years, including a recent

Canada Day concert, and I wondered where exactly he might have sat when he had that idea. I'm sure he never imagined in his wildest dreams that his son, just about seven years old back then, would one day perform in front of an audience of over 20,000 in that very park…

I was born in Vancouver, British Columbia, on March 12, 1959. My parents, Jenny and Heinz, were at the tail end of a short visit from Germany, due to my father's business ventures at the time. We lived in an apartment building overlooking Stanley Park. I still have a small painting hanging in my living room that my father painted of the view from our balcony. Vancouver is one of the most beautiful places in the world, but we moved back to Germany before my first birthday and so I have no vivid memories of it. To this day the city has a surreal edge to it I can't shake whenever I go there. It's as if my mind keeps trying to get a fix on what's a real memory and what's not. When I walk its streets, it's like walking through an enormous movie set with props and building fronts. Vancouver is one huge grey area for me. When they say a place can haunt you, I understand what they're talking about…

The next few years we lived in Maichingen, West Germany, as it was still called back then. The nearest big city was Stuttgart. The Berlin Wall still stood and my father told stories of how he and his family had snuck under barbed wire fences to go from east to west when he was a kid. He didn't tell me until many years later that he was also captured by the Russians in World War II at the age of fifteen and kept in a prison camp for three years. My father's artistic skills had endeared him to the guards, for whom he produced small drawings to give to their wives and girlfriends. He was pretty sure that had something to do with him eventually getting a job in the camp kitchen and going on to live a long and happy life. Of the 20,000 captives that went into the camp, about 2,000 came out alive. Since the day he imparted that cheerful little story to me, I've had a much greater appreciation for art.

SPOONFED

My memories of the early Germany years are about as sketchy as Vancouver. Somewhere, somehow, my brother Gary was born and I had an instant playmate. Our stay in Germany was short-lived and we returned to Canada within three years, to Toronto this time. There, on a short street in the west end overlooking the Gardiner Expressway and Lake Ontario, I have my first real small recollections of childhood. There are shadowy pictures in my mind of friends, their houses and a giant tree at the end of the street that I'm pretty sure I fell out of at least once.

Some kid hitting me over the head with a rake stands out in my memory. I remember my mother holding a cloth to my scalp and seeing the rows of bloody dots. Understandably she was quite upset, but I carried them like a badge of honour. I've heard that in more savage times, nails were similarly hammered into the cranium to relieve patients of their insanity. What effect it had on me, I'm not quite sure. Today, I can still see the end of my old street and that tree from the highway every time I drive to Toronto. A piece of the past perfectly preserved...

My Dad (Heinz) with my brother Gary, Mom (Jenny), and me.

SPOONFED

Within a year we were back in Germany. I was too young to wonder why we were moving back and forth so much. This time we headed to the fairytale setting of Lübeck, the remnants of a feudal town complete with a miniature castle and moat. Lübeck was well known for its marzipan, a crushed almond and honey paste that the town's people must have stockpiled against imminent sieges in earlier centuries. In the 1960s, when I lived there, it had risen to an art form and various shops proudly displayed marzipan sculptures and delicacies of every shape and size in their windows.

The Baltic Sea was not far away, and there we spent every summer on the beach. A wide, wooden boardwalk ran along it, providing passage to marinas lined with rows of shiny white boats and the many hotels and seaside restaurants we were never to visit. Our greatest indulgence was to rent a beach basket, a combination of mini change room, lounger and storage space. They were scattered along the shore like delicate wicker cottages. They became a part of our private summer world where my brother Gary and I would spend endless hours searching for jellyfish and seashells.

My first public school years were spent at a grey and rather dull, old building that was split down the middle with boys on one side and girls on the other. In fact, there was a high brick wall running down the center of the grounds out back where we went for recess, to save us from the distractions of the fairer sex. I have glimpses of walking a long distance through fields and along a busy road to get there. We carried our books in leather satchels strapped to our backs, spent days writing into little notebooks with lined pages and went home again. The highlight of the day was chocolate milk which we could buy in small glass bottles at lunchtime in the school basement. Milk was all they sold, brown or white .

Music hadn't entered my life in a profound way quite yet, but I do remember a few early encounters with it that left a

10

strong impression. The first songs that really stuck with me were from 45s that my mother played on our old turntable. One was *Lara's Theme* from the movie Doctor Zhivago and the other *Puppet On A String* by a female singer with a sexy foreign accent (English, I'd later discover). Their choruses were relentless and wormed their way into my brain. I think I quickly learned twhat a musical hook was. I had absolutely no thoughts of becoming a songwriter then or any time in my life, but the power of those simple melodies was undeniable and stayed with me. I was their little puppet on a string. And a totally willing puppet at that.

Before long I began to make up little songs, out loud, usually as I lay in bed just before falling asleep. They were totally spontaneous songs about animals and castles and whatever else kids had knocking around inside their heads. My voice obviously carried, because I soon had my first experience with audience heckling. The funny thing is, though I remember a lot of yelling from my parents telling me to go to sleep, I had no sense of self-awareness or stage fright. That, strangely enough, wouldn't come until years later. But one thing was certain; I'd gotten the songwriting bug very early on and it made me feel like nothing else could. Words and melodies came and went like animal shaped clouds in my head, painting some pretty amazing pictures. Some kids had imaginary friends. I had a whole made-up world to lose myself in.

The medieval setting of Lübeck, I'm sure, had its part in shaping my imagination. A lot of Germany, like all of Europe, has a lush history and a story to be told around every crooked corner. It's almost impossible for the creative bug to lie dormant. The much bigger city of Cologne on the Rhine River, where my grandparents lived, was like a lightning bolt to my imagination. I stayed there with them for weeks at a time and my grandfather, probably my best friend in the world then, would take me on adventures down its countless cobbled streets, sometimes back in time to what seemed like a whole other century. Cologne's massive cathedral, one of the biggest in the world, stood over us wherever we went like a page out of the Hunchback Of Notre Dame. Its giant bells could be heard for miles when they rung every hour and sent the pigeons skyward. I remember long walks with my grandfather in the ancient shopping district of Hohestrasse, usually to have lunch at some centuries-old pub and stop at a small toy store to search for the latest Dinky Toy car.

I have fond memories of meandering back alleys that eventually took us to our favourite restaurant. There, we squeezed in between rows of old men sitting at long wooden benches, hunched over steaming bowls of delicious smelling mussels. I was adventurous for my age. Once we stopped to see a puppet show in a small, dark theatre somewhere near the cathedral that left me more frightened than entertained. Germany isn't known for its cheerful children's stories. But it was all part of my fairytale surroundings – and fuel for a young boy's imagination.

In comparison, the bustling city of Hamburg, an hour's drive from Lübeck, was seated firmly in the Twentieth Century. I had no idea, as a kid taking his first baby steps in songwriting, what was brewing and about to explode there in the early '60s. We only went there to visit the famous toy store and maybe stay for a dinner of sausages and sour kraut in the local Kneipe, a German pub. A shame that I was just a little boy without the slightest idea what an electric guitar and Vox amplifier could conjure up, let alone what they were. Music history was about to be made in Hamburg. I do remember sitting in my sandbox in front of our house one very hot summer playing with cars and bugs. I overheard my parents talking about some new group of musicians from England called, of all things, the Beatles. I recall thinking how funny that was as I pushed a bug around in the sand. What did insects have to do with music? About as much as spoons, I suppose...

2 Disneyland & The Twilight Zone

In the summer of 1967, the year of its centennial, we moved back to Canada. This time, according to my father, for good. For an eight year old, this came with a massive dose of sadness mixed with excitement. On one hand, I was leaving my friends and all our relatives behind. On the other, we were heading to the land of Star Trek, Kool Aid and breakfast cereals. We were moving to a brand new world filled with twenty-four hour cartoons, peanut butter and Disney.

I'd been raised on the Walt Disney Hour every Sunday evening, aired pretty well worldwide, including West Germany. I'd fantasized about going to Disneyland all through my early television years and had actually watched it being built in installments on the weekly show. And now, incredibly, I was on the same continent as Anaheim, California. Apart from all the cartoons, animatronics and theme park rides, I was as much drawn in by the music of Disney films. The songs in Mary Poppins grabbed me as a young kid when I saw it in a big, old Hamburg movie theatre and never let me go. Too young to read the sub-titles, I was moved by something beyond the words.

Now, Burlington, Ontario was our new home; the town my father had stumbled upon on a trip between Toronto and Niagara Falls. We lived in apartment 303 in LaSalle Towers, a gleaming white tower of 1970s modern architecture. The building still stands today, though I'm sure it's been painted a few times to keep it gleaming. Whole days could be spent playing imaginary games in its fifteen floors, endless hallways and multiple stairwells. When I saw the hotel in the Shining, it felt strangely familiar. I still dream sometimes about secret rooms and wings of the building that never really existed. Some I'm still not so sure about.

There was a huge indoor cement swimming pool in the building that my brother and I would spend what seemed like eternal afternoons playing in. It was often empty, so we had our private little oasis to ourselves. Different friends came and went through the years and two shy girls we sometimes swam with were the daughters of John Munro, Prime Minister Pierre Trudeau's finance minister at the time. He'd rented an apartment in our building and, a fact that went right over our heads as kids, was instrumental in bringing John Lennon to Canada during the whole anti-war love-in period. They'd met a few times and he came back to LaSalle in the evenings while we, quite possibly, were swimming with his daughters. Those bugs from the sandbox days of my childhood were following me around. I just didn't know it at the time.

We moved a lot when I was a kid, finally settling in Burlington.

SPOONFED

Close to the Hamilton Harbour, we had LaSalle Park on one side and the infamous Aldershot High School of our first doomed Spoons concert on the other. But that fateful night was still years away and I wouldn't be going there for a little while yet. The park held our attention for the time being. Like the corridors of our apartment building, we could lose ourselves for whole afternoons in the forest and lakeside of the park. On weekends we'd leave after breakfast and return in time for dinner, without any concern from our parents about sinister consequences. But that was the world then; the innocent '60s.

The park was a very surreal place. In the 1920s it had been the site of a large fairground accessed by dirt roads and also by boat via a dock just below it, the spot where the explorer LaSalle first touched ground. Old black and white photos showed whole families decked out in full Victorian attire and ladies with parasols enjoying Sunday afternoons in what seemed like a much more civilized age.

When we lived there, the ruins of a bathhouse still remained on the lake. A sandy bluff had slowly shoved it out into the water and created a perfect place for young boys to spend afternoons jumping from and building very dodgy tunnels in it. Not one of our better ideas, thinking back. A rumour went around that some kid had gotten stuck when one of the tunnels collapsed on him. But that was just a rumour.

The place that held the most fascination for me was the old pavilion that still stood in the middle of the park. It was all that remained of the ancient fairground, though we once found some faded wooden balls in a small outbuilding that must have belonged to one of the arcade games. Another Shining moment. Croquet anyone? The pavilion was huge, with a boarded up restaurant at one end, a large open dance floor in the middle and stairs that led up to another enclosed ballroom above it. Everything was locked up tight and it seemed like the 1920s

15

were still in there somehow, ready to burst out if someone dared to crack open a door or break a window. It was the first time I recall being struck by the mystery and power of the stage. Here we were, playing games on what had once held musicians and dancers in another age, a magnificent Victorian structure built for entertainment. It was overwhelming – all this ancient splendour, just for music to be played.

The stage. There was something incredibly seductive about that to a boy not quite sure of where he was going in life. It was a world of mysteries and shadows that seemed to call out to me. But for the time being, it simply remained a good place to find cover when it rained. The cement floors were perfect for floor hockey, so we spent many days in our private little arena.

Yet, there was always the feeling that something was looking out at us through those darkened windows. Maybe the lost souls of some big band from the '30s trapped there forever. We didn't bother them and they didn't bother us...

The old pavilion, a source of inspiration and a few ghosts.

SPOONFED

Many years later the pavilion would burn to the ground in a freak accident. I don't even remember it happening. We were most likely on the road touring somewhere as the roof caught fire and the windows finally popped outwards from the heat. Who knows where we were as our old playground turned to ash. Eventually the city would rebuild it and restore the restaurant and upper ballroom to their ancient glory. The old ghosts were sent packing and the LaSalle Park Pavilion was open for business once again, a popular destination for corporate parties and weddings. In the late '90s, Aldershot High School erected a circus size tent beside the pavilion and held their twenty-fifth reunion. I performed there that night and later strolled through the newly refurbished pavilion for the first time. Crammed with drunken graduates and decked out like the Royal York Hotel, I kept thinking, "What have they done with our hockey rink and what are all these people doing here?" I missed our old playground...

But in 1967 the original pavilion still stood and became our little sanctuary on weekends. For the rest of the week, there was school to deal with. The first few months of my first year at Elmhurst Public School in Burlington were pure terror. Somehow, incredibly, my parents had neglected to tell the principal about my non-Canadian background. I remember a lot of red-faced teachers stabbing at the blackboard and mouthing angry incomprehensible words as the kids in the class laughed all around me. I just shrugged and smiled, which I'm sure infuriated them even more. I can only imagine how my teachers felt when they finally called in my parents to discuss their problem child and discovered I didn't speak a word of English.

Self-esteem wise, this little misunderstanding set me back light-years. But it would also encourage me to pick up English at super-human speed. With the aid of big picture books and television cartoons, I relearned the language forgotten from my early youth in Toronto. Thankfully, the old rake injury I'd sustained hadn't stunted my learning abilities...

Like a lot of singers, I got my first taste of performing in front of an audience in the school choir. I didn't find the courage to join until my last year at Elmhurst Public School, which was a shame because, the moment I did, I discovered there was something quite amazing about a group of voices coming together. Something locked inside me was about to be awakened. The harmonized sounds that we created out of thin air and that swirled around us had power.

One voice was great but the more singers you added, the greater the effect, exponentially speaking. I'd never been much for joining clubs. I'd had a short stint with the Boy Scouts, where I never quite fit in. But this was strangely seductive and full of possibilities. This I could lose myself in, body and soul.

I'd always been painfully shy and quiet, something people find hard to believe about anyone who makes a living standing in front of a crowd every night. But I believe a lot of performers start out that way in life. Some, like me, will forever carry a little bit of that introvert deep inside them. It's just something you learn to hide better with age. I admire performers even more when I see that trait in them. Some people call it humility. I believe it's a very good thing.

Being in the public school choir, my first musical group I suppose, made me feel larger and more important in a very unexpected way. I was suddenly part of something that people took notice of. That Christmas, a local radio station recorded us singing carols and, in an indirect way, I made my on-air debut. You can imagine what that did for the self-esteem of a quiet grade-schooler, not to mention a young and tender ego.

Even in a public school choir, I could see a whole new world of possibilities opening up. Like that spinning door suspended in space in the Twilight Zone TV show opening sequence, it seemed to be waiting for me, beckoning me to step through it.

SPOONFED

When I got home each day, after-school television had about as much impact on shaping my view of the world as anything else did. Probably more than I knew. It had enveloped me and acted as a sort of safety blanket after our big trans-Atlantic relocation from Germany to Canada.

Cartoons helped dull the homesickness and distracted us from the dreary real world. It was the thing we ran home to for relief after a day of classrooms and drudgery. It caught us at our most vulnerable and, without mercy, had its way with us – and we loved every minute of it.

Saturday morning cartoons were the first to grab me, but I was probably too dazed and sleepy-eyed that early in the morning to really absorb much. And the cartoons of the late '60s were nothing like they are today. They were as squeaky clean and innocent as everything else was at the time. Then, they would pay homage Mickey Mouse. Today, they'd stomp on him and send him through a meat grinder. Tastes for kids' entertainment were very different then.

After school we were alert and like eager little sponges. Batman, H. R. Pufnstuf, Gilligan's Island, every commercial pushing the necessities of life like Hot Wheels race tracks and Rock'Em Sock'Em Robots; we took it all in. We devoured it. Especially for a kid from Germany, with its three TV stations of bland, grey offerings, this was heaven.

But the television show that affected me most of all, that changed my life really, came much later in the evening. Then the whole household could be pulled in and have their minds messed with together as one big, happy family. That show was the Twilight Zone.

The moment I heard the opening theme, I knew I was in for a bumpy ride. Its surreal, disturbing snapshots of American life shaped my imagination more than any book or movie ever

19

did. Each episode was a roller-coaster ride of dread filled anticipation, often awaking a fear I hadn't even considered yet. In the end, with the help of the show's host and creator Rod Serling, there was often a moralistic but disturbing outcome that wrapped up the whole thing as best as it could.

Some episodes stayed with me for days, weeks, even years. There was enough material there for songs to last a lifetime.

I watched some of the old episodes recently and, though dated in many ways, they still have that affect on me. I have a soft spot for any episodes that dealt with deserted cities or the end of the world as we know it and the few survivors trying to find their way.

A favourite show began with a man and woman waking up in a house in an abandoned town, a town where everything, including the food in the fridge and the squirrel in the fake tree, are all just props. They board a train and try to leave, but always end up back at the same station. The disturbing ending, which I won't give away, left a profound impression on me.

I suppose a psychoanalyst could read something into a young boy's fascination for such bleak views of the world. For me, it was just a comfort zone I could relate to; a world tailor-made for loners like me...

3 Kites, Doors & Magic Boxes

Unexpectedly, I got my first guitar when I was ten years old. And I never asked for it. It just appeared. My father bought it for me on a business trip to Toronto. My brother Gary received a toy car. I thought I'd gotten the rotten end of the deal. It was a cheap acoustic with strings like trapeze wires and almost impossible to play. I wasn't very happy about the arrangement and didn't touch it out of spite for a long time. But one day, thankfully, I snapped out of my mood and picked up the thing and another new door was opened. And not a moment too soon. My father was about to take it back and my life might have gone down a completely different path...

Today, when I explain playing guitar to someone, I compare it to flying a kite. At first it's completely out of your control and a little overwhelming. Then, as you gradually get more and more of a handle on it, it eventually becomes an extension of yourself. It becomes a piece of you that can let you soar higher than you ever could by yourself. And the fact is, there's always more string to let out, always more to create and discover. A guitar is a raw thing that needs to be tamed. But it also changes you.

I took lessons at the local music school, The Burlington Conservatory of Music. A bunch of us sat in a circle with our music stands learning to read from the old Mel Bay guitar method. Songs like Volga Boatman and Twinkle Little Star; a lot of uninspiring nonsense as far as I was concerned. Everyone else seemed to take it very seriously. I didn't.

I needed something more and soon started playing along with records on our turntable at home. Jamming with my first band, I suppose. I had by that time moved up to a four pick-up, blue sparkle electric made by Santron, a local electronics company that decided to try their hand at guitars. I remember getting it for my birthday and the whammy bar snapping off the first day. Jimi Hendrix would have demolished it in seconds. I didn't have an amplifier yet and plugged straight into our old Philips stereo, pretty well just a turntable with a speaker in its removable lid. I still have it in my basement as a reminder of those days; my very humble beginnings.

We left for a family road trip to California one summer and I just quit going to lessons. The only thing that had kept me interested as long as it did was my teacher's collection of nice guitars. She played in a band on weekends and had professional equipment. I'll never forget her bringing a red Fender to class one day and all the kids' eyes bulging out. It was as close as any of us would ever get to a "real" guitar. As far as Volga Boatman went I was at the top of her class and, to my astonishment, she let me play it. It was one of those moments that stick with you forever; the first time you hold a fine instrument.

I recall how smooth and low the strings were and the gentle, seductive curve of the fret board. I'd been trying to hammer out notes on what seemed like a medieval torture device in comparison. This was a completely different kind of instrument than I was used to. I sat there a long time holding it in my hands, just staring at it. Numb in its presence, I felt like it could take off on its own at any moment. This kite hadn't been tamed yet.

For amplification, my teacher usually brought in a big Fender Showman amp. I would often lose myself in the bright green "On" light when I got really bored with the class; some self-hypnosis to escape when necessary. We all ran our cables into a junction box on the floor, which sent a single line to the amp. When you had six or seven kids all playing at once, it was

22

hell. Just go to a big music store on a Saturday afternoon and you'll get the idea. You'd have stared at that green light too.

Our teacher had a beautiful Gretsch White Falcon semi-acoustic electric that she offered to sell me at one point. Maybe she saw something promising in me. Maybe her weekend gigs weren't panning out and she needed the cash. It was a monster of a guitar, way out of proportion to a kid my size and a little eccentric for my taste. The thing had a padded cushion on the back, for God's sake! I decided this was a guitar for geriatrics, not the kind of rock machine that I needed.

Around this time, full of Twilight Zone ideas swirling in my head, I started composing songs again. I'd been on sabbatical since my early childhood bedtime songwriting sessions. I wrote out the notes in little pads of manuscript paper, with the lyrics underneath, like in the music books we used in class. I spent way too much time making the quarter notes and clefs and rests as neat as possible, but gradually filled a few books with ideas. I still remember the very first one, an eleven-year-old's view of the stark, modern world titled *The Concrete City*. Pretty heavy stuff for a kid. I'd forgotten how great it felt to make up songs. And now I had a guitar and some new perspective on the world to take it so much further.

If the Twilight Zone wasn't enough, another TV show that fuelled my imagination was The Prisoner, a British cult series. It had a lot of similarities to my favourite Twilight Zone episodes. A British agent resigns and is promptly kidnapped by his own people. He wakes up in a remote village cut off from the rest of the world, a sinisterly beautiful place where everything is controlled and never quite what it seems. The main character is given the name No. 6 and must fight to retain his individuality. He's constantly watched and put through tests that push him to the limit – kind of a hardcore Truman Show. Watching The Prisoner, I learned about such modern concepts as mind control, drug therapy and control of the state over the individual; plenty of material to fill a young songwriter's head. This was the psychedelic '60s after all. I began to see myself as No. 6, which I'm sure was the show's intent. My lyrics started to take on a paranoid view of the world and layers of meaning. My creative writing in school also reflected this and probably worried my teachers a little. I'd grown up and my songs about castles and unicorns didn't cut it anymore. There was a big, strange world out there to write about.

The first album that I owned, *Canned Wheat* by Canadian rockers the Guess Who, was given to me by a friend as a birthday gift. Until then I only had my mother's record collection to go by, heavy on Elvis, Tom Jones and Engelbert Humperdinck. I don't remember the guitar playing on those records very much, which is a shame, because I'm sure I could have learned something from them. But like my tastes for television shows, I yearned for something a little darker.

One my mother's friends in our building had a strange little album called Solid Gold Guitar that intrigued me. I'd ask her to put it on whenever we visited. There was, as you can guess, a big electric guitar painted gold on the front cover. All instrumental, the music was in the twangy, spaghetti western realm, so I wasn't too inspired song-wise. But, lord, all that washy reverb sure left an impression on me. I was beginning to see a whole other world of possibilities as a guitarist. That golden guitar, dripping with drama and attitude, sounded like it was being transmitted from another planet, a planet I wanted to discover and conquer.

I'd started bringing my guitar to music class when I graduated to Mapleview Middle School. Our teacher was rather flamboyant and had a cheap sunburst electric guitar with plastic flowers tied to the headstock. I think he had slight hippie inclinations beneath the conformist haircut and neat suit and tie he wore. He taught us songs like *Signs* and *You're So Vain*. This was a few years before my ears would be awakened to harder music, so they seemed like radical songs at the time. It quickly became my favourite class and I found the same sense of belonging that I had felt in the elementary school choir. I was about to embark on the next chapter of my musical life. Quite by accident, my first rock group was about to be formed.

Our teacher decided to organize a sort of band within the class. What started as a group of about ten students gradually became just three as kids lost interest and dropped out. A very talented singer and keyboard player named Rod James, drummer Gary Kennett and myself had always been its core. We simply took over the band from our teacher and ran it ourselves.

Rod and Gary both sang lead and I was happy as the guitarist and backup singer. I was way too self-conscious to even consider carrying a song by myself. Being a front man, I was certain, was not in the cards for me, ever. We remained a three-piece and performed at school assemblies without a bass player. It didn't even occur to us that we needed one. It would take a future school trip to change all that.

We called ourselves The Right Side, as in, "Everyone stay to the right in the hallways," something we heard daily over the school intercom or from hall monitors. The band name poked fun at the establishment in our own innocent, adolescent way, perhaps sowing the first seeds in my head for the Spoons' anti-conformity concept album *Arias & Symphonies* we'd record years later: "Little boys in harmony, ringing in my ears..." But those kinds of grand ideals were still a long way in coming.

After blowing out the speaker in our home stereo, my parents finally gave in and bought me a small amplifier actually meant for guitar. I'd also moved up to a much better instrument, a black Ovation semi-acoustic, which my father let me pick out for my birthday at a music store in Hamilton. It was a big step up from my old Santron electric. Things were starting to get serious. Ovation was a make of guitar prevalent on a popular '70s American country music TV show called Hee Haw, a program that combined slapstick comedy with performances by some really fine players like Glen Campbell and Roy Clark.

The Spoons recently appeared as part of a musical gala at our hometown Centre For The Arts alongside other fellow Burlingtonians. One of the performers, an elderly gentleman with an endless supply of funny stories, was Canadian comic Gordie Tapp, one of the key characters on Hee Haw. Sandy backed him up on bass for a song and Rob Preuss, also musical director of the evening, sat in on piano. The spiral of time can come spinning around in very unexpected ways.

The other TV show that hooked me on Ovation guitars was The Partridge Family, a hipper version of the Brady Bunch. They were a family, but also a band that played some very nice musical instruments. Bands in children's shows seemed to be all the rage in the '70s. Between the Partridge Family, The Banana Splits and The Monkees, I'm surprised more young viewers weren't subverted into becoming musicians. Sex and drugs weren't even in the picture, but there was something undeniably seductive about the band lifestyle, even at that level. Right there and then, I chose to be a Partridge rather than a Brady. But my tastes for innocent, perky music were about to get a rude awakening.

The first single I bought, quite by accident, was *School's Out* by Alice Cooper. I found it in a bin of marked-down 45s at the local Towers department store. A random buy, there was something about its title that called out to me. When I took it home and put it on the turntable, the snarling vocals and guitars full of attitude grabbed me right away. This was like nothing I'd ever heard, a million miles from the peppy bands I saw on television and aging idols of my mother's record collection. I'd stumbled through another new, slightly gritty door and I liked where it was taking me. Alice Cooper's *Billion Dollar Babies*, in turn, would be my first album purchase. How I jumped from Volga Boatman straight to Alice Cooper, completely unfazed by Elvis and the Guess Who, is a mystery to me. I appreciate all those artists now, but there must have been something in the darkness and drama of this heavier music that woke something inside me. Finally, music that made sense with my Twilight Zone view of the world.

I was transfixed by those distorted Gibson SG guitars with their bat-shaped bodies that Alice Cooper's guitarists played. My teacher's Gretsch with the pillow on the back was for grandparents. These guitars were the key to something altogether different, something raw and youthful and dangerous. And I hadn't even discovered Black Sabbath yet. That SG wielding band was still lurking around the corner, waiting patiently for me. So many dark treasures yet to be revealed. My parents, as you can imagine, were not impressed.

The first live concert I attended, Alice Cooper at Maple Leaf Gardens in Toronto, was still a long way in coming. And I wasn't going to get there without a few hurdles to jump over first. Ironically, my first exposure to live amplified rock music had come via bands at Disneyland in California on that fateful guitar-lesson-quitting family trip. I stopped taking lessons, but was about to get some proper, first-hand inspiration. Tomorrowland, which showcased technology of the future, had a small stage that featured live music. There I saw a three-piece rock band that was quite heavy, Disney speaking. A nice surprise for a young musician expecting not much more than theme park rides and giant, fuzzy cartoon characters. And the guitar player had something on the stage he kept stepping on for solos that I'd never seen or heard before. I couldn't get close enough to see what it was, but it was the most amazing thing in the world – after guitars and amplifiers of course. My life had been effect-pedal free until that point. The Pre-Stomp-Box Age, you might say. I just assumed that all those great

FED

guitar sounds on albums came from turning the amplifiers up really loud. I kind of got the same result from turning the family's Philips stereo up to 10, until I finally blew the speaker. But true, controlled distortion had been a mystery to me until then. It would be a few years until I had one of those magic little boxes, the distortion pedal, for myself. Then came the phasers and flangers and wah-wahs and other treats that awaited young guitarists – all the sound-shaping devices that would help me make my sound my own; the keys to expressing all the feelings pent up in a young adolescent boy's head.

To be sure, any time I saw a live band, it was the electric guitars that held my attention. I've never been drawn in the same way by acoustic guitar. I would have probably dozed off watching the Hawaiian review at the Tahitian Terrace at Adventureland if it wasn't for the electric guitar and bass.

I even endured watching the Lawrence Welk Show with my parents on Sunday nights because there was an electric guitar in the orchestra. It went way beyond the sounds that they put out. It was something unexplainable, some esoteric combination of wood and wires and electronics that took hold of me.

To this day electric guitars have that effect on me; old Gibson and Fender guitars in particular. Apart from all their history and the culture shifting they caused in '60s and '70s society, I believe they are one of the most perfect creations ever made by man. A piece of wood with six strings on it that has limitless possibilities. For that reason electric guitars have pretty well stayed unchanged for 60 years. They were perfected a long time ago. The only instrument it might be surpassed by for pure, simple perfection is the violin. Just four strings that take a lifetime to master. I can pick up most instruments and get something musical out of them. The violin is like Mount Everest. There's no way of faking your way around that one...

4 High School & The Love Song

Middle school ended with a fizzle, apart from a clandestine maneuver to retrieve some forgotten musical equipment from the gym one night. No janitors were seriously hurt during the operation. High school, like for most people, was to be a game-changer for me. Aldershot High had been waiting all these years, steps away from the apartment building where we lived, just opposite the park and pavilion where I'd played floor hockey on my first stage. After years of walking past it to public and middle school, I'd finally arrived.

I immediately joined the high school band, quite aware by then that I needed a band as a place to belong. I chose the alto saxophone as my instrument. My father had always liked it and suggested the choice, but I'd already developed a soft spot for it on my own. One of my favourite movies, the 1959 comedy Some Like It Hot, featured Tony Curtis and Jack Lemmon as cross-dressing sax and stand-up bass players who join an all-girl jazz band to escape from gangsters in prohibition era Chicago. The cross-dressing part didn't rub off on me – I was much more interested in Marilyn Monroe.

The high school band was like an amazing club for me. I had stayed, to the most part, absorbed in my own private world of music until then. Now, all of a sudden, I found myself surrounded by a whole bunch of other kids just like me.

By high school, most students had pretty well determined what side of the popularity fence they were on, whether by choice or not. A lot of us didn't fit in anywhere else. The school band was our sanctuary. Our music teacher and conductor, Mr. Anderson, a kind, slightly awkward gentleman, took me under his wing. I think he was the grown up version of his students and understood us perfectly. We were like family.

Lunchtime and after school rehearsals became rites of passage, times to look forward to when we could be together with others of our kind. We became very good as a band and put on some amazing school concerts. In many ways, we came to represent our school as much as the football team did. The rest of the school cheered us on at band competitions. Suddenly, the misfits and socially inept were raised to a level of celebrity we could never have reached otherwise. Despite this, I found it very hard to talk to girls, unless of course they were also in the school band. I didn't even look at them as regular girls, but rather as flutists and French horn players and so on. Fellow band-mates. As luck would have it, there was one girl I liked and she wasn't in the band; a dark haired, big brown-eyed creature I longed for from afar. Being outside our circle, meeting her seemed out of the question. I even wrote a song for her, my first love song I suppose, called *Brown Eyes*. Van Morrison, I'm sure, could relate.

I would never have played the song for anyone, let alone her, but somehow the word got out at school. You can imagine the terror I felt. I would have gone into hiding if I could. But, to my amazement, she found out and thought it was incredibly romantic. In fact, she showed up at my sixteenth birthday party in a friend's basement and gave me my first serious kiss. We ended up on the couch and clearing the room. I knew then, beyond a shadow of a doubt, the power of a song. I made up my mind right then and there to be a songwriter. And, of course, to compose as many love songs as humanly possible.

Still, despite that monumental night, I remained girlfriendless and retreated to my bedroom to keep writing. Most people, apart from a particular brown-eyed girl, had no idea of my musical abilities. I was invisible at high school in the grand scheme of things, just one of the faceless teenage crowd. But this was all before I brought my electric guitar to school, before I came into focus a little and started standing out as an individual. When that happened, everything would change...

Our annual summer fair, the Canadian National Exhibition in Toronto, had a free concert series at their Band Shell in the evenings every summer. I saw countless local rock bands there through the '70s and experienced my first whiff of pot smoke. After a day of rides, I'd spend hours watching everything from David Bowie wannabe's and country rock bands to actual big leaguers like Tony Orlando and Dawn. I was probably just as captivated by *Tie A Yellow Ribbon* as a cover of *Suffragette City*. I definitely leaned toward harder music, but a good hook was undeniable to me, whatever shape it came in.

Those hot summer nights were a sort of education for me. Because of the variety of performers, I learned about all aspects of live shows, from how two guitars played off each other to stage presence to clothing styles. I recall the skinny lead singer in pink full-body tights and a plastic hand sewn over his crotch as much as the glorious stacks of Marshall amps. I saw that each element built on the whole impression you were left with. Live shows, I realized, weren't just about the music. There were props around it.

When I finally made it to my first legitimate concert, Alice Cooper at Maple Leaf Gardens, it wasn't without a few battles. I remember my father reading a review of Cooper's demonic stage antics in Time Magazine to my mother in the kitchen, loud enough so that we all could hear. At the time, Alice Cooper was Marilyn Manson ten-fold. There was talk about ripping the heads off dolls and on-stage homosexual innuendo. But to me it was all just more theatre, more parts of the puzzle to a great live show experience. I knew then, though I'd probably never rip the heads off anything, that I'd want to be in a band that had some 'show' to it, something more. Sadly,

FED

when I finally made it to the Cooper concert, it was far tamer and less provocative than I'd hoped. To a kid living in the Twilight Zone, this was child's play.

Our turntable was soon worn out on Alice Cooper, Black Sabbath and Deep Purple. The slightly naughty *Sabbath Bloody Sabbath* album cover with semi-clad women was heaven for a teenage boy, and more cause for concern for my parents. I think my father kept hoping I'd come to my senses and dedicate myself to classical guitar. I remember him taking me to an Andres Segovia concert at Hamilton Place and sitting through it politely. Just a guy with a flamenco guitar; no show, no theater, no Marshalls! What was the fun in that? *The Spoons would play a sold-out show at that same theatre at our peak in the mid 1980s. By that time we were doing quite well and Segovia was a distant memory. Even to my parents.*

I was drawn to the more theatrical and eccentric musical acts very early on. Glued to the TV on weekend nights, I'd watch Don Kirshner's Rock Concert and The Midnight Special with Wolfman Jack. There was always some slightly fringe act near the end of the show that I counted on for inspiration. Performers like Bowie and Cooper usually got those spots, but there were many others: Todd Rundgren, Iggy Pop, Queen and so on. They confirmed my hunger for the more unique and daring and sometimes flamboyant acts out there. Whatever had been awakened at those free Band Shell shows, I wanted more.

My guitar playing also started to change, to become more experimental. I really got my teeth into more serious playing when I discovered Jeff Beck. He was doing things I'd never heard squeezed from the instrument before; much like Jimi Hendrix, but I wouldn't discover him, strangely enough, until years later. Richie Blackmore of Deep Purple was another huge influence. I pretty well played the Machine Head album to death. I must have been on the right track, because their iconic song *Smoke On The Water* still rings true with listeners of every new generation. Blackmore also smashed his guitars on stage at live shows, which affected me to the core. He was destroying something I could only dream about, let alone possess, and just for show. That was more theatre than even I could handle. I found out later he was using cheaper parts and gluing them back together again for the next show. But at the time, you might as well have hit the family dog with a car.

So, while a lot of my friends were content with easy listening bands like the Beach Boys and the Eagles, I gravitated more toward artists that dabbled in the dark notes, the minor keys, the shadowy and dramatic. Looking back, it makes perfect sense for a kid who grew up on The Prisoner and a Rod Serling perspective of the world. Songs have always been more than just words and music to me. They paint pictures filled with props and characters that move in and out like actors in a movie, often stark worlds where people struggle to find their way. From the kid lying in his bed singing about castles to the young adult writing songs for the Spoons, songs have always been like tiny plays in my head. Each one starts with an empty stage. The lyrics fill it up with people and things. My people and things just happen to be a little different.

During all this time, my brother Gary was going through music lessons and instruments at a ridiculous rate; the drums, accordion, trumpet, you name it. He was either trying to follow in his brother's footsteps or just bowing to pressure from our parents. Family trips to Florida and California became a summer tradition. Sometimes relatives from Germany came along and we always packed an acoustic guitar, as well as an assortment of kazoos, wooden flutes and other noisemakers. Little impromptu concerts after a day of driving were quite normal and I'm surprised we never got kicked out of any motels. Maybe we weren't that bad. Gary reluctantly joined in, but eventually convinced us that fishing was his life's passion. Any hopes of a Partridge Family band in our household were shattered. I would have to look elsewhere…

5 The Sound Shop

There was a great little music store in Burlington called the Sound Shop. I'd ride my bike there after school or on Saturdays and just stare at all the goodies. Gibsons and Fenders and Marshall amps; all the tools the professional groups I'd been listening to were using. Here we were, face to face.

I soon learned the distinct smells that different instruments had. The scent of the glossy lacquer of the guitars, the pungent aroma of the wiring, the otherworldly tang of vacuum tubes. I fancied myself a bit of a connoisseur. The grouchy storeowner, Mr. Haywood, would regularly chase me and other loiterers out of his store. My nose was probably getting too close to his merchandise. I started to go on Sundays instead, when the shop was closed, and just sat on my bike and stared at whatever guitar was in the window. A glimpse of my future, displayed behind glass. A particular black Gibson Les Paul Custom caught my eye and held me helpless in its grasp; an object of my rock and roll dreams way beyond the means of a 16-year-old boy who's only income thus far came from caddying and delivering newspapers.

But life sometimes has a strange way of changing course when we least expect it. Now and then I would still brave the music store during regular hours, careful to avoid the evil stares and eventual showing of the door by Mr. Haywood. One evening I'd been so lost in pungent guitar-land that I hadn't noticed the store emptying out. I was the last one left standing.

Suddenly I was knocked out of my daze by a gruff "Hey, kid!" and I, knowing the routine, started heading for the exit.

SPOONFED

Instead, with a slightly less menacing voice, old man Haywood called me over. He pointed out that I was becoming a regular fixture in his shop and that, if I was interested, he was willing to offer me a part-time job. I think he'd mistaken my obsession for instruments for knowledge of some kind. In any case, if I was interested, I was in. The answer was obvious. And my chances of possessing one of the beautiful guitars I'd been having staring contests with was moving ever closer.

By that time the black Les Paul in the window was long gone. But Mr. Haywood had obviously never forgotten. I'd only been working in his store for a short while when he made me a surprising and very unexpected offer. I'd obviously been eying another Les Paul that had come in. "You really want that guitar, don't you, kid?" he said out of the blue one day. I think I just gave him a blank stare and mumbled something like, "Yeah... Sure... What?"

"How much can you afford?" he asked without waiting for a coherent reply. The guitar was about $850 in 1974, a crazy amount of money to me. I didn't really know how to respond and he came back with an offer before I could think it through; a few hundred dollars down, a small amount each week out of my pay and the guitar was mine. One moment of kindness from a man who once kicked me out of his store and my self-esteem skyrocketed. It was a major turning point for me. I was moving that much closer to my guitar heroes.

I decided to order a white Les Paul, like I'd seen at the Alice Cooper concert, but somehow it got sold to someone else when it arrived. They were harder to come by than other colours for some reason. An embargo on rare white rhinoceros pigment perhaps? In hindsight, I'm glad I ended up with the next black one that came to the shop. It's the guitar I used in the *Nova Heart* and *Romantic Traffic* videos and on stages for countless shows. A guitar that I still own today and couldn't see myself without. A Stradivarius, as far as guitars and kites go.

SPOONFED

My father still hoped my musical endeavours were just a hobby, so I kept the new guitar a secret from him for a while. My mother was more supportive and understanding and helped me with the downpayment. She saw, if nothing else, how happy it made me. My father, more practical, would have gone through the roof if he'd seen how much money I was putting into my little hobby. I looked at it as an investment.

Motivated by my shiny new guitar, my songwriting really started to take shape. I'd compose privately behind closed doors, usually when no one else was home. There was something incredibly personal about my own music. Songs brought out my deepest thoughts, like a diary set to music. But I wasn't ready for anyone to see that much of me yet. I poured my heart out at home. I started singing with more and more confidence, as long as no one was there to hear me. I found my voice wasn't really that terrible and even pictured myself as a lead singer performing in front of huge audiences. But I never believed in a million years it would ever be anything more than a foolish daydream, like x-ray vision or super human strength. I still had some serious coming out of my shell to do first.

Then one day, at a Right Side rehearsal, I showed the guys some of my song ideas. They obviously had no idea how prolific I'd been behind closed doors. They loved the songs and insisted we add them to our set list right away. It was a breakthrough moment for me. You can't imagine the gratification I felt after years of closet songwriting. It meant everything.

To this day, I get the same pleasure/pain tingle of uncertainty when I bring a new song idea to the Spoons. It's an incredibly personal thing to lay bare in front of other people, when it's still raw and new and unformed. When everything falls into place and the band gets excited, I'm on top of the world. I may be one of the biggest self-doubters on the planet but, give me an ounce of encouragement, watch out.

But there were going to be consequences. Everything that defined me up to that point was about to change. Blindsided by the effect my songs had on the world around me – in other words, brown-eyed girls and my credibility within my band – I found myself slip more and more into the creative half of my brain. It was incredibly easy to be seduced by it. My schooling and grades were going to be casualties. My classes, except for music of course, started taking a back seat to my new focus. Music, I decided, would be my life. But I would keep that realization to myself for a little while.

A combination of strict German schooling, my persistent parents and the fact that most studies came easily to me, had made me a model student to that point. My life was all about good grades and, of course, my secret alter ego as a guitar player. I recall a few years in high school when a competition between myself and a certain other student had us vying for top marks. We had our respective classrooms behind us as support teams, coaxing and rallying us on. The annual science fair became a battleground. Years later, that other student became one of the youngest doctors in Canada, ever. I, on the other hand, veered off on a very different course in life.

It's easy to see how it happened. Incredibly, I attended only one full-blown party all through my high school years – the infamous night I was introduced to serious kissing. Maybe my reputation had gotten around and my friends' parents didn't want me wearing out their basement couches and banned me from all further parties. But I seriously doubt that. I was a late bloomer in so many ways it would spoil the rock and roll credibility of a biography such as this if I exposed them all. It's probably wiser to file it all under the shroud of "Immersing oneself in one's art... dedicating oneself to their passion." My Grade twelve yearbook photo, with long hair parted in the middle, thick sideburns, mustache and glasses – mercifully omitted from this book – summed it up pretty well.

But that was all about to change when I brought my Gibson Les Paul and my songs to school. When people started to see what I'd been hiding all these years, the world became a different place. I became a celebrity overnight.

Word quickly spread and everyone, it seemed, heard about the guitar. Even to non-musicians, it was a big deal. Girls that would normally give me a wide berth suddenly came ever so slightly closer to see what the fuss was about. A big rocker kid who'd harassed me most of the school year miraculously softened and asked if he could hold my guitar. It turned out he was a closet guitarist like me and we had more in common than appearances suggested. He went from bullying me to wanting to be my friend in a nanosecond. It seemed like everyone started to look at me differently. Who, no matter how humble, could resist falling headfirst into this glorious abyss? For a teenage boy, this was heaven.

Dad, Gary (fishing on his mind) and I jamming at the cottage.

6 The Magic Bus Trip

As is often the way of the world, one door opening leads to others opening soon thereafter, like dominos you didn't even know existed. One day, at rehearsal, I noticed a new girl in the high school band. Every year brought its new recruits to replace those that quit or moved on. The band life wasn't for everyone. She played trumpet and, luck would have it, the trumpet section rubbed up alongside the saxophone section. My choice of instrument had paid off. Depending on where everyone sat, and if it was my lucky day, I sometimes ended up beside this cute little pixie blowing her horn. Her name was Sandy.

Despite my introvert nature, I surprisingly found her easy to talk to. Maybe she saw through my awkward, unpolished appearance. I discovered that twin girls – one a friend of mine in the sax section, the other with the trumpets – lived in her neighbourhood. The very neighbourhood, in fact, that would be the subject of the first Spoons album years later. This loosened things up for conversation even more. Sandy was dating someone at the time, a bit of a troublemaker who bashed away at the kettledrums with a passion and hated being in the band. So anything more than musical chitchat wasn't on the horizon. Or so it seemed.

The school band usually participated in one band exchange every year. We'd travel by bus to another city a few hours away, performed at some big assembly and then stayed overnight at students' homes. On one particular excursion I'd taken along an acoustic guitar and started playing at the back of the bus. Friends gathered around and someone mentioned that there was a girl at the front of the bus who'd also brought her guitar. They asked her to join us and, when they brought her back, there was Sandy. Neither one of us knew it then, but that would be the beginning of a very long and glorious musical partnership.

My drummer Gary Kennet from The Right Side was also on that school outing and suggested we throw together an impromptu band. We promptly designated Sandy as the bass player and I showed her some simple parts to play on the bottom low strings of her acoustic. A bit sketchy I know, but we were using any ploy we could think of to keep the cute trumpeter around. I'm pretty sure that by the end of that trip Gary and I had the new line-up for our band all worked out in our heads. A few days later we asked Sandy to join The Right Side. We'd been bass-less long enough. With her parents' permission, she agreed.

So, in between rehearsals with the high school band, we managed to put together a decent little pop group. Rod on keyboards and vocals, Gary on drums, myself on guitar and our new addition, fourteen-year-old Sandy Horne, on bass. We changed our name to Impulse, perhaps something to do with the teenage boy lust urgency to have Sandy on board. We'd never heard of another group with a girl bassist, so we thought we were unique. It brought us attention very quickly. It would continue to do so for the many years of adventures yet to come.

As fate would have it, somewhere along the line Sandy broke up with her music-class-hating old boyfriend and started dating Gary, our drummer. Just like that. Without warning. I'd just been too unaware and shy to see it happening right before my eyes. Story of my life. Or, my life until I started paying more attention. Gary had no such mental roadblocks and didn't waste any time. Maybe that's why I'm a little suspicious of drummers. I always have to read between the lines with them. I'd just have to bide my time and wait for the next opportunity.

Through my connections at the Sound Shop, we always had the best equipment. Old man Haywood was like family by then and even let us rehearse in his store basement, which soon became a sort of private club for us. Sandy's first bass was a cherry red Gibson EB-O, but she soon moved on to the smaller, more playable Fender Mustang bass. I still had my black Les Paul and had picked up a Marshall amp from the store by that time, which pretty well completed my teenage rock dream. Other kids saved up their money for bikes and records. We put every dime we had into our band.

As Impulse, we played school assemblies and a few outdoor concerts; never for money, just for the "experience." One performance that stands out in my mind was for Canada Day in the mid '70s on the rooftop of Jackson Square Mall in Hamilton, Ontario. We all wore matching white overalls and red T-shirts. Not my idea of fashion cool, but we were, after all, representing the colours of our flag. I recently found a cassette tape of that show and was amazed at how good we were, especially for a bunch of kids still in high school. And my original songs, although not very Spoonsy, showed a lot of promise. I can see now why people took notice.

Impulse (in overalls) on the Jackson Square rooftop stage.

SPOONFED

Our first small break came in 1976, when we entered a local battle-of-the-bands. Down a dirt road that is now Burloak Drive on the edge of Burlington and Oakville, the organizers set up a stage and got a good sized crowd out to cheer on local groups. We were by far the youngest band. There was one group tackling difficult material like Genesis, a band I was yet to discover. Our set was heavy on Elton John because our singer/keyboardist was good at it. Somehow we made it through the first round and weren't sent packing like some of the others. We performed again and incredibly made it to the final three. At this point we were getting angry stares from the more "serious" musicians. It didn't help that we were wearing those same perky white overalls and red T's from Canada Day.

When the judging was complete and winners called out, we were amazed to be awarded second place. The prize, I believe, was a set of proper microphones for the band. Then one of the judges came over and introduced himself. And so we met David Marsden for the first time. I didn't quite know who he was then, but our drummer would bring us up to speed later. Dave had already made a name for himself as a TV personality in the '60s and later for his more infamous stints as a radio deejay. He'd become a sort of rock star in his own right on CHUM-FM, the big rock radio station in Toronto in the '70s. He was known for pushing the boundaries, sometimes more than the censors could handle, which of course made him an even bigger rock star.

And here he was, at a battle-of-the-bands in Burlington, telling a bunch of kids how impressed he was by them. Those ugly jumpsuits we wore had actually worked in our favour. He commented on how he was intrigued by the androgynous appeal of the band. We were confused and a little frightened by this, but decided to take it as a compliment. He gave us his business card and, as he turned to leave, said something I'll never forget: "I have a feeling I'll be seeing you guys again."

42

SPOONFED

Sandy and I didn't know it then, but Dave Marsden would show up at almost every key point in our careers in the decades to come. When he introduced us at our thirtieth anniversary show in 2010, his words meant more to us than anyone could imagine. He'd literally watched us grow up and become who we are over the years. A couple of kids he first saw in a dusty Burlington field in 1976 had come a long way.

We packed up our prizes and gear and headed home. Then, unexpectedly, something happened which would break up Impulse and move us one step closer to the Spoons. I'd obviously liked Sandy since we first met in the high school band, sax and trumpet players rubbing elbows, but had kept that little secret to myself for years. I'd been too unaware to notice she was starting to like me. It was a gradual thing that crept up on us and, one night, sitting in a car after rehearsal, she told me so. I remember not handling it very well. The best I could come up with was something like, "Thanks." Smooth talking has never been my strong suit.

From that moment on, the world was a different place. Suddenly I felt like the nerdy kid in a teen movie that, against all odds, gets the popular girl everyone wants. Not the captain of the football team but me, the quiet, artsy music student. Except this wasn't a movie. There were going to be real consequences and some very difficult times ahead. Since Sandy was still seeing the drummer, this would mean the ultimate demise of Impulse and probably some friendships. But, obviously, I didn't care. I had my first real girlfriend.

I don't remember all the details or I may have blocked them out, but the next few months were a slide show of ugly confrontations, secret phone calls and tears. I think the final nail in the coffin was Sandy and I taking our equipment from the rehearsal space beneath the Sound Shop and moving it to her parents' basement. Until then, her ex wasn't getting the message that it was over. Moving our equipment meant business. Impulse was no more. From then onward it was just Sandy and I. Without a band, a little scared, but free.

But freedom came with a price. All of a sudden there wasn't a lead singer to back up anymore. I hadn't thought that little detail through. I'd been distracted. Of course, I'd been working on my private bedroom-singing all along and knew my own songs inside out. So that, at least, was a starting point. I'd never sung lead on other people's songs, so we decided then and there that we'd only do originals. That way, if I messed up, no one would be the wiser. Doing my own songs was like a huge safety net.

Sometimes the most important turning points in life don't come out of planning or wisdom, but rather from necessity or sheer dumb luck or, as in our case, any excuse to get out of a difficult situation. Thankfully, the luck part was taking care of itself. We were going to be needing it.

Around this time, I happened to meet a kid in school with some very different musical tastes named Brett Wickens. He played keyboards and – there's always one guy like this in school – he had all the new records I needed to hear. Originally from Britain, he turned me onto Genesis and King Crimson and other progressive rock bands like Van Der Graff Generator and Gentle Giant. Van Der Graff's album *Pawn Hearts* knocked me off my feet, with twenty-minute epics about ships colliding in the fog and demented lighthouse keepers. More fuel for my already twisted perspective on the world. Without hesitation Sandy and I asked him to join our new group. This, though we didn't know it yet, would be the first small step toward what would eventually become the original Spoons.

I quickly fell head over heels for progressive music, especially Genesis. For me, they took over from where Black Sabbath and David Bowie left off. They were the culmination of all the dark bits of all my favourite albums. Genesis were the kings of the theatrical and progressive rock realm. When I heard my first Genesis album, I became a prog-rock nerd overnight. I pretty well stayed one for the next few years, right until the birth of the Spoons. I can show you sections in Spoons songs that came directly from those prog-rock-immersed years.

With Genesis and the playing of Steve Hackett, things took a definite left turn for me guitar-wise as well. Like that old Gold Guitar record from my mother's friend's collection. I saw that the guitar didn't have to be front and center. It could be a different sort of paintbrush, one that created landscapes and textures. Sometimes the guitar could be a violin, a flute, even a human voice or something from a totally different universe. Steve Hackett didn't just dabble in other worlds, he broke through to other dimensions. That's how profound it seemed to a young, impressionable guitarist like me. I wanted to learn his secrets, to undo the riddles of his haunting sounds.

Somehow, it wasn't a big leap from writing the pop songs I'd written with Impulse to writing more ambitious progressive works. Since I'd always leaned toward the darker and more evocative cuts on pop albums, like *Funeral For A Friend* on Elton John's *Yellow Brick Road* and years of Alice Cooper and Sabbath, it was just a matter of focusing. The album *Equinox* by Styx had also perked my ears, sort of an everyman's progressive band. And then there was Kraftwerk from Germany, so far ahead of everyone that we didn't yet see that they were the future. With Brett and Sandy at my side, I entered a whole new era. I dove head-first into progressive rock and, right then and there, cut all ties with the mainstream.

Odd key signatures, counterpoint melodies and obscure lyrics lead to me writing some epic gems like *Plague Of The Electric Doorknobs*. This, incredibly, was done drug free. We'd landed a like-minded drummer from another school named Peter Shepard with a basement we could rehearse in. His parents let us leave our gear there, so we practiced constantly.

45

SPOONFED

We called ourselves Tryst, as in secret rendezvous. Considering Sandy and my recent escape from our old band, the name made perfect sense. Brett had a Farfisa organ and a very early synthesizer that recreated some of the sounds of our progressive idols. Sandy acquired a set of Moog Bass Pedals that reproduced the low-end rumble of our beloved Genesis. Those same sounds, little did we know, would fit effortlessly into a whole new wave of music looming just around the corner. We weren't aware of it yet, but we were on the right track.

We did a semi-professional recording of one original song called *Dreamer's Alibi* that actually got one or two plays on a local radio station. I found a copy of it on cassette recently. Very haunting and swimming in pools of reverb, it was undeniable proof that we'd accomplished all our prog-rock dreams. So musically complex and lyrically over-dramatic, it stands out like the thesis at the end of our musical education.

Tryst performed a total of three shows, one in Sandy's basement, one at the Burlington Public Library and one at an Aldershot High School assembly. Apart from some out of control fog from a homemade dry-ice machine, the show in Sandy's basement impressed our friends. Before that they'd only known us as perky Impulse in white overalls. We'd come a long way music and fashion wise. We sold tickets to our friends for the library show and brought in a pretty decent-sized crowd. We had the dry ice machine under control by then. The performance at our school, on the other hand, wasn't as easy…

Rumour quickly spread that we were going to use a flash pot at our high school talent show appearance. Flash pot, as in pyrotechnics. Smoke and things going boom at concerts were all the rage in the '70s. By flipping a switch, an electric spark set off a small amount of gunpowder in a metal box, resulting in a quick, but very efficient and bright explosion. Just like all the big-name bands were doing. Our principal caught wind of

46

this rumour, sat us down in his office right before the show and made us swear we wouldn't do something so irresponsible and dangerous. Of course, we promised, we wouldn't dream of it.

But by that time we'd already bought the thing. This is how we pulled off our high school pyrotechnics and escaped severe consequences:

1. A friend kept the flash pot and cable in a blanket side stage.
2. When our turn came to perform, he discreetly pushed the blanket to the front of the stage while we set up our equipment.
3. He then opened the blanket, carefully unraveled the cable and plugged it in.
4. He waited side stage with small fire extinguisher in hand.
5. At the agreed moment at the end of our show, he flipped the switch, set off the explosion, ran onto the stage, gave the super-heated flash pot a squirt with the extinguisher, rolled up the whole thing in the blanket and disappeared out the back door.

The operation, from detonation to clean up, took all of five seconds. No one was harmed during the procedure.

Tryst perform at Aldershot High.

SPOONFED

By the time our red-faced principal came bounding onto the stage – to the wild applause of the audience I might add – all trace of any evidence was long gone. We played sufficiently dumb and told him an amplifier had blown up. He obviously didn't catch the scent of gunpowder in the air and stormed off the stage in frustration.

This would be the same principal we would have to convince a few years later to let the Spoons perform at the final dance of our graduating year. The one that would get us banned from playing any other schools in Southern Ontario. In retrospect, I can see he had good reason to be concerned.

A student in Sandy's grade named Jim Carrey also performed at one of those school assemblies. He was a big hit, though I think he irked our puritan principal with his slightly naughty impersonation of the "Living Bra", which he achieved by pulling his yellow turtle-neck sweater over his knees and jumping around the stage. Jim only spent half a year at our school and Sandy knew him only casually. He would, of course, go on to become a huge comedic movie star, unlike any other.

Years later, performing in the same city somewhere on the road, Jim came back to our hotel room to wind down. Incredibly, he was even quieter and shier than I was and we hardly said two words to each other. Looking back now, it doesn't surprise me at all. Who we are on stage, and who we are when we're not performing, can be very different things. Sometimes complete opposites.

The stage, though often an incredibly frightening prospect, brings out something in performers that yearns to be released, to be screamed out. Whether at a basement party or high school auditorium or concert arena, it's what we live for. It's what scares us and completes us at the same time. Once you've had a taste of the stage, there's no turning back.

7 Out With The Old Wave, In With The New

Around 1979, things began to shift dramatically under our feet. We'd been so absorbed in our elitist world of self-indulgent progressive music we hadn't noticed that the mainstream was being turned upside-down. Punk was kicking out the old rockers, the New Romantics were bringing back glitz and glam and the New Wave was washing away anything that stood still on the musical landscape as we knew it. I'd lost interest in '70s commercial pop long ago and managed to avoid disco altogether. This couldn't have come at a better time.

Our keyboardist Brett picked up records and turned me onto one new and brilliant band after another. Gary Numan and The Tubeway Army, The Flying Lizards, The B-52s, Orchestral Maneuvers In The Dark, Lena Lovich, The Stranglers, Devo. The list went on and on. Never had I heard so much diversity and originality and pure creativity. I felt my prog-rock legs stumble slightly beneath me. This was something I could wrap my head around. And, most amazingly, with some editing and a few adjustments, the music we'd been making as Tryst wasn't far off the mark. A band I thought was destined for basements and libraries suddenly had a home. We could be part of this.

Around this time we discovered CFNY-FM, also known as The Edge, the Brampton based radio station that changed everything. They were playing all the great bands that Brett had introduced us to, plus a thousand more. Predominantly acts from England, they weren't the regular middle-of-the-road offerings the other stations were still broadcasting. We didn't know it then, but our new friend and The Edge's program director David Marsden was to thank for that. This, I knew in my heart of hearts, was where we belonged.

SPOONFED

Overnight, CFNY managed to nudge Genesis out of my head and fill it up with more than I could ever want. We became such dedicated listeners and pupils of the station that we began to believe it was the mainstream. We cocooned ourselves so well that we scarcely noticed that much of the rest of the musical world was still hanging onto the past. It was probably the best thing that could have happened to us.

Our drummer, Peter, didn't share our enthusiasm for the new music. He was more challenged by the progressive music of our past. Or perhaps he could see the rise of the drum machine on the near horizon. I think his parents had enough of our noise-making anyway, no matter how sophisticated, and one day asked us politely to move the show elsewhere.

Sandy and I began meeting at Brett's house to work out new song ideas. Peter never came along. We remained friends, but the shake up in the band was probably for the best. Being drum-less would open some very different doors for us. We had most of the tools - guitars and synthesizers, even an early chorus effect pedal called the Clone Theory that I used - but the one element we still lacked was the all important drum machine. In the late '70s you couldn't just walk into a music store and buy one. At least not the stores in our town.

Brett's parents had one of those home organs in their living room with built in rhythms; useless goodies like the samba, fox trot and waltz. There were one or two simple straight beats we could use, but we soon got tired of having to crank up the old organ and finding our settings, so we recorded three or four minutes of the best drum beats onto a portable cassette player and there it was, our first drum machine.

The first official Spoons song, though we were still floating somewhere between Tryst and the Spoons, was called *Alphabet Eyes*. I'd call it a Spoons song because it has almost no trace of our progressive past and plenty of the Spoons sound that was yet to fully develop. It's actually quite good and something we might want to look at again, a snapshot of the Spoons just as we were grabbing hold of something new. The recording starts with some strange squawks and garbled tape sounds – me trying to hit the play button on the tape deck with my foot to get the drum loop going. Very high tech.

What followed was some of the most prolific, and sometimes ridiculous, song-writing of my life. Songs like *Highlight* (about an albino girlfriend who needs lots of eye liner so she doesn't disappear in the bed sheets), *The Wreckers' Ball* (a formal and ultimately final bash for demolition experts) and *Picnic On Kitty Litter Beach* (absolutely no idea on that one). The music was angular and brash, more spoken than sung. Each instrument seemed to be in it's own paranoid world. If some young, new band redid these songs today, they'd either be committed or hailed as geniuses. I'd be interested to find out.

The television show Saturday Night Live had become the new testing ground for up and coming bands, as the Midnight Special and Rock Concert once had been. The show usually had a cutting edge musical act that would ultimately inspire me. Devo performing *Satisfaction* was a jaw-dropper. Patti Smith unnerved me a little, or was it Gilda Radner impersonating Patti Smith? The Talking Heads made me run and grab my guitar. What they were doing knocked me off my feet. The lead singer was shy and awkward, they had a female bass player and they were singing about suburbia. They were pretty well us, except they hailed from New York and we were from Burlington. The first seeds for *Stick Figure Neighbourhood* were sown.

My lyrics had always been about small, mundane things blown out of proportion. Who else would build a whole song around rampant killer doorknobs? Or want to? David Byrne of the Talking Heads was the master of making lyrical mountains out of molehills. Just as I was once absorbed by the flowery depths of progressive rock lyrics, I was now held captive by minimalist sketches of suburban life. Suddenly the boring landscape of our own backyards, which we had tried to escape from through progressive music, had become center stage for a whole new generation. And we, all the misfits who had never really fit neatly into the mainstream, had finally found a home.

In this way, I think a lot of artists who never would have made it in another decade, had their shining moment in the '80s. Once the floodgates were open, the outpouring of creativity and sheer bravado was overwhelming. It didn't matter so much how good you were at playing the guitar, but rather what new, unheard of sounds you could squeeze out of it. Knowing how to play wasn't even a prerequisite. Doing something new was. I'm not saying everything that hit the airwaves back then was brilliant, but there was an undeniable excitement I hadn't felt in a very long time. One new interesting and inspiring band was coming along after another. And we weren't intimidated by them. We were drifting right along with all the other eager travelers.

We'd toyed with our home-made drum machine long enough and realized the time had come for a real live drummer, especially if we were going to perform in front of an audience, something which was presumably going to happen one day. The little tape deck with drum loops on it wasn't going to cut it anymore. There were triplets in our school, very popular and notorious for swapping girl friends. Or so the rumours went. Sandy heard that one of them, Derrick Ross, was a pretty good drummer and, even better, had a basement we could rehearse in. That was half the battle. We hit it off immediately, asked him to join and had a band again. It was that easy.

Strangely, apart from Alphabet Eyes, we would not incorporate the drum machine in our music again until two years later. It would be missing completely from our first album, Stick Figure Neighbourhood. A little surprising, considering that drum machines are synonymous with the

SPOONFED

Spoons to a lot of people. It would be forgotten and not introduced again until our recording of Nova Heart, when our future producer John Punter would bring along a little box called the Roland 808 to the studio and drum machines would become an integral part of our sound again. But there would be some more growing pains to go through, musically and personally, before that happened.

How we came up with the Spoons name is a little foggy. I vaguely remember throwing ideas around over lunch at Brett's house. We liked the notion of naming ourselves after something everyday, something utilitarian, something simple that we could attach a whole new meaning to. Bands like the Cars and Martha And The Muffins were on the radio. There was a Toronto group called the Dishes. Something about that simplicity made perfect sense to us. Fate would have it, we were eating soup and the answer was right in front of us. Right in our hands, as a matter of fact.

So, with a name and a band and our final high school year coming to a close, Sandy and I found ourselves sitting in the principal's office trying to sell him on the Spoons. There was enough underground hype brewing by that point to create some excitement among the students, even before we'd done a single show. I think having Derrick in the band had greatly widened our social circles. Our principal must have been aware of this and, though at first reluctant, finally submitted to our wishes. I suspect he'd forgotten about the flash pot incident by then. But the two model students he'd known to that point, the well-behaved trumpet and sax players from his pride and joy high school band, had alter egos that he wasn't aware of. To be fair, Sandy and I didn't really know about that side of ourselves yet either, or the full potential of our little new wave group. Everything about that fateful first Spoons performance at the end-of-year Aldershot High School dance – the one that would get us banned from playing any other high schools in the province – would be utterly spontaneous and out of control.

The big night came. With our trusty Saturday Night Live episodes and new wave album covers to guide us, we somehow stumbled on a band look that entailed sticking a coat-hanger in my tie and bending it upwards so it looked perpetually windblown and Sandy putting wires into her pig-tails in a Pippi Longstocking meets Lena Lovich creation. There was a lot of wire action going on which, alone, could ultimately spell trouble. The result was an edgy, slightly punk vibe that, despite our more artsy musical direction, would be enough to get the ball rolling towards disaster.

We set up in the high school cafeteria, perfectly suburban for our first gig. Sound check went well. Our old drummer Peter volunteered to be our sound man and had set up a small p.a. system and a couple of lights. Everything was running smoothly, too smoothly obviously. It was barely dark out and the doors were opened. Kids started filling in almost immediately, a lot already primed for something to happen. Very soon the cafeteria was jammed with a much larger crowd than we'd ever anticipated. The couple of teachers who'd offered to oversee the party were already looking like they should have made other plans for the weekend. There was a strange electricity in air, as if things could explode at any moment. And they soon would.

We walked on stage, tie and pigtails flying, plugged in and, before the first song was even finished, saw the room erupt around us. As if on cue, a mosh pit materialized, chairs went flying, tables were overturned. Someone brought a carton of eggs and used the cafeteria wall for target practice. One kid climbed onto our p.a. speakers and dove into the crowd. Fists flew. The volunteer teachers tried to do something, anything, but got pushed aside like so much fluff: A full-blown punk fest.

And we just kept on playing through it all. We were scared as hell but, at the same time, took it as a compliment. We thought we'd driven the audience into a frenzy, which wasn't the case at all. We had nothing to do with it. We were just the excuse for something that was going to happen anyway. We could have played Pat Boone or Osmonds songs. It didn't matter. Our fate had been sealed before the doors even opened.

A far as first gigs go, this was a groundbreaker. The kind high school legends are made of. It was also the realization of our principal's worst nightmares. Fortunately, it was the end of school and we never had to meet him face to face. But phone calls were made and word was out that he'd had us banned from playing any high school in the area ever again. I hope it made him feel better, because it didn't hurt our budding careers in the least. We would soon be going on to bigger and better things. Word of our little band kick-off had gotten around.

Ironically, a few years later, when we had hit songs on the radio, that same principal called us out of the blue one day. He'd moved to another high school by that time, somewhere obviously outside of the Southern Ontario region. He wanted to know if we could come and play a concert at his school, at a discount no less! We, to put it politely, declined. What is it they say about revenge best served cold...?

A local music magazine called The Red Shoes heard about the Aldershot show and promptly put us on their next cover. The article inside was glowing, milking the now infamous concert for all it was worth. We did our first photo shoot in the basement of a little house backing onto the Royal Botanical Gardens, on the border of Hamilton and Burlington, where my father had his business. It was so remote and secluded that we started to call it the "cottage." We rehearsed in a tiny room upstairs, often while my father worked in his office with classical music cranked up loud to help drown us out. How he managed to get anything done still amazes me.

My father had an wide assortment of books that he kept in a sort of library at the cottage. I could search through them and, at any point, come across something that would provoke and inspire me. He was interested in a lot of things. We shared a love for old trains and travel by rail. There were plenty of science fiction books to light up the imagination, one of which would one day help inspire the lyrics to *Nova Heart*. I also discovered books on the paranormal, from case studies of ESP to the memoirs of Lopsang Rampa, a westerner who had submersed himself in eastern culture; writings about the "third eye" and "out of body travel." This, as you can imagine, was not your average reading material for someone my age. The Hardy Boys would have been more like it. But I was hooked and absorbed as much as I could from my father's crazy library. Thanks to him, I learned to keep an open mind very early on.

We shot the Red Shoes cover against a wall of old boxes in the basement. Shortly we discovered, being so close to the botanical gardens, that we shared the old house with some ominous wildlife. Rehearsals at our little cottage soon became notorious for giant, mutated spiders sitting in. These were of Hollywood B-movie proportions and seemed to be attracted to amplified music. To this day, I still compare all other spiders to those of the infamous "cottage" variety. I'll see if I can look up the proper Latin name sometime.

One day Brett brought two friends to one of our rehearsals. We'd never seen anyone like them in the flesh before. Two local hairdressers named Reg and Joe, they had more style than anyone we'd ever met. With fluorescent Flock Of Seagulls hair and wild, angular clothes they'd designed themselves, it was a huge wake up call for us. We were way too tame and very much in need of some help in the image department. Reg and Joe loved our music and, then and there, became our style council for many years to come. And it couldn't have happened at a better time. We were about to break out of Burlington. Through the Red Shoes connection, we landed an opening slot for the Diodes at the Riverside Club in Oakville, just east of Burlington. We were taking this fame thing in small steps.

SPOONFED

The Diodes were the first Canadian quasi-punk band that secured a national record deal. Their song *Waking Up Tired* was a bit of a party-all-night anthem back then. Strangely, we fit the bill. We were no punk band, but somehow our quirky pop music was edgy enough to keep the hardcore faction in the audience at bay. It also helped having Sandy in the band. Any thoughts of tossing beer bottles seemed to be squelched by teenage lust. Ironically, there weren't any of the punk antics we experienced at our infamous high school show. This was tame in comparison. I think we would compare all other gigs to that fateful first one for a long time. Kind of like the cottage spiders.

The audience liked us, the club asked us to come back and do a gig on our own, and the Diodes offered us a slew of other opening slots. This would be the pattern for a while. Open and then return as headliner. The next show was at Toronto University, followed by the Edge and Larry's Hideaway, which had us back many times to appear on our own. In this way, the Diodes opened a lot of doors for us. Things would have moved a lot slower if we'd tried to go it on our own.

Not that it was easy by any means in those early years. Time, as I'm fully aware, is very clever at playing with smoke and mirrors. Nostalgia is one of its best inventions. We never made much money, usually just what was collected at the door, and I remember one night at the Edge bringing in just enough to cover our expired parking tickets. We played for the pure joy of it. We were living our dream. Other kids spent their weekends at parties and movie theaters; we played in a rock band. It was our social time, but also the thing that united us and gave us cause.

Sandy, for some strange reason, had started using a Gibson Grabber bass. For a girl of her diminutive stature, it was probably the biggest and heaviest bass guitar available. It might have looked and sounded good, but I'm sure it was taking its toll on her spine. As fate would have it, the appearance of the Grabber was short-lived.

After another show at the Riverside in Oakville where we'd first opened for the Diodes, two male fans were just a little bit too eager to help Sandy load her gear. Somewhere along the line, one of them kept her occupied while the other carried her guitar and promptly stashed it somewhere behind a dumpster at the rear of the club. By the time Sandy realized her Grabber had been grabbed, the two thieves were long gone.

For the next few weeks we kept an eye on local music stores and scanned the classifieds. Sure enough, a Gibson Grabber showed up for sale in a townhouse complex not far from where Sandy lived. All the pieces were coming together. Plans were set into action as we prepared to move in on our fool-hearted felons. Brett and Derrick would knock at the front door while Sandy and I waited in a car in case the culprits decided to hightail it with the evidence. All very Starsky & Hutch. It was a stake out by any definition of the word and probably a pretty stupid idea on our part.

Someone answered the door and, watching from afar, we saw our band mates disappear into the house. It occurred to us that the situation had potential for turning ugly very quickly. What seemed like an eternity slipped by as Sandy and I waited and watched nervously from the car, while our friends had walked into a potential lion's den. We were seriously thinking about calling for backup when, finally, they re-emerged from the house. It was a false alarm; wrong Grabber bass. When we asked why they'd taken so long inside the house, it turned out that they were all having a good laugh about the case of mistaken identity! They'd been socializing while we sweated. Sandy's bass was gone. She'd have to accept that. Somebody else's spine was going to be punished instead.

8 The Rise Of The Mannequins

We decided it was time to bring some show back to our live performances. It'd been a long time since fog machines and flash pots. I'd always been fascinated by the use of black lights, as I'd seen on the cover of the Genesis Live album. I remember Bret and I going to a tiny place in Yorkville, Toronto called the Electric Gallery, which exhibited eclectic works of modern art created from light fixtures and mirrors. We were on a young band's budget, so we improvised and came up with some very simple but ingenious ideas of our own.

One of our better inventions involved stretching lengths of white yarn between wooden slats. The strings were spaced a few inches apart and the slats cut in various sizes. By nailing one slat to the floor and the other to the ceiling (which we could easily do at smaller clubs like the Edge and the Hideaway), we stretched the strings tight and lit the whole thing with long black-light tubes in boxes we had built. Voila, poor man's lasers. When we had multiples of these on the stage, crisscrossing at different angles, the effect was pretty stunning. And all for about twenty dollars.

As we became regulars in the Toronto music scene, building a small following, our fans came to expect a bit of stage production from us. One day our old drummer and technical whiz Peter surprised us with an elaborate effect he'd been working on in his basement. Just as ingenious as our cheap lasers, he'd taken cords of Christmas lights and put them into long, white, flexible six-inch tubing he'd bought at a hardware store. When he hung them like robotic tentacles all over the stage and got the lights pulsating with a small sequencer he'd built from scratch, the result was like a scene from the space ship Nostromo in the Alien movies.

One ill-conceived effect didn't work out so well. Always searching for something new, we came up with the idea of hanging long tubes of fluorescent fluid by thin wires from the stage ceiling. Lit by black lights, the effect would be amazing. Just think of the glow sticks you see at concerts and sports events, but larger. Half way through a show one night at Larry's Hideaway, we discovered that fluorescent liquid has a funny way of expanding under hot lights. You guessed it, the tubes started exploding one by one, splattering their oily contents all over us. End of that bright idea.

Eventually we simplified things and went the safer route of using projections on stage. We played with different ideas and finally settled on a big triangular white screen made out of thick Styrofoam board. It was nice and flat and easily hung from the backdrop. On it we projected all sorts of black and white vintage movie clips, from Godzilla to War Of The Worlds. I worked out a routine of borrowing super 8 films from the public library and editing out the scenes we needed. We would use them for shows over the next few weeks and then I'd splice them back in again. At first I felt guilty about it, but I got so adept at using my trusty splicer that the library was soon getting their films back in much better shape than they'd gone out as. I was doing them a public service.

Somewhere during all this experimentation, our first mannequin made her appearance. The guys from Red Shoes Magazine had formed a small record label. The timeline is a little vague, but we'd started bringing a female mannequin on stage with us and their label was called Mannequin Records. I'm not exactly sure which came first, but it was the beginning of an image that would work its way in and out of Spoons marketing throughout the years. The actual mannequin eventually stopped showing up at shows, but the mannequin head image continued to appear on many of our gig posters. When she returned in 2010 on our Imperfekt CD cover, it was totally by surprise. No one had planned it. She just showed up.

SPOONFED

Two songs that went over particularly well at those early shows were *My Job* and *After The Institution*. They embodied everything we were listening to at the time; the Talking Heads, Devo, a touch of Flying Lizards. Totally in suburban angst fashion, *My Job* tackled hating one's profession, in this case dog grooming. *After The Institution* tried to paint a picture of life after being committed to an asylum. Way too much going on here for a first single. Still, in the naive and stubborn way of young bands, we went ahead and recorded the songs and released our first 45 on Mannequin Records.

The music showed little indication of what we'd eventually become, but it has its screw-the-music-industry charms. There was no way of mistaking this for the other more conservative bands kicking around Burlington. It was weird and raw and it was ours. And it was bound to get us noticed. Only a few hundred were pressed. *That piece of vinyl would go on to become one of the most collectable pieces of Spoons paraphernalia. One went for $200 on eBay recently. I hope the buyer wasn't disappointed. Getting airplay wasn't on our list of priorities back then.*

It would also be the one and only recording we released with Brett on keyboards. He'd leave the band soon after to pursue other interests, primarily in album art design. He created the artwork for our single and would go on to design the *Stick Figure Neighbourhood* cover.

True to our artsy progressive rock roots, the image on that album was inspired by the paintings of Magritte and a short story from the liner notes of an old Genesis album, one that Peter Gabriel used to introduce one of his songs during live shows. Our relationship with Brett had come full circle in a way, beginning and ending with Genesis. Eventually he would move back to England and collaborate on album covers with another future ex-pat, Peter Noble, who we were about to cross paths with very shortly.

61

And the two figures on the front of *the My Job/After The Institution* record sleeve? Our hairdressers Reg and Joe. Not the band. We were relegated to a small photo on the back cover. Us and the indifferent gaze of our trusty, old mannequin, which had become the label's logo. Reg and Joe were still much more fashionable and photogenic than we were.

When Brett left, we needed a new keyboard player and fast. We immediately put a want ad in the local papers. Very practical and to the point. I only remember one reply and that came from a fifteen-year-old named Rob Preuss. No lengthy auditions. No fuss. We met, we played through a couple of song ideas and he was in. The Spoons were now complete.

Rob was, as we soon found out, somewhat of a classical piano prodigy for his age. Which would explain why today he makes a living as main keyboardist and assistant conductor for musicals in New York City. Rob was also a music-obsessed recluse like we were and, of prime importance, owned some pretty decent equipment for a fifteen-year-old.

Incredibly, I'd find out later that he was also the grandson of my father's old boss in Germany and that my parents knew his family quite well. Somehow, by chance, two kids from two different immigrant families that had distant ties ended up in a band together in Burlington, Ontario, Canada. It was by dumb luck that we did, or by fate, depending on how you look at it.

Rob performed his first show with us at the Edge and fit in seamlessly. Because of his age, we had to provide the club owners where we played with a special permission slip. Something worked out between the liquor licensing board and the Musicians Union. It required that he stayed back stage between sets, safe from the temptations of the corrupt adult world. There was really no reason for concern. I don't ever remember Rob having a drink in all the years I've known him.

SPOONFED

At the time, Rob had a new Roland Jupiter IV and SH-2000 for keyboards, miles beyond Brett's older gear. There was a definite further shift toward what would become the Spoons sound. I'd also picked up a white second-hand 1974 Fender Stratocaster, probably influenced by the raw Talking Heads tones I liked, and set aside my old black Les Paul for a while. That pretty well completed the picture. The way we sounded then was the way we would sound for the next year or so.

Between sets at that first show we went upstairs to the Edge change room and congratulated Rob on his performance. He was fitting in very nicely. And then, right out of left field, someone came in with some very shocking and surreal news. John Lennon had been shot to death in New York City. The rest of the night was a daze, a jumble of emotions and pictures that will forever stick in my mind. I still remember the pattern on the dark red couch that I stared at back stage, my head hung low in numb shock. I wasn't prepared for the loss I felt. John Lennon and the Beatles had always been there, from the day I first heard their name playing in my sandbox as a child in Germany. A piece of all of us had suddenly been ripped away. We went downstairs to do our final set and there were people crying in the audience. We half-heartedly ran through the rest of our songs. It was one of the hardest shows we'd ever have to play. The world seemed very quiet all of a sudden. Many of us, I'm sure, feared it would never be the same again.

The Edge was owned and run by a pair of local promoters named The Garys. They'd brought a lot of future superstars to Canada to do their premier shows at their little Toronto club; practically unheard of artists like The Police, XTC and Ultravox. The Garys quite liked us and one of the two, Gary Cormier, became our first manager, pretty well on an imaginary handshake. Soon he had local record company reps coming out to see what the fuss was all about. We never sent out a single demo tape. Gary had good things to say about a little label called Ready Records. They'd released music by some very interesting groups, including the iconic *New York City* by the Demics. Before we knew it, contracts were signed and we had our first legitimate record deal. It happened that fast.

It was time to make our first album. I'd been attending McMaster University in Hamilton and Sandy was taking an accounting course at Mohawk College on the Hamilton Mountain. Unlike a lot of other young adults, we opted to stay close to home and live with our parents. Being a couple and having the band made it out of the question to be elsewhere.

I remember struggles with my father about going to university. He was concerned about his son and his unrealistic daydreams of becoming a pop star. He hoped I would never take it beyond the hobby stage. Ultimately I gave in, finished three years at McMaster and completed my B.A. But, for reasons I can't explain, despite my introverted nature, I knew somehow in my heart of hearts that I would succeed at music. It was one of those rare moments of clarity in life when you know something with all certainty, even though everything tells you otherwise. I'd just have to prove to everyone else what I already knew deep inside.

When we signed our record deal, I think my family took my music career a little more seriously. It was the last year at university, so I suppose they saw I was pretty well in the home stretch anyway.

But finishing my final year, while recording our first album, was one of the most difficult high-wire acts I've ever had to perform. I had to divide my brain into two compartments, one for music and one for my studies. It almost tore me apart. A little voice in my head kept telling me to, "Give it up, forget school... music is your future... none of what you're studying applies to your life." Pretty common conflicts for someone my age.

SPOONFED

But somehow I stayed with it and managed to accomplish both. Good thing because, in the end, university opened my mind to some very different concepts.

My psychology classes would come in pretty handy when it came to lyric writing. So that little voice in my head hadn't been completely right after all.

The song *Red Light*, for instance, came directly out of a behavioural conditioning class. Part of the course required training a pigeon to peck red and green lights for rewards, usually food. I had a particularly nasty bird that pecked me instead when I tried to handle it. I started bringing oven mitts to the lab. I had to protect my guitar playing hands from pigeon mutilation and soon decided to give up on the whole thing altogether. That bird had it in for me. I just applied the same conditioning theory to relationships between the sexes. Somehow it worked. *Red Light* was born.

Another song, *Only For Athletes*, was our anthem for all the outsiders and uncool of the world. Memories of Aldershot High, I'm sure. The words clearly expressed how I felt in university in the shadow of the popular crowd; which usually meant the athletes, specifically football players and their circle of friends. There was still a bit of the old stigma that, even as a young musician signed to a record deal with his whole future ahead of him, I wasn't able to let go of quite yet.

Old insecurities obviously die hard. I realize, looking back now, that was probably a good thing. Feeling like an outsider ultimately makes for much better lyrics than a life of joy and contentment. It's much more interesting in the long run.

So, with my last year of university winding down, we prepared to record our first album. We were ready to make *Stick Figure Neighbourhood* and put our little mark on the world.

9 Building The Neighbourhood

Andy Crosbie and Angus McKay, who ran Ready Records, brought in Graeme Pole to produce *Stick Figure Neighbourhood*. A hotshot student from the Fanshaw College recording program in London, Ontario, he'd sent us some of his work and we liked what we heard. Most importantly, he had a firm grasp on that sparse Talking Heads sound we craved – the sound of suburbia.

We'd heard great things about a little place in Hamilton called Grant Avenue Studios. Only about a ten-minute drive from McMaster University, it was perfect for my music/academics juggling act. Ready Records booked some time for us there while we worked out the songs over a week of pre-production. We were obviously excited about making our first album and working in a proper studio, but doubly so because legendary producer Brian Eno, who's name we knew from Roxy Music, had worked there with the up-and-coming engineer and owner of the studio. They'd collaborated on some high profile ambient recordings. That young hotshot engineer was Daniel Lanois.

I remember Daniel strutting into the sound-booth after we'd already set up our equipment on the first day. Knee-high red cowboy boots stick out vividly in my mind. I recall him being somewhat aloof around us. Not unfriendly, just perpetually distant. Perfectly understandable, seeing who he'd worked with and who he was about to record in the not so distant future. He was, I'm sure, already mentally rubbing elbows with Bono and U2.

That all changed when Sandy's father Terry dropped by the studio one day for a visit. Mr. Horne seemed to recognize

Daniel right away, but wasn't quite sure from where. He sat quietly watching us in the control room for an hour or so, then suddenly yelled out, "I know who you are!" At that time Sandy's father was the manager for Robinson's Department Store at the Burlington Mall. Years ago he'd hired someone at a tiny garage studio in Hamilton to write, record and sing a radio jingle for his store. Something like, "Robinsons... price and quality..." You know how they go. We've all heard them. That guy in the home studio was Daniel Lanois.

After that revelation, Daniel loosened up around us considerably. We recorded *Stick Figure Neighbourhood* over the next few weeks and learned so much, fortunate to catch Daniel just before the word got out and everyone wanted to work with him. Graeme brought some quirky recording techniques to the table, like Sandy's warbled voice in *Only For Athletes*, achieved by sending her microphone through the tremolo in an old Fender guitar amplifier. He also brought in Hugh Syme to play all those haunting choir sounds on his Mellotron, another staple of our prog-rock heroes Genesis.

The Spoons and Sandy's dad – he'd met Daniel Lanois before.

We'd never been able to afford one of those otherworldly keyboards. It actually had tiny loops of taped sounds, like human voices and violins, that played every time you hit a key. Mind-boggling. Hugh was also known for the album cover art he'd done for, most notably, Rush. If our old keyboard player Brett hadn't already put something together, we'd most likely have had a cover designed by Hugh. Mister Stick Figure won out in the end.

We completed *Stick Figure Neighbourhood*, our ode to suburbia, in only a few weeks. No big recording budget quite yet. But, full of flaws and little eccentricities, it captured a moment in time for a young band still finding their way. I saw similarities between our hometown Burlington and The Village in The Prisoner TV series and even put a credit on the back of the album to "No. 6 for inspiration." If you look carefully, etched around the center of the album vinyl are the words "Arrival" on the A-side and "Departure" on the B-side, the opening and closing episodes of that influential television series. I was at the lacquering session when our record was being made and the engineer asked if I had any personal message to add there. You might want to check some of your old albums to see what other bands left as parting words.

Some vivid snapshots stick in my mind from the Grant Avenue sessions: the "adult movie" collection in the lounge upstairs, the very odd Joe Mendelson paintings on the walls and some of Martha And The Muffins' equipment sitting around the studio. Their song *Echo Beach* was getting all sorts of airplay and Daniel was recording their new album. I was intrigued by the Roland JC-120 amplifier Mark of the Muffins was using, a huge part of the '80s sound then. I'd wanted one of those for a long time. We didn't know it yet but, as fate would have it, we'd soon be sharing a stage with Mark and Martha and the rest of the gang. Looking back, it's incredible how one thing lead to another, almost effortlessly, like pieces in a puzzle that would ultimately set us in the right direction.

SPOONFED

Gary Cormier from the Edge had many connections in the Toronto music scene, including The Muffins. They'd played his club a few times before their big song broke, when there were still two Marthas in the band. Calls were made and we were confirmed to open for them at an old movie theatre in Hamilton. It was a step up from the smaller clubs we'd done with the Diodes. *Echo Beach* was fast becoming a worldwide hit. It was a musical marriage made in heaven; two slightly nerdy bands that made minimalist music and sang about life in suburbia. Not very sexy, but that was the nature of the times.

Like many shows, the actual performance is a bit of a blur. It's the peripherals that stay with me. In this case, the fans trying to climb in the change room window – quite the feat, since we were on the second floor. I remember the dusty gloom of the old theatre that had likely featured films like Some Like It Hot when it premiered in its heyday. Old theaters always make me feel a little sad; so many forgotten memories lost in the walls. So much joy and pain and wonder faded away.

I remember the Muffins being quite friendly back stage, especially their bass player, Carl Finkle. He'd been watching us and liked what he saw. Our two bands fit together very well and, as with the Diodes, we'd be asked to open for them again on a mini tour through Ontario and Quebec; our first real, extended out-of-town tour. We were finally breaking out of the Toronto area. Things were moving along nicely.

It was around this time that we met Andrew MacNaughtan, a few years before he picked up a camera and made photography his life's work. We were opening for Martha And The Muffins at a hall in Oakville, Ontario. A bright eyed kid about our age, Andrew was crazy about the new music and full of big ideas for a young band that, like him, were just starting out. He interviewed us for the very first issue of his homegrown Free Music Magazine and ended up giving us the cover story. It would be the beginning of a long and beautiful friendship.

69

Andrew would go on to be our photographer for the next thirty years. As his magazine grew, he soon got tired of dealing with the photographers he hired, bought a decent camera and took charge. The rest is history, having since worked with every big name in the industry, from Bono to Ella Fitzgerald.

Andrew would also become Rush's official photographer. He'd see the world and capture it through his lens. Photo exhibitions, album cover design, music video direction and a book of his work would soon follow.

But I will forever remember him as the eager kid full of bright ideas who came along just as we were starting out. And he never lost that childlike innocence and sincerity in his work. Right until his untimely death a few years ago, he somehow managed to stay himself – quite the feat for anyone in this industry. He was our photographer but, more than that, he was a very dear friend. One whose opinions and big ideas I will miss always.

Ready Records released Stick Figure Neighbourhood and, although no singles were ever worked to radio, two key things happened. The album began to chart on college radio and CFNY-FM – yes, our beloved Edge Radio – took an immediate liking to us. This was a huge moment for the band, especially for Sandy and I, who had practically grown up listening to the station.

I remember someone from CFNY coming to Ready Records to interview us. Our first real, big-time interview. I also recall David Marsden, who was running the station at the time, playing *Only For Athletes* and saying on the air something along the lines of, "Can you believe these guys are from Burlington?" I don't think he'd even made the connection to those perky kids in jump suits at the Burlington battle-of-the-bands yet. That wouldn't happen for some time. But he had been right about seeing us again one day.

So, between touring with the Muffins and support from college radio, we pieced together our first national tour. At the time, our angular, angst-ridden sound was considered "alternative" and we incredibly made it to No. 1 on campus charts. Universities and colleges were the perfect way to see the country. The shows, usually put on in cafeterias, gymnasiums and theatres, really felt more like small concerts. But sometimes getting to the stage from the change room required navigating mazes of hallways, often through the basements of the campuses. One Spinal Tap moment stands out, at Laurentian University in Sudbury I believe. It was a few minutes before show time. We grabbed our guitars and started to make our way to the gymnasium where we were set up to perform. We could hear our intro tape begin somewhere in the distance. We heard the crowd cheering, likely as the lights were dimmed. One small problem; somewhere between the change room and gym, we got terribly lost.

The hallways and tunnels that were supposed to take us to our destination sent us in circles instead. We could hear our intro tape finish somewhere just out of our reach, the crowd chanting and then the tape being started up again, by a very nervous sound man I'm sure. We actually passed the same janitor twice in our loop-the-loop. Eventually we did make it to the stage, feeling like rats that had just escaped a maze. The audience had no idea. We were just glad to find civilization.

And so we toured Canada and left our little mark. Even though we bypassed mainstream radio completely with our first album, we'd started to build a solid base of fans hungry for something different. And different was something we could deliver. We weren't the only ones turned on by the new wave of bands from Britain and America. We were all in this together, the audience and us. And, as far as I was concerned, we were just getting started. I knew we could be something more, something much grander and big and sophisticated. I just didn't know exactly what that was yet.

71

10 Dark Days

Unfortunately, not every twist in the road we were on would be as harmless as losing our way in a university basement. There would be less innocent mazes to get sidetracked by.

As our popularity grew, we soon learned not all attention is good attention. While at home, in between tours, Sandy began to have concerns about a boy our age that would show up at her house. He'd appear at the oddest hours; sometimes early in the morning, sometimes late at night after a gig, standing in the street or hiding in the bushes outside her windows. He'd run off if she or her parents approached him. Things took an even stranger turn when Sandy received a letter in the mail from the boy claiming that we'd stolen all the words in our songs from him somehow, telepathically, through the airwaves.

What seemed funny at first soon became quite serious. There were rumours that the boy had psychological issues; that he'd even been institutionalized. We were starting to have a very bad feeling about this. So many things could possibly go wrong and, eventually, they did. One day Sandy called us with the horrible news. She'd read in the papers that the boy's body had been found floating in the Hamilton harbour. He'd apparently taken his own life.

We were devastated. On our merry road to musical fame and glory, we were blindsided by this terrible tragedy. Overnight, everything that we had thought was so important was put into harsh perspective. Unfortunately, it wouldn't be the only brush with the dark side of celebrity. The road ahead would have all sorts of unexpected twists and turns waiting for us. But no one had warned us about painful ones like this.

SPOON FED

We moved on as best as we could, though I'm sure we all changed a little bit inside after that. We needed something good to happen. We needed guidance and direction, now more than ever. Then, one day, Martha and The Muffins' bass player Carl Finkle gave us a call. He'd decided to leave his band and asked to become our manager. Apparently he'd been thinking about it for quite a while. It couldn't have come at a better time.

Carl had the natural air of a cultured gentleman, someone we believed we could trust with our careers. The typical cigar-chomping, fast-talking wheeler-dealer had never been our idea of a manager. Not only was Carl instantly likable, but he also showed the kind of class we felt we needed to represent us now that things were moving forward. He often wore tweed jackets with elbow patches and I starting thinking of him as our Brian Epstein, the Beatles' manager. With his background in business and his dealings with Virgin Records in London while with the Muffins, Carl was convinced he could help us reach the heights we deserved. Overnight, his home turned into Spoons central.

To showcase the *Stick Figure Neighbourhood* album to the Toronto press, Carl suggested doing something a little different and rented a small theatre downtown. Designed for plays, the building had tiered seating in a semi-circle around the stage - very classical Greek theatre style – and gave us access to all sorts of fancy theatre lighting. We wanted this to be more than just a band playing on any old club stage. If there was ever a time to announce us as an up-and-coming new band, this was it.

Knowing we meant business, Reg and Joe introduced us to a Burlington clothing designer named Judy Cornish. Image, of course, was half the battle. She came up with simple matching grey outfits for the show. Imagine seeing the crew of Star Trek on a black and white television, very industrial and George Orwellian in concept. The only bit of colour I allowed myself was a small rectangular pin I wore on my shirt made out of Lego pieces. My private revolt against conformity.

73

Judy would go on to be our personal designer for the next few years. Such extravagances, like personal hairdressers, were par for the course in the '80s. She, like us, still lived at home and made us clothes out of her basement, pretty much for the experience and very little money. Some years later she would name her clothing line Comrags and have her creations racked in big name department stores. But, somehow, I don't think our cheery grey ensembles made it to the racks.

The theatre show sold well and Carl managed to get the attention of the local press as planned. We performed all the songs we knew, which was pretty well the *Stick Figure Neighbourhood* album in its entirety and a few leftover songs. The show hopefully proved that we could be something more, although it seemed most of the attention was still focused on the fact that we had a cute female bassist. That was inevitable. But, if nothing else, it took us to the next level in Toronto, one above the Edges and Hideaways of the world.

Things were building nicely for us, having broken college radio and finally being properly introduced to Toronto society. Carl decided it was time to take on an assistant. The Spoons empire was growing. That assistant's name was Pat Prevost. With a solid background in indie marketing, she could step in where Carl's expertise ran out. She also brought some street smarts to a bunch of kids raised in the vacuum of Burlington. If Carl was our Brian Epstein, Pat was our Malcolm McLaren. Together, they could take on the world on our behalf from all sides. We were getting a nice, little team together.

Then one night, returning from a show in Brampton, things took a very dark turn. Rob had decided to drive home with me, while Sandy went with Derrick and another friend in their car. The plan was to meet back at the cottage in Burlington to unload our equipment. The first half of the trip was uneventful. Rob and I talked about the gig, thinking the night had gone well. But life can change in the blink of an eye. When we

74

reached the highway and headed westbound onto the Queen Elizabeth Way, our world was turned on its head.

There was a sudden bright flash of light in my rear view mirror, followed by a deafening crash that sounded like an explosion. At least that's how my brain registered it. From there the world went totally and inexplicably still. Time wound right down and seemed to move in super slow motion. Lights streaked by our windows as we spun slowly into a vortex. We were like two time-travelers in a little compartment spiraling through space. That's how surreal and strangely peaceful the moment felt. I heard Rob ask: "Gord, what's happening?"

I'm pretty sure I answered: "I don't know." And I didn't. It was as if we were in a shared dream.

Then everything came to a sudden stop and the real world came surging back. I stared at my hands locked in an iron grip on the steering wheel. My arms would ache for weeks. Rob and I looked at each other, unsure of what had just happened. In the same dream-state voice he asked, "Was that an accident?"

And I still wasn't sure. But we were alive. That was a start. I hadn't yet noticed most of my car's windows were shattered. When I looked out, I saw someone running toward us mouthing incomprehensible words. He seemed distressed and when he reached us, yelled through the window, "Is everyone alright!?"

And then things started to come into focus. All around my car was a disaster zone. Several vehicles had pulled over, including a semi, and the driver had put out flares all along the highway to divert traffic. A small group of late-night travelers had gathered to help. Rob and I got out of the car, looked at it and started to laugh. My little blue Honda was crushed from both ends beyond recognition. We laughed because we realized how lucky we were to be alive and because shock was probably setting in. If we had died in the accident during our surreal little

75

voyage, we'd never have known it. I spotted two cases lying in the dark on the tarmac far ahead of my car. It didn't register that they could possibly be ours. Someone explained that a large sedan had come racing out of nowhere, hit us from behind and sent us spinning across the lanes into other vehicles. They'd sped off down the highway. Some of our equipment had flown out the windows, strewn all over the highway ahead of us. Those two cases I saw earlier were my guitar and Sandy's bass. Bet she wished she'd taken it in her car instead.

The other driver was found a few miles down the road, unconscious and drunk. He'd be slapped with multiple charges. Rob and I suffered no more than stiff necks. We'd been very lucky. My white Fender survived intact, but Sandy's bass didn't fare so well. The flight through the air and impact on hitting the pavement had caused the strings to dig deep grooves into the fret board. We guessed that the wall of equipment packed in the back of my car had probably protected us during rear impact.

It was, I hope, to be my one and only serious accident. Once in a lifetime was enough for anyone. But, considering the surreal and very peaceful moment Rob and I shared during all the chaos, I learned that the mind has a way of cushioning and protecting us. If things got really bad, it would graciously let us off the hook. Sometimes, I was glad to discover, a disconnect from reality can be a very good thing.

Many years later, with a family of my own, I would move into a house right near that highway cutoff where my little misadventure took place. I didn't even realize it until I'd lived there a few years. When we moved again, it was just north of that same location. Maybe I was subconsciously tied to the place where my life could have gone either way. Maybe I'd crashed there for a reason. Maybe, in the Twilight Zone version, I didn't survive that fateful night at all. That might explain a few things.

11 Architects Of The World

We'd made our little mark on the world with *Stick Figure Neighbourhood*, but it was time to think about the next record. I continued to write songs, searching for something that would take us to that elusive, next level. I was becoming less inspired by the Talking Heads of the world and getting more excited about the new British keyboard-based bands. *Stick Figure Neighbourhood* had gotten us respect at college radio, but I always thought we could strive for something more grandiose and sophisticated; more of what Sandy and I had accomplished in our progressive rock days, but new wave elements, like the drum machine, thrown into the mix.

A band on Martha And The Muffin's record label was playing a small club in Hamilton, an ex strip joint turned new music venue; some lads from England called Orchestral Maneuvers In The Dark that I'd heard a little about. That night in 1981 would change everything. I remember finding my spot at the rail on the balcony overlooking the small stage, not quite sure what to expect. An electro-pop group from the States called Our Daughter's Wedding opened the show, all synths and drum machines. Just an appetizer. Then OMD took the stage and I was held captive for the next hour. *Enola Gay, Electricity,* so many great songs that lodged themselves in my brain. Here was a band that embodied all the elements I envisioned for the Spoons and had a sound that was as big and grand as I thought we could achieve. I didn't know it yet, but this would become the model for the next Spoons recordings.

I'm not sure how much I slept that night, but early the next day I wrote *Nova Heart*. I can't remember if I already had Rob's old Elka electric piano or if I grabbed it from him that morning, but it seemed the perfect place for me to begin. No guitar for miles. I can still picture myself sitting on the floor, the morning sun streaming through sheer curtains like a blank slate to compose against, the music just pouring out of me. I'd found the direction for the next Spoons record overnight. When I showed Rob my keyboard idea for *Nova Heart,* he said it was so simple he would never have thought of it. I took that as a compliment. Simple but hooky would be my mantra.

The lyrics for *Nova Heart* were partly inspired by an Arthur C. Clarke science-fiction paperback I'd found in my father's trusty old library at the cottage. It explored a kind of universal oneness we all become part of in the end. I used that concept to lay out all the inventions and creations of our civilized world, the works of all our architects and gentlemen; to show how they, no matter how noble, are just a sideshow to something bigger and better. You can think of it as a love song if you want to, just one that's much larger than life.

Everyone in the band was excited about the new direction. Even my father commented on the improved sounds emanating from our upstairs rehearsal room at the cottage. We'd come a long way since *Kitty Litter Beach.* We quickly recorded a demo of *Nova Heart* and another song called *Symmetry* at Soundpath, a little studio in Oakville, Ontario. The engineer there, Rick Lightheart, would become our go-to guy for all our demos thereafter. There was an urgency about things. We finally had something worth putting our necks on the line for, internationally speaking.

Through Larry Carlton at our distributor Quality Records, the demo would catch the ear of British producer John Punter, who'd made some brilliant records with Roxy Music and Japan. He just happened to be in Canada for a Nazareth tour and Larry slipped our tape into his pocket. As fate would have it, within the year we'd not only be making records with John, but we'd also be touring with Orchestral Maneuvers, the original catalyst for our newfound creativity. Talk about guilt by association! A better script could not have been written.

SPOONFED

It was December 1981 and time to make a proper recording of *Nova Heart*. Andy and Angus at Ready booked us into Sounds Interchange, one of the big three studios in Toronto in the '80s. Compared to homey Grant Avenue, this was a factory for making music. With its multiple studios and endless halls, countless great albums had been produced there through the decades. Their supply of snacks and sweets was definitely up a few notches as well. There were bowls of junk food everywhere; a vital part, it seemed, to enduring late night recording sessions.

The studio sat on a part of Toronto that at one time had been under water, before landfill had artificially added a few kilometers to Toronto's waterfront. I later saw a map of the city showing the original shoreline. It seemed a lot of mystery and strange tales enshrouded what had once been seabed.

According to one bleary-eyed engineer at Sounds Interchange, the studio was said to be haunted, something to do with the building that had sat in the same location previously. Spending a lot of late nights at the studio, he'd become obsessed with the idea. But in all the time we worked there, like the spirits that watched over my friends and I in the old pavilion of my youth, no ghosts ever gave us any trouble.

A major snowstorm had hit western Ontario. Getting to the studio from Burlington was quite the trek, even for those bred on Canadian winters. For others, like John Punter, it was like stepping onto the North Pole. We anxiously awaited his arrival from the airport and, when his taxi pulled up outside Sounds Interchange, he stepped into knee-deep snow wearing nothing but loafers and a flimsy windbreaker.

Rushing out of the storm into the building, we got our first glimpse of our fearless leader accompanied by a barrage of expletives about Canadian weather. We were a little taken aback by the ill-tempered Englishman but then, as he brushed the snow out of his hair, a big smile spread across his face and he embraced us warmly one by one. It was as if he'd returned home after a long ordeal in the arctic. We were happy that he'd survived. After some chitchat and settling in, it was time to see our studio. We hoped everything would be up to John's standards. In our eyes he was the star, having worked with the artists that he had.

Then the in-house engineer Mike Jones, who'd be assisting John, walked in the room and John's eyes popped. Coincidence of coincidences, they'd known each other years ago, having learned their trade together at the old Decca Studios in London, England. Old school chums, so to speak. I imagined cricket bats and old school ties. What a great bit of luck. They'd have no problem working together. They'd also have no problem turning into young boys again and playing old school tricks on us, just like they'd done back in jolly old England.

John Punter at work – producer and master prankster.

SPOONFED

Over the next few weeks we'd somehow manage to make a record, despite shenanigans from our reunited production team. One day Derrick arrived to find his drum shoes glued to the floor beside his kit. Another time we found a young studio intern, who tended to nod off during late night sessions, duct-taped to as chair in the control room, snoring away.

John and his old mate Mike were good, very good. But their masterpiece was yet to come; an intricate gondola system devised out of Styrofoam cups dangling from recording tape. The control room was probably fifteen feet wide, with huge tape machines on either side. They'd spliced one continuous piece of recording tape from one machine, up to the ceiling, over our heads through little hooks, down to the other machine and then back again to the other side. They then attached the foam cups like tiny gondolas, turned on the tape machines and set the whole thing in motion. It was so magnificent and ridiculous at the same time that we couldn't help but applaud. Apparently, this is how they made records in the good old days.

Recording studios are very interesting places. Your senses are naturally heightened, catching you at your most creative and vulnerable as you commit your life to tape. But studios can also be dangerously seductive. Music fills your world all day long, surrounded by the hum and heat of hundreds of thousands of dollars worth of equipment, most of which is still a mystery to me. Back then, when huge two-inch wide reels of tape were still the medium, the very tape itself had a distinct scent that was unmistakable, intoxicating even. It could make you woozy and lead to hallucinations if you weren't careful.

A major hallucination many artists suffer from is the belief that everything they create is brilliant. I've tried hard over the years to be my own quality control board, but nasty things still tend to slip through now and then. When I first started writing music, I wrote the notes out on manuscript paper, like in the old music books in school. I stopped doing that long ago, figuring if it wasn't catchy enough to stick with me without being put to paper, it wasn't worth keeping. Lyrics are another matter. I need to write those out and massage them over time so that in the end they come out as natural and effortless. On rare occasions, they just fall onto the page all by themselves.

Like all writers, when you hit a certain zone, you hold onto it for dear life. I've never been one to follow a daily regime of sitting down and composing songs. I've learned the hard way not to force it. Weeks, months, even years can go by without producing anything worthwhile. I've actually gone so long without creating anything good that I believed my writing days were over. And then one day, out of the blue, the tap suddenly opens and it just pours out. The songs almost write themselves. If I knew what the magic motivator was, I'd bottle it.

Nova Heart, a perfect example, was the turning point we'd all been hoping for. But there was one small problem. Once in the studio, we discovered that John had always assumed *Symmetry* was the single and *Nova Heart* its B-Side. Had the tape fumes clouded his mind? This, as you can imagine, was not what I'd expected. I wanted to trust John's instincts completely but, to me, this was all wrong. I didn't want to start off on the wrong foot and tell him so, but there had to be some kind of mistake. Fortunately, as *Nova Heart* began to take shape in the studio, that idea was turned on its head. The song had a life of its own. Every layer we added did more to solidify the fact *Nova Heart* had something unique and special about it.

Derrick had played real drums on the demo. John, once a drummer himself, suggested we reintroduce the drum machine, something we hadn't done since our home-organ rhythm-inspired *Alphabet Eyes*. I couldn't agree more, especially after my life changing Orchestral Maneuvers night. He programmed the rhythm parts on a Roland 808, relatively new at the time, and had Derrick play along with it. That live drums/drum machine combination would become a major part of our sound.

SPOONFED

The signature loop that John created was one of the very first uses of the handclaps that we all now know so well. The 808 and that key sound would go on to be used by countless other artists and is still employed to great effect in dance music today. John was onto something good.

The original low synth drones that start the song came from Sandy's old Moog bass pedals, another remnant of our progressive Tryst days. Rob built layers on top of that with his Jupiter IV keyboard. There was one problem. For some reason, but only to my ears, the two sounded slightly out of tune and grated on each other to the point where I thought the whole thing was doomed. Like a lunatic, I tried to convince everyone else to hear something that they obviously didn't. I recall a few days where I was so frustrated I decided I wanted nothing to do with the song anymore. It was me against the world.

Luckily my ears eventually got accustomed to it, whatever it was. Magically the sounds sorted themselves out and I moved on. For the life of me, when I listen to it now, I can't hear what I was so obsessed about. A moment of temporary tape-fume induced madness, I have to assume. *Nova Heart* began its life as a twelve-inch vinyl dance EP (extended-play record). Later it would be edited down to its more manageable, commercial radio length. The original clocked in at over six minutes. That was the way of the world back then. Big and bold.

John, our lucky friend, was flying on to Air Studios in Montserrat in the Caribbean to work on another project and talked Ready into letting him finish mixing *Nova Heart* there. You have no idea how hard it was to let go of our recordings. We'd been involved in every step of making *Stick Figure Neighbourhood*. We'd now have to put our complete and utter trust in John. It was a terribly painful thing, staying behind in the snowy Canadian tundra while our producer flew off into the Caribbean sunset. John left for the airport, in the loafers and windbreaker he'd arrived in, and waved good-bye.

12 Towers & Tiaras

It was March of 1982 and time to make a cover for our new record; something to divert our attention while John slaved away at his tropical paradise. Brett Wickens put us in touch with a very creative and avant-garde photographer named Peter Noble. He had a reputation for being innovative with where he photographed his subjects and he wasn't about to let us down. He scouted out locations in Toronto and had the brilliant idea of shooting us in the CN Tower, then the tallest freestanding structure in the world. And he was about to shoot us higher than most anyone else had ever been before.

Somehow he twisted some arms and managed to get permission to take a second elevator from the observation deck all the way to the radio tower at the very top – the part that regular, sensible tourists didn't visit. I'd never been comfortable with heights and the idea of going even higher made me a bit nervous. For anyone who's taken the trip, you know the ride isn't an easy one. Attached to the outside of the tower, the elevators shoot up and leave you suspended in space for what seems like an eternity. A few of us had second thoughts about this photo session half way to the clouds.

But the real agony would be endured by Sandy alone. Reg and Joe had concocted a work of art so groundbreaking that it was sure to become an icon among coiffured creations. One that would cause Sandy to shed tears of pain and endure indescribable suffering. They set to work, starting with a circular wire frame on her head, feverishly braiding and weaving her hair, sewing it in place here and there for stability. The end result was amazing. It was hair architecture. And Sandy's silhouette, shot in one of the circular windows in the tower, would stand out among our photos on the *Nova Heart* cover that you know today. Apart from the glowing orb in the video we were yet to make, that image is probably more synonymous with the name Spoons than anything else. For Sandy, it was the tiara from hell. She had mentioned that it wasn't comfortable all during the shoot, but it wasn't until the car ride home that the full extent of the damage hit her. The moment Sandy began to undo Reg and Joe's handiwork, to cut out the strings and disassemble the wire frame beneath, the excruciating pain set in. The crown of terror, so tightly bound, was now released and the blood in Sandy's head rushed back all at once. She shed tears of agony and cursed the hairdressers all the way home. It would take days until her head made a full recovery. A high price to pay for a bit of new wave infamy.

Sandy and the infamous tiara of terror.

When John Punter's mix of *Nova Heart* reached Canada from Montserrat, all memories of pain and sacrifice melted away with the snow. It was the gift we had hoped for. The end product retained all the elements we'd put into it, a concern when letting a producer take your work away somewhere out of your reach to mix, but it had become so much more.

John Punter had added his indefinable magic, like a coat of polish on a fine piece of furniture, and brought it totally into the realm of the international that I wanted so badly for us. It was the first time I truly believed we had something to put out there alongside the big bands like Duran Duran and Ultravox. We might even make Orchestral Maneuvers proud.

We'd finally achieved what I'd always hoped and believed we could. But it was still unmistakably Spoons. We'd created a little world that belonged to us. When Peter Noble's album sleeve with the CN Tower photos arrived and we slid the twelve-inch vinyl record into it, the package was complete. We were ready to take on the world.

Sandy, Rob and Derrick at late night recording session.

Another British band that I'd heard about was coming to Toronto and, though I didn't know it yet, would give me my next musical enlightenment. That group was Simple Minds. Not only would we be asked to open for them at the Masonic Temple, but they would quickly become my biggest influence of all the bands of the '80s. As we loaded our gear into the hall, Simple Minds were doing their sound check. What I heard knocked me off my feet. I was transformed forever. The guitar playing of Charlie Burchill and sonic landscapes the band created grabbed me more than anything else had in a long time. If Orchestral Maneuvers had started me rolling down a new path, Simple Minds were like a lush, mysterious forest I'd never expected to find.

The change rooms in the Masonic Temple were in the basement. After some exploring, Derrick discovered what had been Masonic meeting chambers some time in the murky past. One large room held what looked like an elaborate throne. The atmosphere was heavy with something indescribably and foreboding. We wondered what kind of rituals and initiations had been carried out within those old walls. The fact that a rock concert was being held upstairs, just above our heads, made the whole thing even more surreal. These were ghosts I didn't want to wake up.

We opened the show with the slow-building *Blow Away*, a song that would eventually close the *Arias & Symphonies* album. But somehow, considering the band we were sharing the stage with, it was a perfect and dramatic way to begin the night. Reg and Joe talked us into wearing white puffy shirts and riding pants with white knee socks and tassels. Very Bohemian and New Romantic. I thought we looked more like Hungarian dancers, but it was the '80s and others like Spandau Ballet were getting away with it, so why not us. I think it also added to the perception that we were a British band; something we'd encounter many times along the way. We'd soon discovered that that wasn't necessarily a bad thing.

Years later, Simple Minds would grant us one of the biggest compliments of our careers. On separate tours in the United States, we'd bump into their tour bus driver in Chicago, parked outside the venue they were performing at. By this time Simple Minds' masterpiece New Gold Dream was constantly playing on our bus as we traveled the States. I think I went through several cassettes. It's still one of my favourite albums of all time. As it turned out, their bus driver told us that the boys from Simple Minds were doing the same with our Arias & Symphonies album, constantly playing it as they traveled America. As far as I was concerned, you couldn't get a better compliment than that.

Mission accomplished, we packed up our puffy shirts and tassels and bid farewell to the old Temple.

Sandy, hair fully recovered from the Nova Heart photo shoot.

SPOONFED

We'd held our own in front of a Simple Minds crowd; an audience very serious about their musical tastes. But much was still being made in the press about our youth and, of course, the fact that we had a girl bass player in the band. We were, it seemed, tailor-made for a whole new generation of kids turned on by the new music that was evolving. We weren't so far from being kids ourselves and our fans could identify with that: our music, our clothes, our hairstyles. In one case, the small scar on my left cheek. A remnant from a childhood accident, I'd always felt a little self conscious about it. One female fan decided to take her admiration to the extreme and cut her cheek, superficially I hoped, to emulate my identifying facial feature. I wasn't quite sure how to react to such an unusual exhibition of fan adoration. To be honest, it made me feel a bit scared.

A few months later we all received letters from the same girl's parents informing us that she had committed suicide. My God, not again! The dark side of celebrity was rearing its ugly head once more. Her parents thanked us for all the joy we'd given their daughter with our music. We'd been a big part of her life and they wanted us to know it. We were devastated and, after the incident with the boy in the Hamilton harbour, we had no reason to question it. What a senseless waste of life. Was there anything we could have done? Were we somehow responsible? Then, incredibly, we would find out that the girl's supposed suicide was just another way of drawing attention to herself, like the self-inflicted scar on her face. She'd written the so-called letters from her parents herself. Apparently, we hadn't been noticing her enough. Well, we did now.

We learned right then and there, regrettably, to never take our fans at face value again, to never take the true meaning of their intentions for granted. I think then too, I first started to close up a little, to set down the first few bricks in the wall that would separate me from the audience. It had started with the boy in the Hamilton harbor. It was now official. A little bit of the innocence of a young band from Burlington had been lost.

FED

Derrick, Sandy, Rob and I, ready to take on the world.

13 The Symphony

When the gang at Ready Records sent out the *Nova Heart* single to radio stations, I'm sure they held their collective breaths. It had never been a regular pop song and what John brought to it took it even further out of the mainstream. Considering what else was being played on the airwaves at the time – Led Zeppelin, Queen, The Who – it was a pretty gutsy move on their part. It was unrealistic to expect much of anything to happen. We were about to get a pleasant surprise.

A remake by Soft Cell of an old Motown song called *Tainted Love* had opened up the ears of mainstream listeners to some new sounds. It was the first song of its kind to make it onto American radio. Drum machines and sparse synthesizers were not the norm then. It seemed that listeners were ready for something different. And we were about to give it to them.

When *Nova Heart* started to climb the charts, I was truly stunned. I'd pretty well resigned myself to the fact that I'd spend my life writing quirky little songs that no one else would understand. When people actually liked our strange and wonderful creation, I was totally blindsided. It was like someone turning the light on and confirming that, just possibly, we might have a future. The first time a car pulled up beside me at a stoplight and I heard our song coming from the radio, I knew anything was possible.

It wasn't long before *Nova Heart* reached the ears of a few major U.S. labels, particularly A&M and Sire Records. The latter was the Talking Heads' label, which of course was a big deal to me, and their president Seymour Stein came to Canada see us a few times. I had no idea then what a major career-maker he was. One of his other little projects was Madonna.

SPOONFED

One night, after watching us at a club in Oakville called Sharkey's, Seymour asked us to join his label. We must have come across as the cockiest bunch of kids on the planet because, on the advice of Ready and our manager Carl, we said we'd think about it. We'd think about it!? It seemed that A&M Records out of Los Angeles was also interested and that we shouldn't make any rash decisions until they came to see us. Oh to be popular! The date was set and in the summer of 1982 a small entourage from A&M flew to Toronto to watch us perform at an all night dance club called the Twilight Zone. Sheer poetry, considering the intimate relationship I'd had with that TV show since I was a kid. Fittingly, the club was in a desolate, old warehouse in an industrial part of the city. The perfect setting for our own private Twilight Zone episode.

We didn't start playing until well after midnight and I remember packing up as the sun started to peek out from behind the skyline. We met the gang from LA briefly before the show and didn't see them again that night. It turned into one of the hottest, sweatiest shows we'd ever done, partly due to the dance crowd packed in to the bursting point and partly due to our own nervous energy. Our manager handed us towels as we came off stage at the end of the night. Then, with a straight face that turned into a smile, said, "They want to meet with you at their hotel in the morning."

So next day, thankfully a very late morning, we headed to the Four Seasons Hotel in Yorkville and anxiously took the elevator up to the A&M suite. I remember feeling very pale and small compared to the tall, well-tanned Californians who greeted us. But the meeting was all smiles and compliments about our show and got to the point very quickly. They wanted to sign us to their US label and would send contracts as soon as possible to get things rolling.

And, if we didn't feel on top of the world enough, it so happened that one of the A&M reps who'd been impressed by our show was David Anderle, the same gentleman who once upon a time saw potential in another little band: The Doors.

Carl hired Peter Steinmetz, the best music lawyer in town and, after some tense haggling back and forth, finalized the deal with A&M. I remember the band sitting in Peter's plush office as he played tug-of-war with the lawyers in LA, making some pretty unprecedented demands. He stood his ground, told them we needed an answer by a certain time and hung up. We were scared he'd just blown the whole deal. I hoped that we still had Seymour Stein's phone number tucked away somewhere. Peter calmly reassured us, "Don't worry, they'll call back".

And they did.

Being under a big American label's wing, we finally had the budget to make an international worthy full-length album. The boys at Ready Records, who still represented us in Canada, were as pleased as we were at the opportunities this afforded us. Their little band from Burlington was finally going to get a proper kick at the big leagues.

We happily brought John Punter back and pretty well replicated the same formula we had for the *Nova Heart* recordings: Sounds Interchange Studios, Mike Jones as engineer, our trusty 808 drum machine, late night pranks. Because we could afford to have the studio block-booked this time, we brought in our equipment and left it set up like we were at home. For all intents and purposes, it was home.

Rob had acquired a few new keyboards, including a move up from the Roland Jupiter IV to the Jupiter VI. We'd also rented a Roland JC-120 amp with its quintessential '80s chorus tone that I'd been pining for so long. The sound of that amp – think of the riff in *Echo Beach* – defined '80s music as much as the 808 drum machine did. The new guitar philosophy was all about textures and that amp could deliver in spades.

93

We'd worked out all the songs during a week of pre-production in Carl Finkle's basement. John had flown in early to get us as prepared as possible before hitting the studio, a luxury we didn't have when making *Nova Heart*. It was a good time to get to know each other better, since our last snowy encounter had been very short-lived. John quickly became part of the family. To this day, I still think of him as an uncle or older brother. I think he'd prefer the latter.

We were seasoned pros by now and got to work making *Arias & Symphonies* with new confidence. We decided early on to begin with the dramatic instrumental *Trade Winds*. It would set the tone for the music to come, complete with a lightning crash at its climax. We agreed that *Nova Heart* would be on the album, having only been released as a single thus far. We would also include two other songs I'd written after my motivational Orchestral Maneuvers concert in Hamilton, *No Electrons* and *Blow Away*, as well as a collection of tunes I'd written or co-written with Sandy and Rob since then.

As I'd discovered with *Nova Heart*, writing on a different instrument such as a keyboard set my imagination in new directions. As a guitar player, my fingers seemed to automatically go to the same places on the neck every time I picked it up. My fingers were well trained and did what they were supposed to do, but they were also very stubborn.

I came up with a solution. Writing on a bass guitar instead, playing only single notes, I avoided the full chords I'd normally play on guitar. My mind filled in everything else until I showed my song ideas to the band. This made writing very free and much quicker. No worries about choosing between a D major or a D minor or a D diminished chord. It was all there in my head, like a phantom limb; details to be fleshed out later. The title track *Arias & Symphonies* came out of this method, a song built on simple bass notes. The song's lyrics were about

94

breaking convention, in this case the preconceived notions of male and female roles. It only made sense that I should break convention in writing it as well.

When the recording sessions began, friends and family would often come to visit us in the studio. We'd usually go out for a big group dinner – the Mr. Greenjeans restaurant on Adelaide Street was a favourite spot – and then return to work, more often than not after a few liquid refreshments. Evenings at the studio became, to put it mildly, very social. One particular night ended up being committed, for all eternity, to tape.

We were working on the song *South American Vacation* and the control room was particularly crowded that night with friends and family. John was getting a bit impatient and, just when I thought he would snap, he yelled out, "Ok, everyone into the vocal booth!"

If we were going to insist on having a party in his studio, he was bloody well going to put us all to work. He passed out what percussion instruments he found lying around – shakers, marimbas, triangles – and pushed us all into the soundproof booth. He started the tape rolling and proceeded to record what you now hear at the beginning of South American Vacation. Think of it as happy hour at the "terrace bar."

The obnoxious tourist intro ended up being toned down in the final mix and doesn't give justice to the mayhem that night, but the attitude was infectious and spilled over into other songs. Derrick yelling "rubber biscuit" at the start of *Girl In Two Pieces* is another gem from that impromptu recording session. I have no idea where it came from. Or what it means. But somehow it made sense at the time. Our friends were happy to be part of our album and, in their own small way, could now call themselves "recording artists." I think John had a different British term for them, one that I'd rather not repeat here.

This was all well before digital recording became the standard, so everything still went onto huge two-inch wide reels of tape. It was preferable not to record over the same tape too often when making an album, though most bands did. After multiple takes of the same song, it was then up to the producer to physically splice the tape with a razor blade and stick the best bits back together again. Here, John showed his skill and steady hand. When it came to splicing, he was a surgeon. On one occasion John had slivers of tape – our precious songs – scattered all over the place. We watched, holding our breaths, afraid to blow away weeks of work. It was madness, really. Today, edits are done as digital cut and paste. Back then, it was real cutting and real pasting. The song *Girl In Two Pieces* soon became known as Song In A Thousand Pieces. I love working with tape, but that part I gladly leave behind in the recording stone age. Luckily John sorted it all out and put all the pieces back together again. But it was a tense time, worthy of reoccurring nightmares. Our future was literally in his hands.

Surrounded by recording gear at Sounds Interchange, I'd been staring at the mixing board in the control room one night and the label on a certain button jumped out at me. It was the one the producer pushed when he wanted to talk to the band in the main studio, kind of an intercom system. Also great for yelling at the band if you were losing your patience, as John often did. The words Talk Back on that button seemed full of meaning; the literal one, but also a metaphor for communication in relationships. Perhaps I'd use it in a song one day.

During long hours of recording we'd come up with alternate titles for our songs. After multiple takes it became necessary, for our own sanity, to have some fun with the titles. We'd even throw them into live performances now and then. The audience never caught on, or at least I don't think they did. *The yet to be recorded Tell No Lies sometimes became Eat Those Fries. Old Emotions often turned into those Moldy*

SPOONFED

Oceans. But my very favorite play on words came from the mind of Rob. I'll always think of *Arias & Symphonies* as Hairy Eyes & Pimple Knees because of him – one of the reasons I'll forever look at him as a slightly silly, younger brother. It also clearly shows how innocent and unabashedly playful we were back then. We were still really just a bunch of kids having fun.

The title track, of course, was anything but silly word play. It was an allegory for how I saw the world growing up as a young adult. From my first song *Concrete City* to being relegated to the Right Side in public school, it put into words the story of a young kid determined to not be pigeonholed. Like the loners in my favourite Twilight Zone episodes and No. 6 in The Prisoner, I longed to be an individual. Arias, moments within an opera where a solo vocalist can shine and stand out, represented that individuality to me. The song begins with the question "Is it hard to be the kind of man you want to be?" Yes, it is. Very hard. But it wasn't impossible.

The lyrics portray young boys and girls and their predetermined roles in society – the symphony – and how they yearn to break free from those roles. That kind of rebellion against the norm became the theme of the whole album. Not your average collection of pop songs. Even songs that seemed to be simple love songs weren't really love songs at all. *Nova Heart* put in their place all the creations of the architects and gentlemen of the world. *One In Ten Words* looked at miscommunication overload. *No More Growing Up* was about holding onto innocence in a jaded society and *Walk The Plank* explored control and dominance of one individual over another.

No Electrons was meant for anyone who thought they didn't fit in, which I think accounted for most of us in the '80s. *Blow Away* was like a big kiss off to the world. If you didn't like us, or understand us, it didn't matter. We had bigger plans. We didn't want to fit in. We finished recording most of the *Arias* album at Sounds Interchange. When John suggested that

97

the vocals and mixes be completed at Air Studios in London, England later that year, and A&M agreed, we realized that things were really getting serious .

But, first, it was time to create a cover that would suit the grand, classical feel of our new album. Peter Noble chose Dundurn Castle in Hamilton as the location for our shoot. Once a very luxurious private residence overlooking the harbour, it was now a museum and tourist destination with daily tours of its many lavish rooms. We wisely dropped by when the old place was closed for business. Just us and the usual ghosts.

Going for a look that would fit the classical theme of the album, we took the over-the-top Bohemian attire from the Masonic Temple show and stripped it of all the excess, silly bits; the tassels and knee socks. The white shirts remained, just not so puffy. Sandy came up with the ballet tutu idea, complete with ballet slippers, I pinned a single red rose to my shirt and the picture was complete. In very anti-rock and roll like fashion, Peter photographed us posing in front of gazebos and rose bushes. The results were so convincingly period in appearance that fans actually picked out the fact that I was wearing a modern wristwatch. Where's the continuity girl when you need her?

For the front cover we considered a few ideas, but when Peter showed up one day with the photo of the Lipizzan stallions entering the Spanish riding school in Vienna, we knew we had our cover. Peter tied the whole concept together by creating the stylized Arias crest, putting the final classic piece into the puzzle. We had an album cover worthy of its title. But one little detail, that didn't strike me until many years later, can be found on the back cover. There, in truly outrageous '80s form, amongst the album credits prominently displayed just below the all-important producer and engineer, is a credit for Reg and Joe. For hair and make-up. Enough said.

14 The Picnic

We knew we had the right people behind us, but when Gary Cormier from the Edge and Carl Finkle managed to get us on the bill for the '82 Police Picnic, they'd outdone themselves. I'm sure the Police having played the Garys' little club when they first took on Canada had something to do with it, as did the fact that the Police were also with A&M Records. They were probably their biggest act at the time. Maybe throwing the new kids in front of sixty-thousand people at the CNE Grandstand was meant to be some kind of test. If there ever was a time to prove ourselves, this was it.

Nova Heart was Top Ten pretty well nationwide by then, making us Canada's new wave ambassadors of a sort. Sharing the stage with the Police, Talking Heads, A Flock Of Seagulls and Joan Jett, we had better not let our countrymen down, let alone Gary and Carl, who'd stuck out their necks for a young band from Burlington. We had one little song that we hoped most people knew and not much else.

We decided to stay with our white wardrobe and soon realized what a good idea that was. Even the people way back in the cheap seats would be able to see us on the giant CNE Grandstand stage. Sandy toughed it out in her ballerina's outfit, complete with tutu and dance shoes, and I wore the now prerequisite single red rose on my white shirt. The new Spoons look was solidified, one that would identify us for a few years.

I recently found that white shirt in a trunk of old stage clothes and it still had the tiny holes were I pinned the rose, and permanent stains around the collar from years of sweat and make-up. There'll be no washing that one.

SPOONFED

Walking onto the stage that summer day for sound check was overwhelming. The biggest show we'd done so far was for hundreds of people at the Masonic Temple. We couldn't even imagine the small city of fans that would soon fill the stadium and grounds before us. We were on first, so we set up our equipment in front of layers of amps and drums of other bands yet to come. Each would be stripped away as the night went on to finally reveal the Police at the end. Consequently, we were pushed right up to the edge of the stage, a stage that felt like a steep cliff you could hang-glide off of.

When we finally hit the stage later that day to play our set, the whole experience was utterly and completely surreal. When asked later to describe the scene from the stage, the best I could come up with was to compare the sea of bobbing heads before us to a field of cabbages going off into the distance. That's the first thought that came to my mind. There were real, human faces near the front, but the rest faded off into fuzzy farmland. Not yet comfortable with huge crowds, that was probably a good way to picture it. Kind of like the old trick of imagining the audience naked. Naked cabbages in this case.

All my life I've felt more like an observer than a participant. It's a rare thing for me to be caught up in something so much that I stop watching it from the outside. I'm chronically self-aware. I'm constantly watching, judging and more often than not, making way more out of the situation than it calls for. Much like the lyrics in my songs, making giant mountains out of tiny molehills. Blame it on years of psychology classes and episodes of strange TV shows if you like. However it started, it's not under my control. Standing on a stage in front of tens of thousands of people was no different.

When I look at anything – a beautiful sky, a city in the rain, crowds on the sidewalk – I don't just see those things. My mind automatically starts filling in the scene with storyline, attaching emotions even to inanimate objects; a lot like the empty stage in my head when I begin to write lyrics. A perfect example is the song *One In Ten Words*. In it, the words spoken between two people become actual solid objects that bounce back and forth, off the walls and furniture, in a self contained little room. My way of seeing the world allows songs to come out of the most unexpected places. Sometimes this is a good thing, but it can also be a source of constant sensory overload.

The curse of the detached observer also carries over onto the live stage. I don't remember ever being lost in the moment so much that I ate up the stardom thing hook, line and sinker. I assume that's what other singers in bands do, unless they're as dumbfounded by the whole thing as I am. Often it seems the audience is more caught up in the show than I am.

I've come to the conclusion that the world is divided into two main parts, those in front of the camera and those behind it. In other words, those who go about their daily lives and consume what the creators of art and pop culture put out there, whether in music or film or television, and those behind the scenes who dream up and make those things a reality, or surreal reality in some cases.

Most people don't see beyond the end product. The performers and creators, in our little carnivalesque back stage world like the Police Picnic, inhabit a parallel universe. Knowing some of the secrets of how this world runs kind of spoils the thrill of the thing, but I love it. I thrive in the shadowy hallways behind the stage, behind the screen. Once in a while we get to pop our heads out through the curtain and perform in front of a live audience. It's what we live for. Then we slip back into the shadows, to write and create some more and feel the anticipation of the next time we hit the stage.

I know without a doubt that we performed at the Police Picnic in 1982, our biggest show to date, in front of almost sixty-thousand people. But I don't exactly remember

101

experiencing it. Any other front man would have jumped headfirst into the abyss. Sometimes literally. Instead, I stood back and watched. I looked at the sea of bobbing heads and said to myself, "Wow, this is weird. Look at us and look at all those people. How is this happening?" Like I was watching TV.

I must have moments of disconnection now and then or, I'm sure, I'd have gone crazy by now. I just don't realize it when it happens. Obviously my mind knows better and sorts it all out. The other thing I've come to suspect, since everyone goes through life thinking they're like no one else, chances are that there are a lot more people like me out there than I'm aware of.

I'm just one of many in a sea of detached observers; or a field of cabbages, depending on how you look at it. Maybe our gazes will meet one day as we pass each other in the street.

The audience starts to gather at the CNE Grandstand.

SPOONFED

As usual, it's the small peripheral things that stick with me. Backstage at the police Picnic was like a trailer park of change rooms and mobile offices, much like you'd find at a big movie production. Big outdoor concerts are a combination of circus freak show and moving city. We spent a lot of time with A Flock Of Seagulls, because they were new and young like us and their lead singer's hair reminded me of something Reg or Joe would have sprouted. I recently found a photo of all of us posing together, as innocent and awkward as a bunch of school kids. I also remember them giving us all buttons that said "Flock Off" on them. All in good new wave fun.

Sting spoke with us for a few moments backstage and seemed to know all about us. We were, after all, label mates now. He was charming and very complementary about our performance.

Then, half way through the show, things got a bit ugly. I didn't see it happen, but a certain faction of the crowd decided to pelt Joan Jett with various fruits and vegetables. I assume this was pre-planned, because average concertgoers don't usually bring produce along. She really didn't deserve the attack. Some people had simply made up their minds that Joan Jett shouldn't be on the same bill as the Police and Talking Heads and that was that. Fortunately we'd been off their vegetable tossing radar. I saw Joan slamming the door to her trailer after racing off the stage mid-set. A few moments later a hand-written card with words similar to those on the Flock Of Seagulls button in big block letters appeared on her window.

Ironically, of all the bands on stage that summer day in '82, she and her simple rock songs are probably the most relevant today. She recently had a movie made about her life with the Runaways with Kristen Stewart playing her character. *I Love Rock 'N Roll* is an anthem for a whole new generation. Young listeners today might well travel back in time to hear her and then throw vegetables at the Police and the Spoons instead.

I was really more excited about seeing the Talking Heads than anyone else on the bill that day. David Byrne's songwriting had always been a big influence, especially for *Stick Figure Neighbourhood*. The first time I saw them on Saturday Night Live had changed my life forever. Gary Cormier knew how much they meant to me and, when he came running to tell me that David was just leaving, I jumped at the opportunity of meeting my idol.

It was getting dark and difficult to see in the mostly unlit backstage area, but we caught David just as he was getting into the back of a car to leave. Gary quickly introduced me and, as I shook his hand, immediately realized I had met someone who actually outdid me in the public awkwardness department. He kept his eyes down, mumbled something incoherent and was gone before I knew it. I had met one of my great inspirers and it was like I hadn't met him at all.

I wish there was some video of our performance, but this was the early '80s, a time when personal movie cameras were limited to bulky super 8 contraptions. It would have been great to see footage of four tiny, white specks bouncing around in front of the massive audience. The strength of *Nova Heart* got us through the show very nicely and, all things considered, I think we pulled off our first mega-concert very well. As the only Canadian act on the bill, the press was right behind us and lavished us with glowing reviews.

I would hear later that, when the Police were asked in a radio interview which Canadian bands they liked, they singled us out. Maybe it was the only name they could come up with on the spur of the moment. Maybe they really meant it. In any case, Sting would continue to pop up here and there in our careers and be instrumental in small ways with our successes. In fact, we'd meet him again, very soon, this time in New York City. But not before a detour to his homeland London, England.

15 Going Underground

A few days after the Police Picnic, Sandy and I, accompanied by Carl and Pat, flew to London to complete the Arias album. Having recorded the bulk of it in Toronto, John suggested we complete the vocals and mixes in England. With A&M support, Ready Records had no reason to say no and we jumped at the chance. You can imagine how international this made us feel. Not only were we going to England, the land of most of our musical influences, we were going to record at George Martin's Air Studios, as in George Martin, producer of the Beatles. We were headed to a place were musical history had been made, hopefully to create some history of our own.

I had even more reasons to be excited about flying to England. From The Prisoner to The Avengers to Monty Python, I had a thousand reasons. The British shows that I watched had that darker element I was drawn to and were infinitely more inventive than what most American television had to offer. It connected with me to the core and, unexplainably, made me feel homesick for a country I'd never been to.

John, the old dear, picked us up at Heathrow Airport and the usual driving on the wrong side of the road jokes started pretty well right away. As we hit the outskirts of London, I felt an electric tingle of anticipation, knowing I'd soon be coming home to a place that, until then, I'd only visited in my imagination.

John had the car radio on and we drove into London with Dexy's Midnight Runners' *Come On Eileen* as our soundtrack. I had my face pressed to the window like a little kid, taking it all in. Every street corner, every old church, every pub reminded me of something I'd seen in a movie. If Emma Peel had pulled up beside us in her little powder blue Lotus Elan, it couldn't have gotten any better than that.

We made a quick stop at the London A&M office and picked up our keys for our accommodations in Putney Bridge. *In west London on the Thames, I recently learned that Putney Bridge was home at the time for one of our future keyboard players, Steven Sweeney. He was probably there as Sandy and I rolled into town to put the finishing touches on the Arias album. They say it's a small world, but music makes it infinitely smaller still.*

Our temporary home was in a u-shaped apartment complex with a central garden accessed by a small iron gate. Not quite Baker Street, but it had its charms. The apartment, or flat as the English call it, was rented out by A&M for visiting bands. I was immediately hit by the smell of cooking gas that, as I would find out later, is part of everyday life in Europe. I was also struck by the fact that a lot of dodgy activities had probably transpired within those walls, after years and years of harbouring rock bands and their little excesses. By imagining they were groups we'd grown up listening to, we were able to adjust to the edgy vibe of our rough new digs. We were, after all, stepping into a part of living history.

Our hairdressers Reg and Joe had put us on a mission to find a shop that carried clothes as worn by Boy George and the Culture Club. Very colourful work by a local designer with a distinct urban/tribal edge, we needed to track some down and bring it back home across the Atlantic. We were vaguely aware of Boy George, about as much as anyone else was, due to his already infamous androgynous persona. But that was the extent of it. We had no idea that the following year, by a strange twist of fate, we'd be doing Culture Club's first North American tour. We'd be getting close enough, in fact, to nab one of those loud frocks right off George's back.

SPOONFED

The first place we hit on our shirt quest was, naturally, Kings Road. We'd hailed down our first London cab to get around town and quickly learned that this was a prerequisite to the London experience. Dropped off on Kings Road, we came face to face with our first bona fide punkers. Compared to our tamer Canadian counterparts back home, these were the real deal. Kings Road, after all, was the place where punkers were first born and bred.

The neighbourhood oozed style and rebellion and we soaked it all in as we spent the afternoon walking its well trodden sidewalks. We didn't find the clothes Reg and Joe wanted but, during our search, had our eyes opened wide to all sorts of possible stage styles for the Spoons. It was time to drop the plain white uniforms and go for something more adventurous. Our friend Judie Cornish would take her cue from what we saw here and go on to design her own take on urban tribal. As I've found in every great city we've recorded in, a bit rubs off on you; musically, emotionally, sometimes even, as trivial as it sounds, its clothing and hair styles.

The main reason Sandy and I were in London, of course, was not to shop, but to finish our album. A half-hour Tube ride in the city's Underground took us from Putney Bridge to Oxford Circus downtown and we were immediately hit by the enormous crowds of people. Kings Road was one thing, but central London was a madhouse. Never in my life had I seen so many pedestrians clamouring for space on the sidewalks. I felt like we were constantly walking against the flow and soon wondered if pedestrian etiquette in London had it's own unique logic, like driving on the left side of the street.

Finally making it to the front doors of Air Studios was like reaching an oasis. Stepping inside from the mad outside world, we entered the cool, stone interior of one of the great all-time edifices built to create music. It looked older and statelier than anything from the recording age and had probably been a bank

107

or government building of some kind in another era. In any case, this would be our home for the next few weeks.

John Punter met us, signed us in at the reception desk and took us up the elevator. We were in his house now. After a short tour, he showed us the studio that would be our workspace. The tiny room was just big enough for a huge Neve mixing board and a small vocal booth. Oh, but the history in those walls!

Countless great recordings had been made there throughout the decades. In fact, the big, old Sennheiser vocal microphone in the vocal booth was so caked with grime from years of singers and their historic performances that it was not allowed to be cleaned. I've heard that the English have the same strange habit with their teapots. There was pent-up magic in that smelly old thing and we weren't to question it.

The infamous microphone at George Martin's Air Studios.

SPOONFED

We set to work laying down our vocal tracks but, being at Air Studios in London, England, there were bound to be distractions. George Martin dropping by to say hello was, to put it mildly, extremely surreal. He was John Punter's boss on one level and obviously, as the Beatles' producer, someone bigger than life on another. He'd, I'm sure, seen a thousand young bands like us come and go through his hallowed halls. We were humbled and honoured to be one of them.

After other bands had left for the day, we'd often inspect their equipment and recording set-ups. I have a vivid picture in my mind of The Pretenders' gear lying around one of the larger studios, like so many abandoned possessions at the end of the world. Everything powered up and running, just as it was left, untouched until work resumed the next day. When in a creative zone, the flow of creativity cannot be broken at any cost.

Big Country was set up in the largest room at Air Studios, more of a soundstage really, perfect for live off-the-floor recordings. Our eyes bulged when John informed us that this was the room George Martin used for all the big Beatles orchestral sessions. *Sgt. Pepper* worthy productions. Paul McCartney also laid down *Live And Let Die* there. Oh, to have a time machine.

We really got sidetracked when one of John's other bands came by the studio one afternoon. When several members of Japan walked into the room, we were more than a little star struck. Here was one of the reasons we were working with John Punter in the first place. When lead singer David Sylvian came in, I literally couldn't find words to say. He, David Byrne and I could have had one hell of a conversation.

For some reason Sandy and I hit it off with Japan's bass player Mick Karn and his Californian girl friend. She invited us to go shopping on Carnaby Street one day. Kind of odd, an LA girl showing us around London. She warned us not to expect the legendary street it had been in its swinging '60s heyday. Sadly, she was right, and we hurried through its endless rows of leather shops and stalls offering bargains of everything imaginable. And still no luck with the Boy George shirt. The little quest Reg and Joe had set us on was becoming tiresome.

Once the vocal tracks were complete, John began the mixes. There was a games room at Air Studios where Sandy and I often spent time off playing pool. I got my first snooker lesson from Mick's girlfriend there. It was time to put down our cues and head back to see what John was up to late one night when we bumped into what I would, politely, call a very colourful personality in the hallway. Displaced from another, more flamboyant time, dressed like she just left a party that finished decades ago; a musical Norma Desmond. She surprisingly showed a lot of interest in what we were doing at Air Studios. This was rather ironic, considering that she was probably the most interesting person there. Her name was Angie. Angie, as in the Rolling Stones song, who'd hung out with Jagger and wed Bowie. Probably held court with Andy Warhol. She seemed a little sad and lonely and it touched me in a strange way, meeting her wandering the halls by herself that night. In a way, she was like Carnaby Street. A little sad and grey, past the prime of her life, but her head filled with enough stories and experiences to fill several lifetimes.

Daytimes, when we were not working in the studio, were filled up with the required sightseeing of a London visit: Buckingham Palace, Hyde Park, Piccadilly Circus and the Tower Of London, where we gave up waiting in the endless queue and had a monkey thrown on us by a street vendor peddling unwanted candid photographs. I wonder if the Queen was aware of such goings-on? I have wonderful, surreal memories of London at night, half asleep in the back of an old cab, watching the city lights streak by as we headed back to our flat. *Save A Prayer* by Duran Duran, which seemed to be getting a lot of nighttime play, soon became my theme song for the city. Like every great place, London had a personality that at first seemed foreign, then slowly crept up on me, took me in and finally left its indelible mark on me. Sometimes it's as hard to leave a great city, as it is to leave a lover. A piece of it stays with you forever. And a piece of you stays behind.

Cities also have a way of manifesting themselves in your work. Every place we recorded left it's own personality on our songs. Although we started the *Arias & Symphonies* album in Toronto, there is something undeniably London about it. It's complexity and layers draw you in. If you're lucky you might get lost for a while, like a walk through foggy streets that takes you further and further from where you thought you'd be. Somehow you make it home again as the fog clears and the morning light creeps back into the sky. There's a beginning and an end, and hopefully a worthwhile journey somewhere in-between.

And so, as all good things do, two weeks in London went by much too quickly. Once again we would leave John to finish the mixes, but we'd become unquestioningly trusting in him since *Nova Heart*. Mick Karn's girlfriend gave us her number in Los Angeles, if we should ever be in the neighbourhood, which we would be sooner than we knew. And, as we packed up our things in our little room at Air Studios, John informed us that, sadly, we'd done the last recording on that ancient, iconic Neve mixing board. It would now be replaced by a shiny, new one. I took several buttons off the volume sliders as mementos of our time recording in London. I recently found one in a drawer in my music room at home. I imagined how many times that little button had slid up and down throughout the decades, bringing up Brian Ferry's vocal or Mick Karn's bass line or, perhaps, the performance of a Beatle.

So, our luggage smelling of cooking gas and our hearts a little heavy, we bid farewell to London and to our friend John once more and made our way back to Canada.

16 The Orb

At the end of 1982, the *Arias & Symphonies* album complete, we were contacted by CityTV to tape a live performance at the Concert Hall in Toronto. Our first time in front of television cameras, we didn't know what to expect. The *Arias* album hadn't been released yet, but on the strength of *Nova Heart* and the residual hype of the Police Picnic, we filled the hall to capacity. We'd play the whole album, plus a few unrecorded songs like *Neo Natal* and the instrumental *Young English Gentleman*, written with John Punter and our London trip in mind. We kept the all white look, including Sandy's tutu, which now concealed a weightlifter's belt to support the weight of her bass guitar. We had to, after all, stay in character with the image we'd created for the album about to hit the airwaves.

We'd also perfected the use of movie projections by then. We hung a giant white triangular screen between Rob and Derrick and, for the opening song *Trade Winds*, ran a time-lapse film of clouds flying by at high speed I'd shot on my balcony using an old super 8 camera. When smoke machines filled the stage with their own billowing clouds and we emerged though the mist dressed all in white, it was as if we were walking out of the movie itself.

The show also marked the first on-camera appearance of the orb that would become a key part of the *Nova Heart* video. Its actual origins go back even further. One of our favorite venues, Ballinger's in Cambridge, Ontario, always had potential for something extravagant happening. It was so vast, the ceilings so high, that once trapeze artists performed over the audience as we played. Yes, as in circus daredevils. We'd recently met two radio personalities from CFNY named Live Earl Jive and Beverly Hills, a husband and wife team who set the template for many other on-air duos that would follow.

SPOONFED

We soon became good friends and, one night at Ballinger's, they gave us a special and very memorable surprise. Earl, with his usual showmanship, introduced us with a flourish on his trumpet and then joined Beverly on the balcony at the back of the hall to watch the show. When it came to *Nova Heart*, something magical and unexpected happened. Bev and Earl, unbeknownst to us, had inflated very large white balloons and set them out to float slowly over the audience. It was such a simple thing, but watching the crowd gently tap the balloons back and forth over their heads created a beautiful image that stays vividly with me to this day. We never forgot that night and tried to recreate the magic of that moment for the CityTV broadcast. Its smaller cousin, the glowing orb, would of course appear prominently in the *Nova Heart* video. That image has pretty well become synonymous with the name Spoons. Almost fifteen years later it would reappear in the video for *Sooner Or Later*, directed by Andrew MacNaughtan, back in its much bigger, village-guarding Prisoner form. I'm curious to see where and when it might pop up again. Like our persistent mannequin, I'm sure it will.

Sandy in a tutu, performing at the Concert Hall.

113

The Concert Hall performance would end up on a live concert DVD as part of a series of shows from that era. I wouldn't find out until thirty years later that it was also instrumental in Moses Znaimer, the mastermind behind CityTV, acquiring the license for an all music video channel, something he would call MuchMusic. Our television broadcast tested the waters and helped convince the TV higher-ups that there was a market and demographic eager to consume this sort of entertainment. It may also explain why *Nova Heart* would be one of the videos aired on the very first broadcast of the new and eventually groundbreaking show. A whole new era was launched with the words, "Welcome to Much Music. Coming up we have brand new videos by Duran Duran, Howard Jones and the Spoons."

When we made the video for *Nova Heart*, we were justcatching the wave of a new medium that was about to explode. The timing couldn't have been better. Ready called in Champagne Productions and director Rob Quartly, who pretty well had the whole concept laid out when we arrived for the shoot. Our white outfits fit in perfectly with the dreamy, New Romantic images he envisioned. And, whether he'd seen our Ballinger or CityTV performances or not, the orb quickly became the visual anchor that tied it all together. This time, it glowed and throbbed to the beat.

The orb was just a funky table lamp Rob found at a modern furniture store, with the power cord concealed down Sandy's sleeve. Someone backstage simply played with the dimmer to make it pulse. And, in case you wondered how we got the frets on my guitar and keyboard on Rob's synthesizer to light up, the answer might be a bit disappointing: bits of reflector tape. Being creative with what little you had to work with was part of making videos back then. We were all feeling our way through uncharted territory. Seeing it now, my favourite parts in the *Nova Heart* video are the dream sequences: me looking through a window into a secret garden,

Sandy on a swing in slow motion in the background. Very surreal and extremely un-rock and roll. I'm sure we confused a few MuchMusic viewers with that image. But it fit perfectly with the feel of the song and album that was about to be released. Because it was such a new medium, and because music television was glad to get whatever they could find to fill programming, the video for *Nova Heart* got plenty of airplay. In the end, it was a good thing that we hadn't tried to be like everyone else. Overnight, people across the country knew exactly who the Spoons were.

The timing coincided perfectly with the launch of the U-Know Awards. Later called the CASBYs, they were CFNY's answer to the overly commercial Juno Awards and voted on by actual listeners. Held at the posh Royal York Hotel in Toronto, we arrived never expecting to leave with any statues in hands. We were, I'm sure, the youngest bunch in the room and sat uncomfortably at our table, surrounded by our peers and music elders. Many probably wondered why these kids, dressed like they'd walked out of a high school prom, were even there.

Suddenly, inexplicably, our band name was announced and, like in a dream, we were ushered up onto the stage in front of the same crowd who'd moments before thought we'd taken the wrong door to the wrong party. Now they took notice. We'd received the Best New Band Of The Year award. We said a few awkward, unrehearsed words and were just as quickly pulled off the stage again and taken to an adjoining room for a quick photo shoot and interviews. Flash bulbs flashed. Questions flew. Our old friend David Marsden watched on proudly. How did it feel being the new darlings of indie radio?

Is that what we were? Well, so far it felt pretty good. We returned home to Burlington that night with a shiny and very heavy U-Know Award, one to share between all of us. I'm not sure how much we admitted it to ourselves, but that chunk of wood and steel meant more to us than anyone could imagine.

17 Go West Young Band

And so, with the release of the *Arias* album and a bona fide hit single under our belts, we set out to tour Canada once again. This time there was buzz about this strange little indie band from Burlington that had cracked the mainstream market. And that, strange as it sounds now, is what we were back then; indie and alternative. A bunch of youngsters making very un-mainstream music that had somehow broken through.

Heading west and finishing the Canadian part of our tour in Vancouver, we crossed the border to embark on our first venture into America. It was really more a reason to finally get us to Los Angeles and meet our new record company family. Bob Garcia of A&M Records, a very jovial rep from artist relations, met us stateside and guided us on our first baby steps into the great new unknown. First stop Seattle, Washington, the very same city that would be the demise, a decade later, of all things new wave. But that was still a lifetime away.

A&M really knew how to impress and had arranged a lush meet and greet dinner for us at a restaurant overlooking Seattle; one of those first impressions of a city that sticks with you like a shadowy dream. Candlelight glinting off wine glasses, strange faces coming in and out of focus, the lights of Seattle spinning all around us. Food and drink make it all a little blurry. Several of the A&M team had flown in to meet us and I remember a lot of encouraging talk and high hopes for this young, new band from Canada. The tour would start the next day. Things would then take a slightly less cheerful turn.

SPOONFED

We were booked into a small, but renowned showcase room in downtown Seattle called Astor Park. We set up our gear, did sound check and left for our hotels until show time, as we always did. But when we returned, ready and eager to win over our first American crowd, we soon discovered that our initiation into the US wasn't going to be as welcoming as our happy meet and greet from the night before. There was some prerequisite band hazing to go through first.

The opening band had set up in front of us and were just finishing their set when we arrived. A lot of our equipment was moved, which can happen in tight quarters. But these guys had done it with a passion. Things were a mess and needed sorting out before we could even think about going on. Every cord that could be unplugged was unplugged. When Rob turned on his keyboards, one didn't work at all. After some troubleshooting, we found someone had removed the main fuse from the back. Sabotage of the highest and most cruel order. The opening band really had it in for us. They were as methodical as they were ruthless.

We couldn't delay going on any longer and, new fuse in place, took to the stage. We looked out at the crowd and wondered how many of them were in on the little joke. I hadn't checked my amp, distracted by all the fuse hunting. This would be a major mistake. I plugged in my guitar, turned the main power switch on and all hell broke loose. Feedback squealed and probably burst a few eardrums in the audience. Someone had turned everything on my amp up full blast. I scrambled to get it under control. But, judging by some of the faces in the crowd, they would have happily helped me strangle whoever was responsible. Welcome to America.

The rest of our first US tour down the west coast, thankfully, went by sabotage free. When we finally rolled into Los Angeles a week later and stepped out of our van outside the A&M Records offices on La Brea Avenue, any traces of tour misgivings were quickly dispelled by California sunshine and the feeling that we'd finally "arrived." The Spoons were in LA, the land of impossible dreams, both real and surreal. The picture we presented, tumbling like pasty white Canadian vampires out of our van, wasn't quite as impressive.

A woman, another rep from artist relations, had come out to greet us, took one look and whispered something to Bob Garcia. Discretely, she suggested that she'd better arrange an emergency shopping-trip with the label stylist. These Burlington kids needed a serious LA makeover. I gather that traveling in a cramped van for a week didn't mean anything to her. But her mind was made up. We weren't beautiful enough to be introduced into California society quite yet.

I'd been looking forward to seeing the A&M offices. Bob had told us ahead of time that they were housed in the old Charlie Chaplin film studios. Being the classic movie buff that I was, the scenario couldn't have been better. To enter the grounds, we passed through a large gateway with a security booth and arch over it, just like in old black and white movies. Inside was a large complex of offices and old sound stages left over from the golden era of film. I half expected to see stagehands rolling backdrops of clouds along or a squadron of Roman centurions march by. Bob pointed out one row of rooms that had been Mr. Chaplin's personal offices. I was in heaven. My two passions, music and film merged into one.

I'd also been looking forward to our motel on Santa Monica Boulevard that Bob had bragged was full of rock and roll pedigree. Even the name Tropicana evoked images of style and old Hollywood glamour. Everyone had stayed and partied there; Led Zeppelin, David Bowie, the list went on.

Now, drunks and drug addicts were apparently the new tenants. The place was a run-down disaster. The swimming pool that Marilyn Monroe probably swam laps in at one time was now a green swamp with ducks waddling in it. This, I concluded, had to be some sort of test to see how hearty and tour worthy we were. If we could stomach this, we could handle anything the road could throw our way.

We'd kept Mick Karn's girlfriend's phone number and decided to give her a call. By chance she was in town, not off with Mick on the road, and she offered to pick us up and show us around town. Just like she had in London. Embarrassed, we told her were we were staying. She chuckled and said she knew the area well and wanted to show us something nearby before we went off to dinner. This sounded promising.

We met outside the motel as the sun set and our tour guide informed us that we'd have to walk a few blocks to get to our destination. We were not, to put it politely, in the high rent district of Santa Monica Boulevard and soon were outnumbered by prostitutes, male and female, young and old, at every turn. One boy, probably in his teens, followed us and made several persistent offers to Sandy and I as a package deal. Wherever we were headed, it had better be worth it.

When we finally reached our destination, our jaws dropped. Mick's girlfriend had taken us to the Pleasure Chest, a sex shop. But not any old sex shop, no. This one was the size of a grocery store, complete with shopping carts and turnstiles. She laughed at our innocence and convinced us to go inside. It was massive, with endless aisles of machinery and contraptions. There were even cubicles to try out intended purchases. One devise, the size and shape of a canister vacuum cleaner, with attachments, still boggles my mind. Sparkly lubricant gels could be bought in small jars or five-gallon drums. Shopping in bulk. This was the COSCO of adult stores.

We'd seen enough and, as we left, the elderly man in bondage gear at the checkout smiled and said, "Come again." Very clever.

After such an adventure, we had worked up an unusual appetite. Mick's girlfriend said she knew just the spot to make up for her little joke, a restaurant from which the view of LA at night was incomparable. Taking a long, winding road up through the hills in her little red sports car, we emerged in front of a Chinese palace. It was by far the most spectacular Chinese restaurant I'd ever seen. Pillars and dragons and, she was right, an incredible view of the city lights below. Santa Monica Boulevard and its little diversions were soon forgotten.

After a long and memorable dinner, we wound our way back down the mountain to firmer ground. We were dropped off in front of our motel and said our goodbyes. Tired after our big meal, we went straight to bed. It had been an interesting night, to be sure. But it was about to get even more interesting.

Lying in bed, with the curtains partially open, we observed a small group of men walk by our room. We heard the door to the room right next to us being unlocked and the men enter. And then it began. For the next hour we had to endure loud moans of pleasure, which gradually built into horrible screams of agony. After what we had seen on Santa Monica Boulevard, our minds reeled with the possibilities. Had they bought that mysterious vacuum cleaner device and were they trying it out on their poor victim? It didn't sound like it was going very well.

If it wasn't for the lulls and quieter moments filled with contented moans, we might have dialed 911. Thankfully they were on some kind of schedule and decided to move the show elsewhere. Suddenly we heard the door next to ours open and watched the men walk past our window. Like nothing had happened. Maybe they'd worked up an appetite and were going for Chinese food? Anything, it seemed, was possible in LA.

Next day the label stylist took us, as promised, on a shopping spree along Melrose Avenue and some of LA's other trendy strips. A&M Records was footing the bill, so we were quite happy to play along. A prize find for me was a vintage tuxedo jacket, circa Rat Pack era, glossy blue with black lapels. Had it made it to the Oscars in decades long ago? Perhaps some old Hollywood cocktail party way up in Hills? I could only hope. It sure smelled musky enough, like old film stars.

By night, dressed appropriately thanks to our stylist's efforts, we were escorted around town and made short appearances in various dance clubs. We really hadn't made a splash in Los Angeles yet, but we signed a few albums and shook a few hands never the less. You never knew who might be famous or not in this town.

A&M had booked us at the Lingerie Club on Sunset Boulevard for our LA premiere. A big deal was being made about the fact that scenes for the Eddie Murphy/Nick Nolte movie 48 Hours had been shot there.

All I remember was a ridiculously high stage and a lot of pink neon lighting. We were more nervous than usual that night, performing in LA for the first time, in front of a crowd that had no idea who we were. If there was a time to impress the A&M gang, this was it.

We got through the night unscathed, despite a very vocal Sandy admirer, packed up our gear and trendy new wardrobe and headed home the next day. A show that had seemed so important was over in the blink of an eye.

Red Light from *Stick Figure Neighbourhood* received honourable mention in Billboard Magazine in a review from that night. America, surprise surprise, had eclectic tastes. But we were in progressive California, after all. The rest of America, to be sure, was going to be a bigger challenge. It was time to strategize our next plan of attack.

18 The Boys Club

When we returned home, Ready Records informed us that we'd been nominated for Best New Band in that year's Juno Awards. Maybe Canada had missed us being in America and feared we'd defect. The Junos were perhaps more prestigious, but infinitely less credible an honour than the U-Knows in our eyes, but we were happy that we'd finally been invited to the party. Wearing space age Judy Cornish creations, we performed *Nova Heart* live on television for the show, but ultimately lost to The Payolas in the new band category.

Some people thought we needed consoling, saying we'd just missed taking the "kiss-of-death" trophy, since many past recipients had supposedly gone on to disintegrate soon after receiving the award. But I, for the most part, was comfortable being the underdog. We were, I suspected, always going to stay just shy of the really big leagues. We'd made too much of an effort writing songs that were different than anything else on the radio. If we weren't going to play along with everyone else in the mainstream, it was our own fault. The title of our song *Unexpected Guest At A Cancelled Party* pretty well summed up how I felt then; like the uninvited guest.

That summer, a particularly hot and dry one, we were booked to play a big outdoor festival on a dusty farmer's field near Hamilton. The bill was very eclectic, from Teenage Head and David Wilcox to Mountain and The Joe Perry Project, heavy on rock and blues. For some odd reason the organizers decided to have us and Rough Trade close the show. Kind of like putting Kraftwerk on after Jimi Hendrix at Woodstock. The audience was decidedly of the we-want-to-party rocker variety. We were lucky to make it out alive.

The crowd was polite, considering, but it was the one time I ever remember a piece of fruit landing on stage. I think we held things together pretty well until the tape deck we used to play drum-loops suddenly went berserk during *Nova Heart* and sped up into chipmunk territory. At that point, some Aerosmith fan understandably lost it and let fly. Thankfully, he missed, but only by inches. We got off easy compared to what Joan Jett had endured.

Backstage before our set, feeling like outsiders, we'd stayed safely to ourselves. The scent of fruit already hung ominously in the air. Fortunately Jeanne Becker and J.D. Roberts from the pre-MuchMusic TV show The New Music interviewed us before, not after, the concert. Theirs was the relevant entertainment program to be on back then and we were glad to get the national coverage. Mercifully, the camera crew packed up and left well before the lights went down and things turned ugly. It would have made for some very compelling footage.

J.D. would interview us again from time to time over the coming years and always helped us when he could. It was good having friends in high places. He would keep in touch with Sandy when he eventually moved south of the border, used his full name and became lead anchor on the NBC news. But John Roberts would always be J.D. to us.

Fortunately, we'd leave the dusty farm fields of the world behind and got back on track. There were a few years where everything moved forward so quickly we hardly had time to think. Some badly thought-out bookings were inevitable. It must have required some planning and effort on our part, but it seemed like most things just fell into place all by themselves.

When A&M asked us to join Culture Club on their first American tour it was beyond uncanny. When the cosmos hooked us up with Orchestral Maneuvers, I had at least seen them perform live. With Boy George, apparently, we just had to look for his shirts on Kings Road and our stars were made to align. Maybe, if we concentrated hard enough, anything we wanted was possible.

It was a chilly morning in early 1983 when we all congregated in LaSalle Park to load ourselves and a few belongings onto our first official tour bus. The old pavilion still stood then, before it would burn to the ground years later. I wonder if the old ghosts inside were frantically waving goodbye to us for the last time. We hardly gave them a second thought. A brand new horizon awaited.

The gleaming black and silver bus arrived from California the night before. The driver had parked and slept in front of the infamous cottage where we rehearsed. We'd all gone by to sneak a look but hadn't dared wake him. Bee-lining it from Los Angeles to Burlington wasn't your average pick-up. He now greeted his passengers with the gruff demeanor you'd expect from a road-weary bus driver running on fumes. He'd just finished carting the all girl Go-Gos around America, so I'm sure he wasn't very impressed by his new Canadian passengers.

Our parents and a few friends had gathered to say goodbye that early morning. They might as well have been seeing us off to summer camp. Things were still slightly Partridge Family then, innocent and pure as the driven snow. My mother, bless her heart, even brought along a care package in case our bus broke down in the middle of a snowstorm somewhere, so we didn't have to resort to cannibalism. Mothers are thoughtful that way. The band would shamelessly devour the emergency supplies within days.

We took a few last photos to commemorate the occasion. The bus driver already had the engine running, giving us impatient glances from his seat. It was time to get going. All of a sudden a car came racing up the road, pulled quickly into the

LaSalle Park parking lot and skidded to a stop on the gravel. The driver's door flew open and out jumped none other than David Marsden. He'd made it just in time to bid farewell to his kids from Burlington that early morning. He was, it appeared, as proud of us as our own parents were. Hugs and kisses ensued, final goodbyes were made and we were finally off.

Looking back on that day, what lay before us might as well have been a long distance sea voyage. We had a new ship, a captain to guide it and miles of uncharted territory awaiting us. This was no trifle holiday. We were going out to conquer new worlds.

About to board the tour bus for America.

When the bus started rolling and our eyes adjusted to the dim light, we realized we were in one seriously well-appointed penthouse on wheels. Laid out with black velvet couches, brass detailing and rows of tiny lights running along the floors, it felt more like a nightclub than a mode of transportation. There was a large front lounge with a television, wet bar and kitchen where we'd end up spending most of our time together. The center area contained bunks for sleeping, a communal washroom with shower and one private bedroom with a proper bed and separate bathroom. We would take turns claiming that luxury. The back of the bus held another smaller lounge with another TV. This would eventually become crew central and that place down the hall to go to if you were in the mood for a little game of poker or a blue movie.

Our road crew had left earlier in a truck carrying all our musical equipment and, once over the US border, would take turns joining us on the bus. Once they'd seen the inside of our posh transportation, there was no stopping them. We'd pretty well had the same stage crew for years. Scott Pollard was our soundman and road manager, Tom Allison was stage tech and handled the monitors and Dino Gazzola ran the lights. They worked for us, but soon became part of the family. We were, after all, going out on this big adventure into the great unknown together. The further we got from home, the more it felt like the seven of us against the world. There was strength in numbers.

I still remember the first day of our first big tour, sitting at the bus window, looking out at the world going by.

The weather was so drab that morning that all the cities we passed through were in black and white. I imagined that the colour would gradually seep back into things the further south we went. Our first show was on Rhode Island, so we wouldn't be south enough for truly vivid colours for a while. We'd have to be patient as we slowly inched toward it.

SPOONFED

We met the boys from Culture Club for the first time at what seemed like a huge airplane hanger of a venue. It might have been an arena, but I'm not a hundred per cent sure. The ends of the building faded off into darkness. There were small crowds of people everywhere. It wasn't exactly clear who was who, so Sandy and I stayed on the sidelines watching, to get the lay of the land, so to speak. It was the first day of a tour. The lines were still a little foggy.

Our crew got to work unloading our equipment and jumped right in. Road crews are like the front lines. They're the first to make contact. If our and their crew clicked, we were off and running. In the case of Culture Club, it turned out that they were slightly under-equipped and asked to use some of our drums. They also hired our stage tech Tom to help out. Before we knew it, we were all standing on stage together sorting out the first gig wrinkles. The ice was broken.

I remember our first performance being dark and chilly, not as in audience reception, but because the giant venue was too big to light and heat properly. Apart from possibly *Nova Heart*, the crowd would have been oblivious to our song list, but that wouldn't stop them from liking us. Never, as I look back on that whole tour, did we feel unappreciated.

We would soon discover that American audiences assumed we were also from Britain, having come over with Culture Club. Our music not only sounded that way, but people often mistook the inflection in my singing voice as an English accent.

One newspaper review confused Birmingham, as in Duran Duran's hometown, with Burlington. Another interviewer, seeing my last name, asked if I'd been the singer for Depeche Mode. Of course I was. I wasn't going to argue with him. Being British by association had its perks. Strange that no one noticed my speaking voice didn't sound British in the least.

127

We did a handful of gigs on the east coast, but the one that really mattered, of course, would be our first show in New York City. We were booked to perform at the Palladium, a big old theatre that would eventually be renovated and made into a dance club. Now it was still a grand old building, replete with arched ceilings and steeped in New York entertainment history.

I recall rolling into town on our bus late the night before, crawling through some very dark and ominous neighbourhoods. I think our bus driver had taken the scenic route on purpose; a bit of sideshow entertainment for his naïve, young travelers, for which the admission price included burnt-out cars and shadowy mutants closing in around our bus. This was the Escape From New York ride that Disneyland never had.

When we finally reached our hotel it was, to our great relief, in a much more civilized part of town. A few blocks, like in all great cities, made all the difference. And then we got off the bus. I was immediately hit by the overwhelming enormity of New York City. It bore down on me like a huge weight. Endless rows of skyscrapers in the night. A million lights and lives behind a million windows. The city of twenty-four hour anything and everything. There were more things to do and see here than any one of us could ever hope to scratch away at in a lifetime. It was almost hard to breath. Never before in my life had I felt so small. How were the Spoons ever going to tackle this one!?

We checked into the Milford Plaza Hotel and literally fell into our beds. I slept very little that night, the few hours that were left of it. When I awoke, I pulled back the curtains and daytime was no less intimidating than night was in New York City. In fact, it looked even bigger. Great.

We had a bit of time before sound check and attempted to explore a tiny fraction of what the enormous city had to offer. Between traveling, sleeping and the almighty sound check, there was rarely ever time to properly take in the places we visited. I have fleeting memories of rushing through Times Square and lunch at a very authentic Jewish deli, with us asking a lot of stupid questions about matzah balls and gefilte fish and the elderly waitress walking away, shaking her head. I'd already done the Empire State Building and most other tourist duties with my family on a short trip to New York when I was younger. But that was all a distant blur now. This time was completely different. We were here for business, to leave our little mark on arguably the greatest city in the world.

When we finally hit the stage that night we were, as expected, more anxious than usual. This was the one show we needed to absolutely nail to the wall. The audience was jammed right up to the edge of the stage, eager to get their first glimpse of Boy George, primed for something to happen. Because of New York's reputation in movies and the special tour we'd gotten of mutant-town the night before, we assumed anything could happen. And it did.

The lights went up in the beautiful old theatre and we started to play. We began with *Smiling In Winter,* like we always did. So far so good. It all seemed to be running as it should. Then, halfway through the song a scuffle broke out in the crowd at the front of the stage. I kept an eye on it while singing: "We drive on salted highways, in our warm automobiles..."

Then, before security could intervene, someone jumped onto the stage and ran head-on into me, almost knocking me off my feet. I tried to keep playing as he put me in a submissive hold and swung me around to face the spot in the crowd he'd emerged from. The rest of the band kept playing without me as he waved angrily at someone in the crowd. Was I in the middle of a case of mistaken identity? What had I done? Then a flash went off. My assailant posed for a quick photo with me as his girlfriend snapped away. Before security could grab him, he released me from his iron grip and dove back into the crowd. Welcome to friendly New York City.

Our performance was a big success. And, considering the extra pressure we'd put on ourselves being where we were, it paid off in spades as far as band self-confidence went. We also learned, as I have to remind myself over and over again even today, how important it is to jump headfirst into things that scare you. It's almost guaranteed that you come out feeling much better about yourself at the other end.

We'd just gotten back to our change room after the show when Scott, our soundman, pushed open the door and announced, "You have visitors."

And in walked Sting. He'd come to compliment us on our show – perhaps to report our progress back to the A&M lads in Los Angeles – and to introduce us to a friend of his, Nile Rodgers. The night was getting more interesting by the minute. Sting happened to be in town and had brought Nile along to see us at our New York debut. I don't think we fully grasped the gravity of the fact that one of the biggest rock stars in the world and one of the most relevant producers at that point in time were backstage to see us. Nile was particularly impressed with how well Derrick played along with the drum machine. Grooves, as we'd soon find out, were a big part of his signature sound.

As guitarist and songwriter for Chic, Nile had written hit songs such as *Good Times, Le Freak* and *We Are Family*. As a producer, he'd recently taken a foray into the new music, having collaborated with Debra Harry and about to work with David Bowie. Unbeknownst to us, he had his sights on a new band of youngsters from Canada. He and Sting said their goodbyes and returned to their seats to watch Culture Club. But by then, the seeds for another future collaboration had already been sown.

SPOONFED

All the shows on the Culture Club tour were a big success. The after parties were an even bigger deal. One thing we quickly learned; everyone was curious about Boy George. In New York there was Mariel Hemmingway, in Boston Ric Ocasek and The Cars, in Los Angeles Rod Stewart. Each night after the show was like an Andy Warhol party. All the artistic elite was out to be regaled by the imperial Boy George. Sandy and I usually just sat back and watched the people file in and out. The after parties became shows in themselves.

And so we saw the America for the first time as a band via back-stage parties, some of the most beautiful old theaters in the country and a tour bus window. Very quickly all our clothes took on the smell of diesel fuel. It became a part of life, like the smell of gas in English kitchens. When I drive behind a truck or bus now and smell diesel, I think of touring. It's not a very pleasant smell, but sometimes I miss it. It's the smell of adventure.

Most destinations were close together, but there was one outrageous stretch our driver had to endure that I will never forget, a deadhead from St. Louis, Missouri to San Francisco, California. Culture Club had it in their budget to fly. We drove thirty-six hours straight. Or I should say, our trusty driver did. We did get a little sleep along the way. But the logistics for getting to the show on time were so tight that it's amazing how we made it at all.

As we entered the San Francisco city limits after a day and a half of straight driving, we were only about half an hour from show time. Our crew, who had arrived ahead of us and had already set up our gear, were communicating with our driver via ham radio and getting a little concerned about our progress. This was before cell phones. Since a stop at our hotel was out of the question, we quickly started putting on our stage clothes. San Francisco's notoriously bumpy streets made make-up a big challenge. Eyeliner became lethal.

SPOONFED

Before we knew it, we were pulling up to the back of the Roxy Theater, a theatre already packed with people. The calls on the ham radio had started coming in more frequently and urgently. It was only a matter of minutes to show time. There were, no doubt, some very anxious gig promoters pacing back and forth inside as we jumped off the bus.

We were quickly ushered through the back door. Someone slung our guitars over our shoulders and we were immediately led to side stage in the darkness. The theater lights had already gone down! Someone announced us and we were pushed without further delay onto the dark stage as the crowd began to cheer. We really had cut it *that* close.

All I had to go by was the small red "On" light on my amplifier. At least I had something to orientate myself with. It was my tiny beacon in the void. I just walked toward it, groped around in the dark until I found my guitar cable and plugged in.

I just hoped that everyone else had found their way like I did. Mercifully, the drum machine for *Smiling In Winter* started up. Rob had obviously made it. Then the stage lights sprang on and a world materialized around us.

Suddenly we were on stage at the grand, old Roxy Theatre, packed with people all the way up to the multiple balconies. The dome of the ceiling was so vast it might as well have been the Pantheon. It was one of the most amazing magic tricks I'd ever witnessed, a miraculous transformation out of pitch black.

We could feel the communal sigh of relief backstage push against our backs like a gust of wind. And the audience would never know that we'd just driven 3,300 kilometers non-stop and made it by sheer minutes.

The tour finished in Los Angeles at the renowned Hollywood Palladium. A big wooden auditorium, it had once

132

been home to Tommy Dorsey and Frank Sinatra and eventually the Lawrence Welk Show that I'd watched with my parents as a youngster. That night, the grand old lady opened her doors to some kids from Canada and a boy from England and graciously allowed us to put on our final US show.

A large contingent from A&M Records attended, including the gang that had flown up to see us at The Twilight Zone not so long ago. I remember mingling with them after our set during the Culture Club's performance and trying to have a conversation over the music. They were already talking next album and hinting that Nile Rodgers would be a good choice for producer and, something I'm surprised hadn't happened before, suggesting very politely that we try writing songs that were a little "poppier", a little more American radio friendly.

I, after all, had been as surprised as everyone else that a non-mainstream song like *Nova Heart* had caught on as it did. I nodded politely, but inside felt my ego bruised ever so slightly. This was the first time someone had, albeit in their own pleasant way, questioned our direction or, on a more personal level, questioned my song-writing abilities. It was quite ridiculous, just finishing a hugely successful tour, having taken America by storm, that it should end with that little seed of doubt planted in my head. And you know what that can grow into. You give me an ounce of encouragement and watch out. Give me a gram of self-doubt and who knows what creative skid row I could land in?

In the end, I would turn that doubt on its head and write songs for the *TalkBack* album that tackled mainstream radio in our own Spoons way. We were never going to sing obvious love songs or songs that glorified the clichéd rock lifestyle. Not if I could help it. But that didn't mean that some listeners, including the boys at A&M, couldn't think they were hearing what they wanted to hear. It had worked with *Nova Heart*. It could work again. I was up for the challenge.

19 Don't Talk Back

As far as producers were concerned, I'd always assumed and hoped that we'd be working with our old friend John Punter again. It was probably our manager Carl's job to tell him that A&M had other ideas. It was a horribly difficult thing to do, especially after *Arias* had been such a success in Canada. We all felt like we'd betrayed him and I still wonder sometimes what those songs would have sounded like if John had produced them. A lot, I think, were written with him in mind. But it was not to be. We'd have to be patient and wait five more years until things came back around full circle.

In the meantime, to add insult to injury, the *Arias & Symphonies* album had gone gold in Canada. We all received very nice mementos to hang on our walls. There's nothing like it, your first gold album. But it was bittersweet, the way John Punter was rewarded for his role in making it happen. I still have it, along with a few others, hanging in my music room at home. For anyone born in the CD age, they must seem like objects from a museum of ancient history. To us, they meant everything.

We discovered that when making gold records, the manufacturer didn't necessarily use the piece of vinyl that corresponded to the artist. I thought something was afoot when the track lengths on some of our gold albums didn't jive with the lengths of our songs. Depending on the day, the guy on the assembly line just took whatever was lying around, dipped it in gold paint and slapped our name on it. Sort of like painting over old artworks. I still wonder whose record is really under there. One day I'll have to crack open the old frame and throw it on a turntable and find out.

SPOONFED

We wrote songs for the next album and recorded demos at our trusty Soundpath Studios in Oakville almost continuously. It was a comfortable workplace that allowed us to put down ideas quickly and painlessly. It led to one of the most prolific periods we'd ever see. The studio is now long gone and I still miss it sometimes. If you should ever find a creative outlet like that, hold onto it for dear life.

Making a small concession to being more commercial, we began to write more songs in major, rather than minor keys. I don't know if this was an all-together conscious thing, but it was a start. A lot of the *Arias* album had a definite minor feel, adding to its darker and more serious tone. The shift toward a lighter feel also came out of some of the new music we were listening to. It was hard not to be drawn in by the hugely successful pop songs bands like Duran Duran, ABC and Culture Club were releasing. If *Arias* was our big, grandiose epic, this album would show our lighter, more fun side. Plus that little A&M guy with the devils horns was sitting on my shoulder and whispering in my ear. But it didn't mean we couldn't have some fun with it.

The original version of *Old Emotions* was inspired by a theme song I'd heard on a Canadian vintage movie television program called Magic Shadows. Hosted by Elwy Yost, the show introduced me to all sorts of old film classics. In the original demo, I even tried to recreate a 1920s gramophone-affected vocal by singing through a cardboard tube. That, of course, didn't make it to the final recording. The swing rhythm stayed, quite unusual for a modern pop song at the time. I bet my old ghost buddies from the LaSalle Park pavilion would have approved.

Lyrically, I just took the whole *Red Light* conditioning concept to the next level. The song described how everyday experiences, like the sensation of wet sand below your feet on a beach or the scent of a forgotten perfume, can trigger old, sometimes forgotten memories and the emotions that come with them. Our "private library" is really the subconscious, the place where all these memories and emotions are kept until reawakened. My psychology classes were obviously still paying off.

John Punter had programmed all the drum machine parts on the *Arias* album. Rob must have been paying attention and had gotten pretty good at it himself. He quickly came up with some very clever patterns for the songs *My Favourite* Page and *Quiet World. Old Emotions* also began with a bouncy little drum machine, but that would end up being replaced by real drums for the album. The direction and feel for the new record was starting to take shape; a good mix of *Arias* type songs like *Time Stands Still* and *Don't Shoot The Messenger* along with more poppy tunes such as *Talk Back* and *Camera Shy*.

In the end, it was a good thing that we'd expanded our horizons a little. New influences were driving us to explore as many directions as possible. We were still making our own music, but we weren't averse to soaking up a little bit of what was happening around us. That openness to ideas was the perfect starting point for recording our next album with Nile Rodgers.

I think Mike Jones was as surprised as anyone else when John Punter didn't return to Sounds Interchange when recording commenced in the summer of '83. No more old school chum to play pranks on the band with. But Nile came with such a huge reputation and track record, that any misgivings were soon set aside and everyone involved was eager to see what the new chemistry would lead to. It certainly hadn't done David Bowie any harm.

I'd flown to New York for a few days to meet Nile at the Powerstation Studios before he came to Toronto. He was still working on Bowie's *Let's Dance* album at the time. I remember staying quietly in the background as Nile recorded someone's guitar overdubs. I was too busy waiting for Bowie to arrive to notice that the guitar player Nile was recording was Stevie Ray Vaughn. He wasn't nearly as well known then as he soon would be. I didn't realize it, but I was standing in the same room as a future legend.

When Nile finally arrived at Sounds Interchange, he made his grand entrance wearing a three piece tailored suit, looking like he'd just walked off Savile Row. You couldn't help but take notice and he immediately had everyone's attention. His tailor obviously knew what he was doing. By his side, also from the Powerstation, was his assistant and secret weapon Jason Corsaro. Jason, we would soon find out, had his own set of special talents.

Nile was instantly likable. Like directors of movies, in a way, record producers all have their own definitive style. Graeme Pole, who'd done *Stick Figure Neighbourhood*, was like Woody Allen, letting the talent pretty well direct themselves. John Punter was more an Alfred Hitchcock, with a vision that he adhered to steadfastly and a strong will that appeared when needed if someone deviated too far from that vision. Nile was like a new breed of modern film makers, using few words to influence, now and then touching a dial on the mixing board, in the end creating something minimalist, but with his style written all over it. The foundation for Nile's sound came from the drums. This is where Jason Corsaro came in. One whole day was spent erecting elaborate props around Derrick's kit. Jason was the architect. One contraption entailed building a huge extension of the kick drum, so it resembled a crawling tube at a children's day care. By putting a microphone at the end of it, Nile could achieve the big kick thump he was known for. Nowadays they have software to do the same thing. Back then it was construction playtime. Soon there were "Do Not Touch" signs everywhere. One false move and the whole house of cards would come crashing down.

Working with Nile felt like a lot of playtime. For the group vocal in *Camera Shy*, he set up a microphone and had us all sing in the men's washroom. Apparently the acoustics from the tiles were the only way to get the effect he was after. He'd also brought along a box of effects pedals all the way from New York for me to play with. He obviously knew the way to a guitar player's heart. I used one distortion pedal aptly called The Rat for the slightly nasty guitar dives in *Old Emotions*. I wasn't convinced it was the right direction for a Spoons song. I'd never used such a saturated, almost heavy metal sound before. Of course, since then, my tones have evolved and the Rat makes perfect sense. Now the stuff around it in *Old Emotions* seems tame in comparison.

Songs like *The Rhythm* and *Out Of My Hands* ended up with the distinctive big-drum Nile sound, similar to the one he employed on Bowie's *Let's Dance* album. Others like *My Favourite Page* and *Quiet World*, where we held onto the old 808 drum machine, stayed more on the same track we'd established with the *Arias & Symphonies* album.

Sandy and I with Nile Rodgers at the Powerstation.

138

Nile was letting us hold onto some of our roots. There was a tug of war going on between the old and the new sound of the band, but a very amicable one. Or so it seemed as we were making the album. Once we finished bed tracks at Sounds Interchange, Nile and Jason disassembled their drum creations and flew back to New York. As with *Arias*, Sandy and I would soon follow to lay down the vocals at the Powerstation. That way, New York City, like London, England, had its chance to inject some mojo and personality of its own into our album. And that it did.

If you didn't know it was there, you'd walk right past the studio. Situated in an old warehouse district in Manhattan, the only things to identify the Powerstation were a street number over a plain steel door, a small button on an intercom and a tiny overhead surveillance camera. If Air Studios in London was a factory for making music, this was just a factory. All attempts possible were made to hide the fact that hundreds of thousands of dollars worth of recording equipment were inside. Once we were let in, after identifying ourselves to a faceless voice, a small elevator took us up to the main studio floor.

The elevator opened up into a small lounge with a bleak view of New York outside the grimy windows. Beyond the control room was the Powerstation's main studio, renowned for its incredible acoustics. A lot of hardwood and high, vaulted ceiling made it one amazing natural reverb chamber. Nile hinted that, if we should work together again, the whole record should be done there, especially the drums. We could see and hear why. Standing in the middle of the room and clapping our hands got some pretty impressive results. "Live" couldn't even begin to describe it.

Over the next few days, cocooned in the studio, Sandy and I recorded our vocal tracks and had very little time to see the city. Walking from the hotel to the Powerstation in the mornings was fine, but leaving the studio at night, we emerged into a whole other world. The deserted, gritty streets and alleys of gangland movies lay between us and civilization. Even the common yellow New York cabs rarely ventured into that neighbourhood and had to be chased down. I missed their jolly black cousins that had taxied us around London. Our stay in New York went by incredibly fast. Before we knew it, it was time to head home to Canada and prepare for the album release.

Back in Toronto, art director Dale Heslip and I spent hours in his Ready Record's basement office sorting out strips of coloured paper and photos for the *TalkBack* album cover. An earlier idea, depicting rows of Egyptian hieroglyphics with the characters holding musical instruments, had been nixed. We decided to go with something simpler and more colourful, something that would pop out on the racks at the record store.

The first single off the album, it was decided, would be *Old Emotions*. But I wasn't so sure we were doing the right thing. How could we, after the grandiose creations of the *Arias* album, return with something so unashamedly cheerful, so blatantly pop? To be truthful, when it came time to take our new single to radio stations, something that was still done in person by the artist back then, I was more than a little scared to walk through the door. It wasn't supposed to feel that way. Would listeners even think it was the same band?

Of course, I was wrong again. I'd forgotten how I second-guessed myself with *Nova Heart*. Welcome once again to the world of the chronic self-doubter. People loved the strange little song with a bouncy beat and never once mentioned that it was a big departure from our previous work. To me, they were light-years apart. I was amazed we'd gotten away with it. It's still a favourite for many fans to this day. Live and learn, I suppose. But, knowing me, I probably never will.

When it came time to make a video, the outdoor footage for *Old Emotions* was shot on a chilly afternoon at a remote beach somewhere near Oshawa, Ontario. We're wearing heavy woolen sweaters for a reason. The little black dog running around was my mother's and I have no explanation why he was even there. Maybe I was dog-sitting that day. There was a lot of innocent frolicking on the beach and a scene where Rob and Derrick crash their bicycles into the waves. Rob Quartly was directing again, obviously trying hard to maintain our clean, wholesome image.

The indoor scenes were shot on a soundstage in Toronto, where a sort of floating library was built - the "private library" from the song lyrics. It was all very sweet and innocent, although someone noted years later that a copy of The Exorcist could be seen sitting on a shelf. But a scene that would push us to the very brink was yet to come. Something that looked so harmless on paper would quickly turn into unendurable torture.

For the end of the video, Rob had the brilliant idea of shooting us inside a small cubicle having, of all things, a pillow fight. How Mickey Mouse Club squeaky clean did he think we were? The moms of our fans who'd grown up on Annette Funicello and beach party movies would love it. He convinced us that, played back in slow motion, it would create a striking image. Little did he know that we would almost choke to death on the bags of feathers that the crew rained down on us from above. Embarrassment was the least of our worries.

Every few minutes one of us would jump out of the room hacking, trying to force the feathers from our lungs. Slow death by eiderdown. It was pure hell. My singing days were doomed. At the very least, I saw myself on stage with feathers randomly flying out of my mouth like some Marx Brothers routine. How could one of the most innocent and silly looking things we'd ever done end up being so horrendous? Someone was obviously giving us the proverbial slap on the side of the head for submitting to something so utterly ridiculous.

But, just as I'd needlessly feared the repercussions from releasing *Old Emotions* as a single, the video was added by MuchMusic without hesitation. I was wrong again to question the order of things in the cosmos. Our quirky little song and video caught on quickly. Even the ridiculous feathers went by audience's critical eyes without a hiccup. Either we were getting away with murder or my understanding of our fans needed some serious realignment. Their and my universes needed to sync up, big time.

TalkBack and *The Rhythm* would also go on to be released as singles but it was the darker, edgy songs that were my favourites. *Time Stands Still* and *Quiet World* were still more in my comfort zone and the older Spoons domain. *My Favourite Page* has some of the least commercial and yet most personal lyrics I've ever written. A song about losing oneself in a book didn't make for your average pop song. The progressive rock nerd inside me hadn't died completely and still fought becoming too mainstream. We'd somehow managed it with *Nova Heart*, doing it on our own terms. But now the edges, I was afraid, were becoming a little blurred. An uneasy feeling was starting to nag away at me.

When I flew to New York to hear the final mixes of the album, I sat politely and listened and flew back home again. Nile had done a masterful job, but I was convinced it was all wrong. These songs had been written with John Punter in mind and hearing the end product made that crystal clear. I'd always imagined *TalkBack* as the sequel to *Arias & Symphonies*, with lighter moments yes, but still grand and epic. I'd been fooling myself. That was never meant to be.

No one else in the band seemed to have a problem with it. To make matters worse, while I wallowed in self-loathing for having sold my soul to evil pop music, the execs at A&M in Los Angeles didn't think the album was mainstream enough! How, on God's green earth, was that possible? *Arias* and

142

TalkBack were like night and day to me. I felt like I was losing touch and drifting away from planet earth in my own private little bubble, disconnected from everyone else. Something had to give. To start with, I needed to stop looking over my shoulder to the past, the *Arias* age, and start looking forward. Nile had so much to offer us and I hadn't taken full advantage of it. The sooner I got to terms with that fact, the better for everyone. I wasn't going to give that A&M devil on my shoulder the satisfaction.

I immediately set to work writing songs that made sense with the Spoons/Nile Rodgers pairing. Songs that capitalized on Nile's talents, but still sounded like Spoons songs. Surprisingly, it didn't take very long. One night it just happened and I found myself sitting in our den at home churning out ideas on an old, beat up classical guitar a neighbour had left on his balcony after moving out of the building. Obviously, my new lucky guitar. Like the OMD inspired night that led to *Nova Heart*, suddenly the basics for *Romantic Traffic* and *Tell No Lies* started to pour out of me. Effortlessly. Like a new door was opening. Just by lowering the walls around me a little bit.

Nile had played us *Original Sin* at the Powerstation, a song he'd just produced for a new Australian band called INXS. The simple hook and way the track was put together was brilliant. It had, without knowing it, stayed with me and indirectly led to the attitude behind *Romantic Traffic*. Even on my old, weatherworn acoustic, I could see where this was going. The future looked a lot brighter all of a sudden. As long as I could stay original, going a bit more commercial wasn't going to be as painful as I thought.

Tell No Lies followed and was our first attempt at funk, but funk the way the new British bands were interpreting it. Hidden in the middle breakdown was a syncopated riff that came straight from an old Tryst song. Yes, Tryst, as in our high

143

school band that played ten-minute progressive rock epics and set off flash pots at school talent shows. It was very gratifying to let a bit of the old me slip quietly into a new Spoons song; a song that would probably be more mainstream than anything we'd ever released before.

We'd begun experimenting with some subtle use of brass instruments in our music. Very un-Spoons like in retrospect, but I can see now how things evolved to that point. We'd just toured with Culture Club, whose trumpet player added a lot to their live shows. Other bands we admired made good use of the saxophone: ABC, Roxy Music, Martha & The Muffins. Even my hard-core progressive rock mentors Van Der Graaf Generator deployed saxophones. And, not to be forgotten, Sandy and I first met in the high school band as trumpet and sax players. Like it or not, it had to sneak into our music at one time or another. *Tell No Lies* was that time.

After plying the services of some local Burlington players, we eventually met Phil Poppa and Toni Carlucci. Our official new brass section, they became a staple of our live shows for the next few years. Their colourful characters added a whole new fun element to our performances and helped loosen up the old, stiffer Spoons. Just compare the two shows on our live concert DVD from the Concert Hall in Toronto and the Spectrum in Montreal. We're like two completely different bands.

And so, we entered into a whole new era of Spoons music. What took a recalibration of my mindset – and likely a little adjusting to from our audience – led to a sunnier and more upbeat period in our evolution. If I close my eyes and picture it, *Arias & Symphonies* feels like wintertime, *TalkBack* creeps up like a warm spring and *Romantic Traffic* and *Tell No Lies* play out like a scorching summer. Like the progression of most things, there was a natural arc to what we did. The fall and following winter albums, in turn, were yet to come.

20 Gardens & Snowstorms

One day Rob announced he was going on a little family vacation to Florida, probably to clear his lungs after the *Old Emotions* video shoot. We had a bit of down time and decided we could be Rob-less for a week. Naturally, within days of booking his flight, we were offered the opening slot for Hall & Oates at Maple Leaf Gardens and the Bell Centre in Montreal. Rob's return flight was on the day of the first show, but he was confident he'd get there on time. Of course, that's not the way of the world when it comes to the music business.

The Gardens, one of the best-known hockey arenas in North America, was also the largest and most recognized music venue in Toronto at the time. It was, after all, where I'd seen my first full-blown rock concert with Alice Cooper. Where I'd gone as a kid still longing for a Les Paul and a Marshall stack. We had finally made it after all these years, to step on the same stage as our idols. But it wasn't going to be easy.

The day of the show arrived and our crew set up Rob's keyboards, fully expecting him to join us very shortly. We'd assumed that he probably wouldn't make sound check and went ahead without him. Then the dreaded call came. Rob's flight was delayed. Depending on customs and driving conditions from the airport, it would be tight. A horrible realization was starting to grow deep down in some part of my brain I didn't want to confront. Finally, an hour before the show, our manager Carl walked into our change room and confirmed the worst. Rob wasn't going to make it in time.

There was actually a moment when we thought we couldn't go on without him. We were a band; we had a routine and a safety-net way of doing things. This was way out of our comfort zone, especially since Rob not only filled out a huge part of our sound, but also ran the drum machine. I've learned to become much more flexible and improvisational in my outlook on things since then. Throw me a curve ball now and I get excited to overcome it. Back then, it hit me square in the face and knocked me temporarily unconscious.

Fortunately, coming to our senses, we jumped into action and came up with a plan B. Our crew quickly retrieved the rest of Derrick's drum kit from the truck so he could play without the almighty drum machine. Our brass section, Phil and Tony, quickly wrote out some basic charts to cover the important keyboard lines on sax and trumpet. We could do this. And that we did – in glowing fashion.

We walked out onto the huge Gardens stage before a sold out crowd, plugged in and played one of our most urgent and energetic sets ever. Probably running on adrenalin, endorphins and whatever other 'ins' there are, we jumped into the abyss. Periodically we would have the light man train his spotlight on Rob's keyboards and I'd assure the audience Rob would arrive at any moment, carrying his suitcase onto stage. In the meantime, Phil and Tony churned out all the keyboard melodies on trumpet and saxophone and no one seemed to notice.

Incredibly, when I asked everyone to stand up at the beginning of *Old Emotions*, most of the fifteen-thousand plus in the crowd did. I was stunned. It was the most profound moment of audience/performer connection I'd ever experienced. In the middle of a show that had "doomed" written all over it.

Of course, optimistically putting the spotlight where Rob was supposed to be on stage didn't help one bit. The last song in our set, *Nova Heart*, arrived and still no sign of our sun tanned synth-player. But by that point it didn't matter any more. We were in the homestretch. We finished our show to great applause and headed backstage quite pleased with ourselves. It didn't even faze us when Rob greeted us in our change room. He'd arrived just in time to watch us perform *Nova Heart* from the back of the arena. He said we were very good. More than good, I would say.

A few weeks later Carl arrived with the news that we'd been asked to perform at the Commonwealth Games. Not quite the Olympics, but an honour nonetheless. This sounded quite tame and straight forward at first, until we heard where exactly they were being held that year: Frobisher Bay, Baffin Island, north of the arctic circle. As in extremely remote and unimaginably cold. Considering where Rob had just come from, this seemed like cruel and unjust punishment. In the end, it would be an adventure of a lifetime.

Right out of Indiana Jones, we boarded a cargo plane, the front half carrying our equipment and other supplies bound for the tundra, the back half arranged for human passengers, including four Spoons. We'd all dressed for the journey in heavy fur-trimmed winter coats and long underwear. Derrick decided it would be funny to arrive in the great white far north wearing Bermuda shorts and a Hawaiian shirt. The joke was short-lived on arriving, when he was met by the frigid air and ran for dear life toward the van that had come to pick us up on the tarmac. But it became the focal point in a story that made good reading in Maclean's Magazine that month. Those young, foolhardy Spoons.

We were immediately struck by the great expanses of infinite whiteness. Horizons were non-existent. With no point of reference, we seemed to be suspended in space. I couldn't imagine trying to survive beyond the town's limits. We were soon informed that the local jail had very little security. Anyone trying to escape would certainly meet a frigid doom.

It was also the time of year blessed with almost 24-hour daylight. It was suggested by our driver that we improvise something to cover our hotel windows to help us sleep at night in the unrelenting brightness. This part of our trip wasn't mentioned in the travel brochure.

We arrived at our hotel and, on entering the lobby from out of the cold, were greeted by a horrendous sight. Blocking our way was a giant of a man wearing a caveman beard, clad in ragged clothes and covered in horrible, nasty looking sores. We stopped dead in our tracks before him and, seeing our shock, he broke out a big grin and said: "Don't eat the fish here."

Frozen Spoons in Frobisher Bay.

148

SPOONFED

Then we noticed the other people milling about the lobby and put two and two together. Judging by the gear they carried, they were part of a film crew and, hopefully, this monstrous character blocking our way was an actor. Sure enough, the BBC was in town shooting a film about the Scott Expedition to the South Pole. Apparently poles, North or South, were pretty similar, film wise. The actor covered in sores had just returned from filming a scene, ravaged by frostbite and hypothermia. Heading to the hotel bar for a hot toddy, I'm sure.

That actor, as I would learn later, was an ex-wrestler and one I'd seen playing tough guys in James Bond movies. I'd see him again years later, mean as ever, in Indiana Jones and The Temple Of Doom. It was good to see he had a sense of humor.

Another up and coming actor who was out on a frigid set somewhere, undoubtedly dreaming of warm hotel bars and hot toddies, was Hugh Grant. Movie star or not, once outside, everyone's identity was lost under layers of winter clothing. And outside was something we tried to avoid at any cost.

Hugh Grant relaxes with Sandy during BBC film break.

SPOONFED

Prince Charles was also invited to the Commonwealth Games but had to cancel. A huge impending storm had made all incoming flights impossible. When the snow hit full force, there was no leaving. We'd have to wait it out.

Apart from our performance in the local community center, there really wasn't much to do in Frobisher Bay. Picnics and strolls in the park were not going to happen. There were no malls to hang out in, only a small Hudson Bay Company supply store. The hotel restaurant had just two things on the dinner menu, arctic char and caribou steak. Soon the two would be indistinguishable. Our three-day trip quickly turned into a weeklong stay.

We watched movies continually in our hotel rooms to pass the time. One almost sent Derrick through the roof, literally. It was probably an unwise choice, but we decided to watch The Thing by John Carpenter. The movie, set in a remote arctic research station, was obviously a bad idea. A shape-shifting alien terrorizes the characters and things turn gruesome very quickly. What were we thinking?

In one of the best reactions to a shocking movie scene I've ever seen, Derrick went from lying flat on his bed to bouncing to his feet and almost hitting the ceiling in a split second. It was horror movie audience gymnastics at its finest. I've never seen it replicated.

When the storm finally cleared and takeoffs were safe again, we boarded our little cargo plane and headed back home to warmer and safer climates. Regular Canadian winters would never seem the same again. Like the giant spiders in the cottage we rehearsed in, we would compare all other snowstorms to this one.

21 You Spin Me Round

Ontario Place, opened in 1971, was a place I'd visited every summer with my parents as a kid. It was about as close to Disneyland as we'd get in Canada. An innovative and technically ground-breaking park on the waterfront, it featured a giant geodesic dome that housed the world's largest IMAX screen, sci-fi inspired pods connected by bridges suspended over the water and other various modern installations and children's play areas.

The Forum, innovative above all, was a covered outdoor stage on the Ontario Place grounds that rotated a full 360 degrees every two hours, so that the audience in the circular seating around it could see the performers from every angle. Not something recommended for bands prone to motion sickness or stage fright. Like the inspirational Band Shell nights at the Exhibition grounds, I saw a lot of free concerts there as a young and impressionable musician. It soon became one of our favourite venues to play every summer.

In 1984, the first year we performed at the Forum, I don't think any of us were prepared for the huge crowds that were already pouring in for the afternoon sound check.

Until then a portion of the audience was still allowed onto the floor in front of the stage. That would be the last year for that bright idea. Spinning crazed fans around in circles, it seemed, only drove them into a bigger frenzy. I suspect that the ensuing nausea and complaints of the nightly clean up crew also had something to do with it.

Our first show at the Ontario Place Forum.

We played the Forum every summer for three years running, culminating in a three-night stint followed by a fourth encore performance later that season. We were also apparently the band that caused barricades to be erected for all shows, after a mass swarming of our stage one hot, steamy summer night. I remember fans spilling over the walls like ants and Derrick suddenly pulled backwards off his drum stool and disappearing into the hoards. Sandy and I threw our guitars on the ground and ran for the tunnel to the safety of our change rooms.

The Forum was torn down in the 1990s and replaced by a much larger music venue called the Molson Amphitheater. A lot of good memories went down with the rubble that day. The new stage, sadly, didn't spin, but it would bring in bigger acts and, more business. For us, it was the end of an era.

SPOONFED

Years later, when I had children of my own, we'd go to Ontario Place every summer. I'd tell them stories about the adventures their dad had there in the crazy '80s. We went regularly until 2012, when it closed its gates so the city could decide what to do with the old place. It wasn't bringing in the crowds like it used to. Perhaps it had something to do with the demise of our beloved Forum. I was surprised to see how many other people missed that infamous spinning venue. Like the old LaSalle Park Pavilion of my youth, it held a special place in my heart, a stage filled with memories. I recently heard that plans for a future rebuild of Ontario Place might include a new version of the old Forum. That would be very good news indeed. Back by popular demand, I suppose. A place, I hope, to make some new musical memories in.

Somewhere, somehow, during this time of spinning stages and whirlwind adventures, Sandy and I started to drift slowly apart. We'd been together as a couple, as band mates, as kids growing up, for almost eight years. The people we were now were very different from the two Aldershot music students sitting side by side in the high school band. We'd pretty well grown up within the world of the Spoons. It had taken over and become our lives, bigger than any personal relationship. As the band grew, we simply grew apart. While other musicians fought the temptations of road life and fan adoration, we ran the band together as a couple and as business partners. In a way, the band kept us focused. But it also drove us apart. To the astonishment of everyone around us, one day we broke up.

It was a tense time and I'm sure Rob and Derrick saw the end of the band just around the corner. Who wouldn't? Incredibly, as a testament to our mutual respect for each other and dedication to what we'd worked so hard to build, we managed somehow to keep the Spoons together and moved on. There was no down time, no cancelled shows, no embarrassing scenes played out in front of audiences. Apart from a lot of avoided eye contact we, against all odds, put our personal

153

feelings aside and let something bigger than us carry us forward. A band, we discovered, is more than just people making music together. A band is a miniature universe; sometimes your closest family, sometimes a security blanket, sometimes a fortress against the rest of the world. It becomes an alternate reality you cling onto for dear life. Because, no matter how much you try to tell yourself otherwise, you know it won't last forever.

The winds of change must have been in the air because, around this time, I decided to finally leave home and go out on my own. I wouldn't find out until years later from my mother that it was the only time she ever saw my father cry. Looking back, I was probably going through some long overdue growing-up. I was approaching my mid-twenties but, because of our European background, my relationship with Sandy and our constant touring, living at home for so long had never seemed strange. All of a sudden it did.

The Forum with Phil Poppa and Tony Carlucci.

154

I moved right into the thick of it, in downtown Toronto near Queen and Spadina, on a little street behind Queen where all the clubs were: the Horseshoe, the Rivoli, the Bamboo. I could stumble out of the back door of any of them and pretty well be home. I shared a newly built townhouse with two other musicians, one per floor. I remember a few great parties there, when the house was jammed with people, but most of the time we were off on different tours and rarely saw each other. If you watch the video for *I'm An Adult Now* by The Pursuit Of Happiness, you can see my silver Honda parked out front of the house in the scenes shot near the famous graffiti-covered parking-lot wall on Queen Street. It was early morning and I was inside sleeping through it all.

So, when Sandy and I returned to a chilly New York City to record *Romantic Traffic* and *Tell No Lies* in 1984, we arrived as separate people. How the irony of those two song titles and what we were going through personally eluded us is astounding. I suppose we were so deep in it, we didn't see it. We flew down and stayed at the infamous Gramercy Park Hotel. It was eerily quiet for a place in the middle of Manhattan, but there was lots of rock 'n' roll history in those drab, brown walls. It reminded me of the gloomy apartment building in the film Rosemarie's Baby. If there were ghosts, they'd moved out long ago. But the clouds of our recent break-up were still hanging over everything. That tends to suck the colour out of the world, no matter how vivid. Somehow Sandy and I put our emotions aside and got to work.

This time, the entire project would be recorded at the Powerstation. Nile pulled out every stop and brought in some of New York's heaviest hitters to make this the Spoons release, Nile style, that *TalkBack* should have been. For the Linn drum machine parts and crazy Sinclavier keyboard intro to *Tell No Lies*, he called on the local expert techy on these still very new instruments. Looking more like a silicone valley computer geek, he came in, methodically set up his gear, churned out his genius, then packed up and left. The Simms Brothers were called on for background vocals. They'd just sung on Bowie's Let's Dance album and were going on to do his *Under The Mysterious Moonlight* tour. The Asbury Jukes brass section dropped by and laid down their horn parts in one afternoon like the seasoned pros they were. A few of them performed with the Saturday Night Live band. They'd also worked on Bowie's record and would go on to play on Duran Duran's next album with Nile. It was a veritable revolving door of amazing talent.

One afternoon. Nile's bass player from Chic, Bernard Edwards, dropped by. He brought along something he thought Sandy might like to see. When he pulled his pink Spector bass guitar out of the case, her jaw dropped. Nile suggested she use it on our recordings and the rest is history. Not only did the Spector sound great, it was the perfect size and weight for her. No more weight-lifter's belt for this girl. As fate would have it, it was also the make of bass we'd seen Sting use at the Police Picnic. These instruments were only custom made to order back then. Sting's white model was serial #1. Sandy's would be #2.

There was a definite chemistry for these recordings that had been missing during the *TalkBack* sessions. With the right songs and mindset, working with Nile now made perfect sense. Recording *Nova Heart* with Nile would have been as wrong as John Punter producing *Tell No Lies*. There's a time and place and producer for everything. When we finished the songs, I knew we had something really good. If the making of *TalkBack* had been a way to lead us here, then the journey had definitely been worth it. But the big question was, had we gone mainstream enough for the boys at A&M? The little devil on my shoulder seemed satisfied. Would his life-size cousins in LA feel the same?

22 Sex, Lies & Videos

Feeling pretty good about ourselves, we left New York and flew back home. It was time to get our new songs ready for release. We had to start thinking about making videos again, but first we needed an album cover that reflected the more playful and less serious image that went along with our newfound direction.

Calling on Peter Noble once more, he devised our most elaborate photo treatment yet. Except, perhaps, the CN Tower hair-torture escapade. With some convincing, he shot us individually, shirtless, against a blank wall. Using a technique I'm sure he invented, he then placed our photos in a shallow tray of water, threw in some ice chips for good measure and froze the whole concoction. After a few attempts and getting the results he was after, Peter reshot the iced over collage and, voila, there was our new cover. Spoons uncovered. About time we worked a bit of sex into our marketing. Photos in front of gazebos and rose bushes weren't going to cut it anymore.

A&M also saw the marketing potential of a good-looking young band with a female bass player and wanted to capitalize on that. I'm surprised no one had really taken advantage of that angle before – perhaps because, in Canada, we'd tried so hard to downplay the whole bubblegum pop image. Our American record label had no such concerns. They quickly flew us back to New York to do a press junket of all the teen magazines. Imagine, the Spoons in Tiger Beat. We were in deep.

A lot of weight rested on the success of the new songs. We anxiously awaited the verdict from A&M. It was a nerve-wracking time for all of us. I phoned our manager Carl every day for a week until he had something to report. And, when it finally came, the word back from Los Angeles was good. More than good. It was what they'd been hoping for. *Nova Heart* had found success in the more progressive coastal markets like New York and LA, but A&M wanted all of the USA, including the conservative squishy center. *Tell No Lies* and *Romantic Traffic* were the songs we needed to break America.

It time to think about making videos again. *Old Emotions* had been the only song with a video off the *TalkBack* album. We needed to get our faces back on Canadian music television again quickly and make up for lost time. A rep at our lawyers' office had entertained inquiries from Maxell, the recording tape company, about us doing an endorsement deal. After some negotiations, it was agreed that part of the contract included them footing the bill for the *Tell No Lies* video.

Spoons, my mom and the dog from the Old Emotions video.

Maxell would pay for our video as long as they could use bits of the footage in their television commercial. We agreed and went on to make our most elaborate and costly video yet. Why wouldn't we? First things first, we had to edit down the song to a more reasonable length for radio. The original was somewhere close to original *Nova Heart* size. We were still insisting on doing things backwards then. The extended dance mix first, edited version for radio later. We returned to Sounds Interchange without Nile and, assisted by John's old engineer Mike Jones, cut the song to a more manageable length. We also replaced a guitar solo that somehow hadn't made it into the Nile mix. That alone was worth the studio time for me. The song was now ready for radio and video.

With the song title in mind, video director Rob Quartly drew up a storyboard involving a South American airport, a flight carrying a wide assortment of strange characters and, finally, us dealing with customs back in Canada. Your not-so-average family vacation gone wrong. The video became a mini movie with a huge cast that included many of our closest friends and family, cameo appearances by some local celebrities, a few real actors and a petting zoo of creatures that entailed at least one boa constrictor and a lama. Cecil B. DeMille should have been directing. And then, of course, there were those long Pinocchio noses we wore. True to epic movie form, they were custom made and applied to our faces by the same make-up artists that had just finished working on Quest For Fire, a major film release about cavemen in prehistoric times. We were now, in the prosthetic proboscis world at least, running in the big leagues.

The airport scenes were shot in a downtown studio and Toronto International Airport. The interior flight segments were filmed in an old DC-3 at a small airport outside of Toronto; once Air Oshawa, or something like that. In case you've never been on a small jet, the plane sits on such an angle that the aisle actually slants downward toward the back of the plane and

159

tends to give you air sickness without even leaving the ground. Flight attendants must have been part-time gymnasts back then.

I enjoy watching the video just for the cameo appearances alone, from Live Earl Jive as the pilot to Pete & Geets as customs officers. There are more sight gags than a Mel Brooks movie, including the prerequisite shaky model airplane dangling from a string in front of paper clouds. There's even a crazy Mariachi band as on-board entertainment, us doing some real fine acting, and a lie detector that travelers have to submit to at customs. If we could think of it, no matter how ridiculous, we used it and filmed it. It was utterly crazy and over the top, and the most fun we'd had in a long time.

Tell No Lies was already getting attention at radio and the video was quickly picked up by MuchMusic. The touring phase of our musical arc now awaited. Strangely, there was still no word on a US release for the single from A&M. A little odd, considering their excitement about the new songs, and more than a little frustrating for a band eager to finally conquer America. Fortunately there was enough north of the border to keep us busy. But now a big grey cloud of uncertainty had replaced the little devil on my shoulder. What were they thinking? Why were they waiting? Something didn't feel right.

Somewhere, probably in some desolate stop on the road, we got the call from Carl. Jordan Harris, the main man in our court at A&M had left and gone elsewhere. The new guy was coming in and clearing house. And that included us. The Spoons were being tossed out with the bath water. A&M would not release *Tell No Lies* or *Romantic Traffic* in the US. The new rep had a different vision for the label that didn't include us. Our new songs, so full of potential and already on their way to being hits in Canada, would never see the light of day south of the border. They were getting shelved. One very large rug had just been pulled from under our feet. The world, the way we saw it, changed overnight. Not only were our songs getting dropped, no one else in America would be allowed to release them instead. They might as well have been boxed up and buried. Unless we rushed like hell to record something new and found another distributor, the US market was pretty well a gaping, empty hole for us now. A bitter pill to swallow, especially when we knew our master tapes were just sitting there on a shelf at A&M, deep in the bowels of the former film studios that Charlie Chaplin built. I think I would avoid black and white movies for a long time. As far as scripts were concerned, this one had the worst possible ending.

How we managed to perform over the next few weeks, I have no idea. Sandy and I having just parted ways and our chances at breaking the American market dashed to smithereens, I think we sleepwalked through most days. It was the first big valley in our, so far, smooth and steady climb to international success. A valley shrouded in long shadows and storm-cloud emotions. Thank God we had our Canadian fans to keep us going. I learned very quickly that sometimes performers need their audience more than their audience needs them. This was our hour of need.

The success of *Tell No Lies* mercifully kept us busy and was quickly followed by the release of *Romantic Traffic*. What followed is the video we are best known for and, without a doubt, the most revealing about us as individual people that we ever made. Without A&M to back us and no major Maxell style endorsement deal, we needed to produce something on a much tighter budget. Ready Records found an up and coming young director named Robert Fresco who was accustomed to working on a shoestring. The Champagne days were over. No more elaborate storyboards. No big film sets on sound stages. No feathers. Just us and a hand-held camera in the subways of Toronto.

Permission was granted to shoot our video by the transit authority with the stipulation that, if too large a crowd of onlookers gathered, we would have to move the show elsewhere. Needless to stay, we spent the day being ushered around by a TTC rep from station to station, endlessly evading commuters and overzealous fans. We finally gave in and used some of them in our video. We were, after all, making things up as we went along. I still meet people today who say they were there. Some even made it on camera. One girl, who'd married a friend of mine many years later, didn't tell me for a long time that she'd been featured in the candy bar scene, still a young girl then. She, and the others that contributed their personalities to the video, had no idea how instrumental they were in writing the *Romantic Traffic* script that day.

There are some funny moments, my favourite of Derrick doing his famous Derrick dance, bouncing off a cement pillar on a subway platform. I loved that side of him, a natural and uninhibited comedian. But it's the more somber and serious scenes in the video that truly reveal some truths about that time in our lives. Particularly between Sandy and I. Even I didn't see the obvious distance between us on screen until years later. The title of the song and location for our shoot couldn't have been better chosen.

There's something sad and almost fragile in our expressions as we look off into the distance, Sandy traveling alone on a subway, me with my hands in my pockets waiting uncomfortably on the platform. *Romantic Traffic*, whether we knew it or not, was about us. It was symbolic of the crossroads we were at, going our own separate ways after so many years together. Because we had gone into the making of the video without a script, the story of our lives had taken over and written itself all over the screen; a wide-open picture window into our personal lives. It came out in every glance, every movement, every unsaid word. Some parts are hard to watch for me. Some make me smile. Some make me wonder, what were we thinking!? But it is and will always be my favourite Spoons video.

23 Sandy & The City

Like most bands, our lives followed a repeating cycle, which entailed a year of writing, recording and making videos, followed by a year of touring, followed by another year of writing, recording, making videos and so on. We pretty well did business like that for ten solid years.

It wasn't an exact science, but it became as regular as the changing of the seasons. Sandy's accounting background from Mohawk College came in quite handy. Very early on we set up a system which allowed us to draw regular salaries, like a company, whether we were working or not. This way we could stay afloat, business as usual, even during the creative periods. Pretty good royalty cheques had also started coming in and that certainly helped. Apart from the odd self-given bonuses here and there, we were very careful with our money and never lost sight of the big financial picture. No unnecessary limos, no penthouse apartments, no pet tigers. A little boring, but extremely sensible in the long run.

I'd always thought that our music was tailor-made for film. Instrumentals like *Trade Winds* and *Unexpected Guest At A Cancelled Party*, particularly, had the drama suited for movie soundtracks. Some songs, like *Walk The Plank* and *Time Stands Still*, were like little movies all by themselves.

I continued to approach songwriting as I always had, by filling empty little stages with props and characters. Visuals always made perfect sense alongside the music that we made. It had worked to great effect, after all, for a few Godzilla and sic-fi flicks.

When director Ron Mann contacted us to provide music for his new film Listen To The City, I thought it was about time we were asked. The film, about the economic disintegration of a small town, had small roles for Martin Sheen and P. J. Soles and featured the New York musician/poet Jim Carroll.

Ron saw a potential part for Sandy that would eventually grow into a major role. She definitely had natural acting talent that we never knew about. Ready Records decided that the film would be a perfect vehicle for *Romantic Traffic* and *Tell No Lies*, which had so far only been available on an extended EP, not a full-length album. And so Sandy, the actress, started rehearsing her lines and I jumped headfirst into scoring my first soundtrack.

A large rehearsal space in a strip mall on Brant Street in Burlington had become our new home away from home. At one point we finally decided to have mercy on my father and moved out of the cottage to let him work in peace. I would find out later that he missed us bashing away upstairs. He had, after all, been there to witness all the growing pains and tribulations of a young band. But it was time that we left the giant spiders behind and moved into something bigger and less exotic.

Sandy performing Sundown in the film Listen to the City.

SPOONFED

I spent nights after Spoons rehearsals working on the background music for Ron Mann's film. Various out-of-sequence scenes were sent to me on VHS tape and the privacy gave me a chance to experiment with all sorts of crazy sounds and recording techniques without anyone looking over my shoulder.

The film had an undeniable dark mood enveloping it and I decided to go ambient in my approach. I used drum machines as a starting point. Not being a keyboard player, this was a good chance for me to explore that uncharted side of myself, the frustrated wannabe synth-player side. I got hold of an old Roland JX-3P and went to town.

I recorded various percussive instruments and played with the tape speed to get some pretty eerie effects. Rubbing the drum skin of a tambourine and slowing it way down created the haunting moans in the background of Jim's post coma walks though the desolate city. The opening track, *Theme For A City*, was played almost entirely on a multitude of differently effected bass guitars. I was out stretching musically and having a bit of fun in the process. This wasn't a proper Spoons album after all, so I left a lot of my old preconceptions behind. In a way, it was my first baby step outside the Spoons, my first solo project.

When it came time to put down proper tracks at Soundpath Studios, Rob and Sandy added their magic and made it complete. Sandy's haunting vocal and Rob's drum loop in *Sundown* stand out to me. That song became the theme for the movie, Sandy's character's reaction to the desperate fate of the city and people around her. *We recently performed that song for the first time in about twenty-five years. It still captured the dark mood of that strange little movie all those years later and remains a perfect snapshot of that time in our lives.*

One day, during shooting of the film, I arrived on set to watch Sandy in a scene, as I often did. I hoped to catch Ron afterwards for a few moments to discuss soundtrack ideas. Suddenly a script was thrust in front of me. Either the intended actor hadn't shown up or the screenwriter had added a last minute new page, but there it was, a small cameo for me. I really didn't feel comfortable, but I had little choice. I wasn't about to hold up the making of a motion picture with my little insecurities. Quite possibly, the movie buff inside me wanted to at least give it a shot and be immortalized on celluloid forever. The chance may never arise again. I played Sandy's music teacher, which was ironic in itself. But seeing my performance on the big screen at the Toronto Film Festival later that year confirmed the fact that acting was not in the stars for me.

Around this time we were approached to consider another product endorsement deal. We'd done promotions with music related companies like Maxell tape and AKG microphones, but this was entirely different. A chain of clothing stores called Thrifty's wanted us to be their spokesmen, or spokes-band. Our initial reaction, understandably, was pretty negative. How would this look on us? Was this the ultimate sell out? We were about to find out.

Our finances and relationship with Ready had become more and more strained, especially since the departure of A&M Records in the arrangement. Our management and lawyers advised us that we needed to do something to bring in money and help keep us afloat while the business side sorted itself out. This was that *something*. We were venturing into new and potentially risky marketing territory here, but had little choice.

We reluctantly agreed and jumped head first into a series of elaborate photo shoots for the advertising campaign. The results were huge colour posters of us in Thrifty's clothing, one for each season of the year. As far as photography went, they were quite good. Until I saw them out in the real world, that is.

SPOONFED

The ad campaign was national, but the full impact of it didn't hit me until I drove by their flagship store on Yonge Street in Toronto and saw our giant images covering the whole front of the building. How I didn't slam my foot on the brake and cause a pile up I have no idea. It would be the same embarrassing scenario in every major city across the country, not to mention the radio ads and television commercials. There was no hiding from this one.

As expected, the criticisms were harsh, especially from the normally sarcastic music industry types. Much of it was warranted. But, as predicted, the yearlong Thrifty's contract kept our heads above water as we stopped recording and negotiated to get out of the Ready Records deal. It helped us through a period of uncertainty and financial juggling acts and most of our fans didn't seem to mind or notice one bit. As it turned out, the in-store record signings we did for Thrifty's across the country were bigger than any we'd done in record stores. Except perhaps the one at Sam The Record Man in Toronto, where fans waited several blocks down the sidewalk the day of our Maple Leaf Gardens show.

The ad campaign pretty well subsidized a tour across Canada. We'd take a lot of ribbing for our precarious brush with the product placement world but, before long, everyone was doing it. Today, no one would blink an eye at any celebrity product pairing, no matter how ridiculous. Endorsement wise, it was a different, much less forgiving world back then.

But it was the beginning, in its own small way, of a slow downward spiral for the band, the first hint of things coming undone. Sandy and I had survived our split relatively unscathed. That alone should have sunk us. We'd also managed to overcome the loss of *Romantic Traffic* and *Tell No Lies* to the great, big gaping American void. But there were other more dangerous and unexpected things lurking around the corner on this ever-winding road. We probably didn't see it at the time, being in the middle of it, but a domino effect of wrong decisions had been set in motion.

One of the last happy memories I have of the original band, with Sandy, Rob, Derrick and myself, was the 1984 New Year's Eve show at Maple Leaf Gardens. We were at the height of our careers, having achieved more than we'd ever dreamed we would. But, as is the nature of things, we were about to bring it all crashing down.

That New Year's Eve, shared with Corey Hart and Platinum Blonde, was one big party. I was surprised once again how less intimidating the legendary Gardens looked from the stage compared to up in the rafters where I'd sat as a kid watching Alice Cooper. I recall Platinum Blonde's hydraulic drum riser getting stuck in the up position, leaving their drummer marooned high above the stage for half the set. A classic Spinal Tap moment come to life.

I also remember Heather, my girlfriend at the time, kidnapping me for an hour before the show and taking me on a whirlwind limo ride around downtown Toronto that I'm sure had the rest of the band a little worried about my return. There was champagne and, naturally, the prerequisite hanging out of the sunroof driving down Yonge Street. To everyone's relief, I made it back alive and we proceeded to put on a great show.

And that was it, the last clear memory of happiness for quite some time. The year that followed this last hurrah would be filled with one wrong turn after another. It's not always drugs and alcohol that spell the demise of a rock band. The devils can come in much subtler and more sinister forms.

Someone should have asked us then, like in the first line of our song *You Light Up*, "Why don't you leave what's good alone?"

24 New Spoons In Old Order

We were being courted by several managers at the time, by those who thought they could do more for us than the status quo. One that managed to capture our attention was music business wiz Bob Muir, president of Virgin Records Canada. Very charismatic, he'd won several JUNO Awards for his work in the business and easily won us over as new clients. The Virgin Records offices, walls plastered with one gold and platinum album after another, were based in a funky old house in downtown Toronto. I recall a lot of very effective, ego-massaging meetings and one or two wild parties there. We were being seduced, and quite willingly. Someone had to tell Carl Finkle the bad news.

Over a very somber meeting we let our manager of four years go and, if there was ever a first domino to be dropped, this was it. He took it like the gentleman he'd always been, though I'm sure it hurt him a lot. And there, looking back, went the finest manager and one of the best friends we ever had. It's incredible the kind of decisions and choices we make when at the top of our game, whether out of greed or arrogance or sheer stupidity. We always thought we could achieve more, which we might potentially have done with someone else, but we didn't realize how good we had it. Our little fortress was falling apart. One stone at a time.

We played our last show as the original Spoons on December 31, 1985 in Calgary, Alberta. It was New Year's Eve, but it felt nothing like the previous year's celebration at Maple Leaf Gardens. What should have been a new beginning would instead mark the end of the band as the world knew us. Sandy and I had got it in our clouded minds that we needed a new drummer. This messing with band chemistry was really

169

gaining momentum now. We had no idea what we'd started. When we finally told Derrick our intentions, surprise surprise, Rob Preuss announced his departure. All this in our local Burlington pizza hangout that would never feel the same again. For some reason Rob didn't feel comfortable with our prospective new manager and wanted to pursue orchestra work in musicals. Since our record deal with Ready was winding down, Rob saw the perfect opportunity to step out of the band.

As hard as it was letting Derrick go, Rob leaving was a huge shock for me. There had been no signs of his discontent that I could see. None whatsoever. But, then again, our vision was evidently not very clear during this period all around. I went home feeling completely numb. It would take a very long time for that empty feeling to wear off. Things were never going to be the same again.

In the span of an afternoon, the Spoons, as our fans had known us, were no more. It was just Sandy and I again, reminiscent of the time our old high school band Impulse split down the middle and we moved all our gear to Sandy's basement to start anew. It was incredibly frightening and knocked us off our feet for a few months. But, incredibly, time heals all wounds, even severed bands.

Once the storm clouds and emotions cleared, the future didn't look as bleak. It was time to get to work auditioning for new Spoons. Something we hadn't done in a very long time.

We met with only a handful of keyboard players. I recollect one well-intentioned hopeful flying all the way from Winnipeg with stacks of road cases and racks of gear. Another arrived at audition wearing full '80s make-up and stage outfit, a bit too enthusiastic for our taste. In the end, it was Scott Macdonald's simple approach and gentle personality that won us over. He'd come from a local cover band called York Road and did more with his one little synthesizer than the others did with Genesis-worthy mountains of equipment. It also helped that he was from small-town Ancaster, Ontario, in the Burlington neighbourhood. He fit right in.

Drummer auditions were more extensive and required us to rent studio space at a music store in downtown Toronto that had a drum kit at the ready. Whatching one drummer after another set up and tear down gear would have taken years off our lives. For some reason, drummers were more abundant that year than synth players and we went through our fair share.

We'd met Steven Kendry several times on the road over the previous year performing with rockabilly legend Ronnie Hawkins. I recall one tour where Ronnie's dates pretty well synced up with ours schedule-wise and his band often stayed in the same hotels as we did. Ronnie soon took us under his wing and treated us like family. His own son and daughter were in his band and we'd usually join them at after show parties in his hotel room, at what would be some of the most entertaining evenings from all my '80s memories.

Ronnie was a natural comedian and held court in his suite like the rock and roll royalty he was. We soon discovered he had a strict routine he followed every night. Usually a lot of unexpected guests would show up, tag-alongs and castaways, and Ronnie would quickly dispense with them by hurling out a few colourful one-liners. These were quite effective in chasing away anyone faint of heart. Once they were out of the way, he'd proceed in earnest with entertaining. He was a sweetheart underneath, but he could be ruthless with the uninvited.

One night at the Calgary Stampede stands out in my mind. We were all playing the Cattle Dome that week and Ronnie invited us to come see his show, opening for none other than Jerry Lee Lewis. I'm always glad at the opportunity to see one of the greats, no matter what the musical style and went with an open mind.

After the show, Ronnie surprised us and offered to take us to meet the man himself. Without any warning or introduction, we simply walked backstage into his dressing room. Jerry was alone with his new, young bride, and Ronnie, in true Ronnie form, went right into his comic routine. Not-so-subtle jokes about under-aged girlfriends and watching our step around "the killer" ensued. Jerry wasn't amused and never wavered from his cold, unemotional stare. He reminded me of our old Aldershot High School principal, right down to the black marble eyes.

Ronnie must have gotten a whiff of the tension in the room and suddenly grabbed Sandy and suggested a photo with Jerry. Jerry seemed to brighten up at that idea. Once she was in place between the two of them, Ronnie proclaimed, "This is what you call a western sandwich." It was the one and only time I saw Jerry smile.

Imagine the look on poor Sandy's face, reduced to a southern snack between these two old charmers. Jerry's wife looked on from across the room. There was something in her eyes that made us want to leave. Soon. And that we did.

So, when Steve Kendry showed up at auditions, we pretty well knew each other from our shared road trip adventures. Essentially we stole him, but I think Ronnie would in time forgive us for that. Now that Steve and Scott were officially in, the Spoons were complete once more. Part of me still felt the loss of Rob and Derrick, for the old routine and unspoken connection between band members that only comes from years of playing together. But the new guys picked up the old songs quickly and brought us back into the comfort zone that we needed to move forward. We did, after all, have to start thinking about a new album. We rehearsed constantly in Bob Muir's basement. It seemed that we were back on track again and ready to take on the world as a new band.

SPOONFED

And then, unexpectedly, things took a horrible turn for the worse. As far as unforeseen tragedies went, this would be the most cruel. We got the call one morning that our manager had taken his own life. He'd been instrumental with the transition of our new band and was just getting things rolling toward our new future. We were devastated. I was never given all the details, but there were many emotional and personal elements that drove him to that sad and final end. It would literally stop us dead in our tracks. I don't think, as a band, we could have taken much more.

There was a period where we floated, disconnected and unsure, without management. If grey areas had grey areas, this time in our lives was it. We desperately needed redirection.

Then one day, out of the blue, I received a call from the offices of SRO. They were a Toronto management company that represented a handful of select artists, including a little band from Canada called Rush. Their manager, Ray Daniels, wanted to talk.

He and I met several times, usually at some of the finer dining establishment around Toronto. I didn't realize it at first, but I was being courted by one of the biggest managers in the world. It would turn out that it was Rush who'd actually mentioned us to him. *Many years later, through our mutual friend and photographer Andrew MacNaughtan, I would learn how much they admired our Arias & Symphonies album and Neil Peart my lyrics. Easily some of the highest praise you could get in this business, from a band raised on serious progressive rock like I was.* Of course, I was oblivious to all this as I noshed on truffles and Cornish game hen at Fenton's with Ray.

Ray had a cool and logical game plan for the Spoons and got straight to the point. He was convinced he could break us in America. Obviously Ray had been keeping tabs on our past misfortunes in that elusive market or been reading our minds. In any case, he was well aware of that little thorn in our sides and got our attention. In signing with him, we would also be part of Anthem Records. That way everything would be under one all-encompassing roof; management and record label as a package deal. We decided to put our careers in his golden hands and signed the dotted line.

Anthem had a history of working with heavier bands. Ray believed we could crack the US market by changing our sound ever so slightly, primarily by bringing the guitar and drums more to the forefront. He introduced us to producer Tom Treumuth, who'd just finished working with Honeymoon Suite. I started to get that feeling in the pit of my stomach again. I knew where this was going. We'd expressed our desire to work with John Punter numerous times but, as with the *TalkBack* album and A&M Records, it seemed our happy reunion would be delayed once more. I knew John would be as disappointed as we were, but we had to trust Ray and go with his instincts.

The new Spoons, with Scott Macdonald and Steve Kendry.

We all agreed that a small shift in our direction was worth making further inroads into America. To be honest, I was excited about the idea of bringing out more of my guitar playing. Songs like *Radio Heaven* and *Like A Memory* were written specifically with that in mind, others were pieced together from older ideas and made to work. A good example was the merging of *In The Hands Of Money* and *Unpremeditated Love* to create the love child and title track *Bridges Over Borders*. And, somehow, mysteriously, the drum machine vanished. I don't think it was even a conscious band decision. It simply got lost somewhere between demo time and the recording of the album. Perhaps there's an island of misfit beat-boxes out there somewhere.

We sorted out arrangements and our newfound direction in the basement studio of one of Tom Treumuth's friends. That friend, Arnold Lanni, would later form and be lead singer for the band Frozen Ghost. He'd also contribute some nice guitar bits during our recording sessions at Phase One, a studio just north of Toronto. It was the era of guest appearances on albums. Local session player Howard Ayee dropped by one day and laid down some fancy fretless bass tracks on *Walk Across The Water*. Anthem Records also had it in their minds that we needed a heavy-hitter for the drum parts and brought in Roxy Music's Andy Newmark from New York City. Anthem obviously was unaware of Steve's abilities. On a mission to prove them wrong, he convinced everyone to let him have a shot at the album. Needless to say, he blew the roof off the place. In the end, only one song, *Be Alone Tonight*, would remain with Andy on the drums.

Around the same time, our old hairdresser Reg Quindinho asked me to produce a record for a band he was managing. Reg and Joe had great taste in music and were well connected in the local scene. Having your hairdresser manage you was about as logical as anything else in the '80s. That band was Tall New Buildings, fronted by a singer named Jian Ghomeshi.

SPOONFED

Rehearsals were held in a dark and chilly church hall in Toronto. I'd done a little record production before, once for Curtains, a Burlington punk band, and for some friends of Sandy and I from Hamilton called Tula. I'd learned a lot about recording from John Punter and Nile Rodgers since those days and saw in Tall New Buildings something very much along the lines of what the Spoons were doing. It would be a natural and easy fit. We hit it off right away, got to work and, once finished preproduction in the church hall, headed to our trusty Sound Path Studios in Oakville to record the masters.

Jian would go on to form the band Moxy Fruvous, but is best known today as a talk show host on CBC radio. I've met him at many functions through the years, but it wasn't until something emerged from our mutual past that some forgotten memories were stirred up.

Our old manager/hairdresser friend Reg was also an artist of not insubstantial acclaim and, as part payment for my production duties, allowed me to choose one of his paintings. I found it recently, tucked away with other art that hadn't made it on my walls and was surprised at what I saw. The acrylic painting, very large and abstract, had scattered throughout it stencils of machine guns and a certain silhouette in duplicate. It took only a moment to recognize that profile. Willing model or not, Jian had been committed to canvas for all eternity.

Recently Jian joined us on stage for the 30th anniversary of the *Arias & Symphonies* album release party in Toronto. He performed *Walk The Plank* alongside Derrick on timbales, with Rob looking on from across the stage. Sandy and I were in the middle, taking it all in. The old gang was back together again. Sadly, Reg passed away quite a few years ago, but I'm sure he was looking on; enjoying the music, critiquing our hair. I was reminded again, as I am more and more as time goes by, what a wonderful but fleeting world we live in.

25 Submarines In The Fog

Some of my greatest and most unforgettable memories through the years come, without a doubt, from life on the road. One of the perks of touring is seeing the country from a very unique perspective. Not only from stages in concert venues in front of our fans, but also during late night arrivals and early morning departures when most cities are still asleep. New York is an exception, because it never sleeps. But I have some of my fondest and most haunting memories from the wee early hours, whether you consider them late night or early morning.

I will never forget pulling off the ferry in our tour bus and slipping slowly through the early morning mist in Victoria, British Columbia. Half asleep, I peered out the window at one of the most beautiful and surreal places I'd ever seen, as if in a dream. Someone had told us that Vancouver Island was known for its high concentration of witches and cults. This fueled my imagination even more. We passed tiny gingerbread cottages right out of Hansel and Gretel, turned a corner down a street of high-end boutiques a la Rodeo Drive and turned again onto the next avenue to witness a monk in robes chopping wood outside a crooked old church. It was a place of paradoxes and strange juxtapositions and was totally mesmerizing.

I also recall waking up much too early one morning at the grand, old Hotel Nova Scotia in Halifax, to watch a submarine glide slowly through the fog into the harbour below. Another morning I couldn't comprehend what I was seeing, when what appeared to be a small city-block of buildings emerged gradually from the haze over the water. I stood transfixed, eyes wide, until more of the mystery came into view. A giant oilrig was being towed in for maintenance. I've always had a soft spot for Halifax, a city so rich with history and ghost stories. A devastating explosion in its harbor in 1917 that killed thousands is not something that slips away quietly. Shadows always remain. Walking its steep streets leading up to Citadel Hill, I feel like I'm walking through a movie set full of unexpected twists and turns. There is a quiet sadness that hangs over the city, but also a sense of excitement and dark possibilities.

One night in Halifax, involving a visiting Russian circus, stands out above all others. We were performing at the infamous Misty Moon, a large music venue that'd once been a department store. You could actually still see traces of where the escalators once were. Halifax hours were unique from any other place and our shows started at midnight and finished around three am. And that's when the fun usually began.

On this particular evening, our road manager brought backstage a few performers from a Russian circus that were in town and had caught our show. Their English wasn't very good, but it was soon arranged that we'd join them afterwards for a little party. They were, after all, staying at the splendid Hotel Nova Scotia like we were. It was bound to get interesting.

What I experienced that night could best be compared to walking into a Fellini movie, full of strange and wonderful characters fading in and out of focus. The circus troupe pretty well took up a whole wing of the hotel and each adjoining room revealed yet another curiosity. Greeted by clouds of strong tobacco and the smell of vodka, I entered another world.

I passed a woman draped with a giant boa constrictor reclining on a sofa; walked past mustached strongmen flexing their arms robotically like overwound wind-up toys and, on entering the final room, was met by a dwarf in a top hat, who bowed curtly at my arrival and ran off. It was one of those absinthe-induced romps you read about in Bohemian novels. Pure magic. A night of memories I shall cherish always.

SPOONFED

Even Toronto had its surreal images and carnivalesque nights. I recall one roller coaster of a ride through the city with a friend from CFNY that began with Australian hard rockers AC/DC and ended with the cross-dressing dance music sensation Devine. It was still possible in those days to throw around names and sneak in the back door at Maple Leaf Gardens. And so we did, just as the giant cathedral bell was being lowered and rung over the stage as AC/DC kicked into *Hells Bells*. I got caught up in the moment like everyone else, watching Angus run up the huge ramps above the p.a. system in full school boy garb. They were great showmen, just like Alice Cooper and Genesis had been. Just as I was starting to lose myself in the whole spectacle, I was whisked away to the next attraction. No time to dally. My Alice In Wonderland rabbit was on the move.

Suddenly I found myself slipping in the back door at the Diamond Club. Devine was just about to go on. *You Think You're A Man* was a big hit and I was curious to see how he'd pull it off, considering he performed solo with backing tracks. Because of me, he almost didn't make it at all. My CFNY friend wanted to take me backstage and meet the man himself. And that I did, in glowing fashion. As we entered the small staircase leading up to the change rooms, I swung open the door and heard a muffled grunt behind it. My worst fears were realized when, from behind the door, Devine appeared, attempting to pop out one of his bra cups. A wardrobe malfunction of the highest order due to my careless door push.

All I could get out was an embarrassed, "Sorry." He just glared at me and, without a word, headed to the stage. I had to give him credit; he proceeded to put on one of the funniest and most entertaining shows I'd seen in a long time. He was as much a showman as AC/DC had been. Schoolboys or divas, it didn't make a difference that night. Like the Russian circus troupe in the Hotel Nova Scotia, they were just more characters in a cloudy and ever-shifting dream world.

26 Surviving The League

Once *Bridges Over Borders* was completed, three songs went on to be released as singles off the album: the title track, followed by *Be Alone Tonight* and *Rodeo*. Rock videos by that time were becoming more expensive and sophisticated than the experimentation and silliness of the early '80s and Anthem had the money to fund them. *Bridges Over Borders* was filmed completely on a sound stage in Toronto, pretty well just us performing on a stylized spinning set. The other two videos had more interesting stories in their making.

Once again, the album title reflected my life at that moment more than I knew. It seemed to becoming quite the nasty little habit. The video for *Be Alone Tonight* aligned perfectly with the chaos that was brewing in my life. I'd met someone new through mutual friends and the relationship with my girlfriend Heather ended badly. Just as *Romantic Traffic* had offered a glimpse into the break-up that Sandy and I went through, the video for *Be Alone Tonight* coincided with my current personal dramas.

There's a similar distracted distance in my expression in many scenes, my mind obviously elsewhere. Whether reading a painful goodbye note tacked to a door or throwing my guitar in frustration off a bridge, a lot of underlying emotions come through in that video. I was feeling what a lot of people feel in the painful transition from one relationship to another, the need to just be left alone for a while.

With the making of the *Rodeo* video, things lightened up considerably. We had just arrived in Halifax to perform a two-night run at the Misty Moon, when word came in from SRO that we'd been invited to join the Survivor tour in America. Their song *Eye Of The Tiger* was still huge and we'd be playing arenas and large theatres. Perfect for our new rock and roll direction and not an opportunity to turn down. Only one problem: We needed to film a video for *Rodeo* immediately, with no time to return to Toronto before the tour.

Improvisations were made, logistics sorted out, schedules juggled. A director was flown to Halifax, where he assembled a local crew and set out to shoot a script I'm sure he wrote on a napkin on his flight. He would recruit extras at our Misty Moon shows and film in the daytimes at a local country and western bar. He was after a sort of Blues Brothers band-booked-at-the-wrong-bar scenario. All that was missing was the protective chicken wire on the stage. The video was a lot of fun to make, although some of the extras looked a little too in character for my liking. Luckily the hard-core audience warmed up to us and we lived to tell the tale.

The video was shot, the gigs were played and we headed to the US to start another tour. Because the new album was more guitar heavy, we decided to bring along our friend, Hamilton guitarist Colin Cripps, to fill things out. He would later go on to join the band Crash Vegas and become an accomplished session player. We were lucky to have him for a short while. We'd also acquired Tony Crea as our soundman by then, a master of that big '80s "wall of sound" and the all-important gated-drum effects that we needed. We were ready to take on America, this time as a heavier, rockier Spoons.

Bridges Over Borders was already getting play on MTV in the US and, combined with older material that American audiences seemed to know, the reaction at shows to our music was surprisingly good. I have to admit, I'd never expected that a Spoons/Survivor billing would work, but it did. Ray Daniel's game plan to conquer the US seemed to be on the right track.

181

SPOONFED

It was quite amazing to stand in front of crowded arenas every night. We were starting to feel more like a rock group than the electro-pop band we'd been before. With two guitars and a bass on the front line and Steve's heavy drumming replacing our old drum machine based rhythm section, we were entering a whole new realm. It was easy to be seduced by the new direction, by the sheer energy of it, but things were starting to shift unintentionally below our feet. Even the older Spoons songs were taking on some of the new elements and, consequently, starting to sound less Spoonsy. This was all well and good in the States, where we were relative newcomers, but the reaction back home would be altogether different.

Canadian radio and press weren't so sure about *Bridges Over Borders* and the new revamped Spoons. One interview actually started with the question, "What happened?" That woke me up a bit. Actually, it zapped me like an electric shock. We'd been so wrapped up in making a big rock album that we hadn't stopped and considered whether we really should.

In the end, the *Bridges* album sold substantially more copies in America than Canada. Mission accomplished, I suppose. But at what cost? When we returned home, we quickly adjusted our live set lists and went back to playing mostly the older songs. That's how our old fans remembered and wanted us. One radio station even questioned our lack of gratitude for our success in Canada. Apparently they took our song *Radio Heaven* too literally. The song's lyrics were cynical about celebrity and the music industry in general, not Canada in particular. But, like it or not, the image of us as the pop music darlings we'd been for so long seemed to be changing. The innocence was fading a little. We'd wanted to conquer the US market so badly that we hadn't considered the subsequent fallout. I never in a million years felt we turned our backs on our home Canada. Apparently, some people did.

SPOONFED

The Spoons and Survivor, rocking the arenas.

Fortunately, the shows in America were a huge success and we finished the Survivor tour on a high and particularly spectacular note. We were about to jump ship and join the Human League tour starting in Los Angeles, but not without a fitting goodbye. It is tradition, usually on big tours, to have some fun at the opening band's expense on the final night. The boys in Survivor weren't going to let us go without a proper, and very elaborate, farewell.

To the best of my recollection, here is how that fateful night transpired:

The lights went down and we made our way onto the stage in an arena packed with fans. I grabbed my mic-stand to adjust it and immediately knew we were going to be in for a bumpy ride. Something hard and greasy was attached to my microphone. When the stage lights came on, I saw that all our mic-stands had chunks of fried chicken duct-taped to them. It was such an odd and cryptic prank, my mind couldn't digest it.

183

Maybe it was a thoughtful gift in case we got hungry during our set. I suspect it wasn't supposed to make sense at all.

We began our set – mercifully our equipment hadn't been tampered with – and then things really got going. Some of the band and crew had rented full size rabbit outfits and one by one appeared on the stage. A lot of naughty bunny activity ensued. One bent over toward the audience while another, with a whip, went to work on his tail end. One particularly tenacious bunny paid extra attention to Sandy. How she continued playing was a true test of years of hardened training. All the while, the audience was loving it. To them it was part of the show, some extravaganza worthy of a Tubes concert. They applauded louder than any audience had all tour long. Not quite the Genesis inspired show I'd long hoped for, but it would do.

Then, when it seemed the bunnies were losing steam, the piece de resistance was set in motion. Slowly, right out of the classic This Is Spinal Tap movie, a miniature Stonehenge was lowered onto the middle of the stage. Perfection. This would, I'm sure, go down as one of the most well executed band send-offs in music history. But the show wasn't over yet.

On our way back stage after our set we headed down the long hallway that led to our change rooms. It occurred to me how odd it was that a large section of wall near a bend in the hall was covered in large sheets of plastic. I got my answer very quickly. Out of nowhere we were ambushed by an assault of cream-pies. Survivor and their crew, apparently very quick at changing out of bunny outfits, had one more kiss goodbye, the literal icing on the cake. It was certainly memorable – and extremely messy.

Time to join the Human League tour in Los Angeles. Much more suited for each other than Survivor, I was very excited to work with them, but our time together would be short-lived. Our first appearance was a two-night stint at the old

Pantages Theatre in Hollywood, once host to the Academy Awards in some more golden age. Bob Hope had been king there. All the screen idols I'd ever watched as a kid had sat in its seats and walked its lavish halls. But we were never to meet the boys and girls from the League. No friendships were made, no afternoon tea with cucumber sandwiches; which was probably a good thing, considering that the tour would be over as soon as it started.

I recall a young kid waiting for us at the Pantages stage door with his *Stick Figure Neighbourhood* album in hand. How that obscure little album had made it all the way to Los Angeles I couldn't imagine. He happened to mention that he worked at Disneyland and, of course, my ears perked up at that. I was on tour, but a bit of childhood regression is never a bad thing. He invited us to come down the next day, as a treat to his beloved Spoons. A better start to a friendship I couldn't imagine. That same kid, now a grown man, still flies up from California at least once a year to see us perform. He recently joined us for the thirtieth anniversary of the *Arias & Symphonies* album and brought us all monogrammed Mickey ears as a little reminder of those early days. We will always refer to him as LA Dan.

We did just a handful of shows with the Human League on the west coast, ending in scenic San Francisco. There, the word would come in that the remainder of the tour was cancelled. Despite the Human League having a number one hit on the Billboard chart with their song *Human*, a huge achievement, the shows were not selling.

It seemed that America still wasn't totally comfortable with quirky new wave Brits treading their soil. Or young Canadians, for that matter. Tried and true songs like *Eye Of The Tiger* were obviously still more in their comfort zone. Our big venture into the USA had been thwarted once again. We returned to Los Angeles, stayed a few more quiet days and reluctantly flew back home again.

27 Rocky Fields

After months of living out of a suitcase, I found myself back in my hometown Burlington. It was incredibly humbling, like any return to reality after a tour; a difficult but necessary part of every musician's life. My girlfriend Carol and I were married in 1987 and for a short time rented an apartment in LaSalle Towers; the same, now slightly faded, white tower of my youth. I had grown up and the charms of the old pavilion in the park and my high school opposite it had long been forgotten. Like so many things, their significance in my life wouldn't become apparent until many years later.

I had returned home a changed man. Working so hard to make inroads into the US and paying a price for it with our image in Canada was bound to do that. Maybe it was time we paid more attention to our old fans and not be so concerned with winning over new ones. Remarkably, despite all that we'd gone through, there was still that wide-eyed kid lurking in me that would forever feel the thrill of making music and never give up hope of all its possibilities. That kind of determination or foolishness, depending on whom you ask, is indispensable in this business. Without it you can sink very quickly. One of those possibilities was about to become a reality.

It had become clear, even to our manager Ray, that the magic years had been the early ones with John Punter on board. Perhaps it was time to finally bring him back as producer and try to recapture some of that lost glory. Everyone agreed. I was a little nervous to ask, after so many years of false hopes, but when we did, John accepted the invitation like a gentleman and we moved forward with new optimism in our stride. This was, after all, what we'd wanted all along.

SPOONFED

John had the brilliant idea of recording our next album at Rockfield Studios in Wales, one of the classic residential studios that churned out so many great records through the years by Led Zeppelin, Queen and Mike Oldfield's haunting *Tubular Bells* theme from The Exorcist. Despite the huge cost of relocating a band to Wales, Anthem agreed and set it all up. I was thankful to be heading across the ocean once more on another great adventure. Maybe, if we were lucky, we'd get back a little bit of the magic we'd found the last time we worked with John. Maybe, just maybe, we could get the Spoons back on track.

We flew into Heathrow Airport and were greeted at the baggage claim by an old, English gentleman who would transport us by van to Wales. Miles of beautiful countryside slid by our windows, but sadly were we so jet-lagged that it seemed more like an afternoon nap filled with fleeting dreams. Since we were heading to Wales, the shooting location of my beloved TV show The Prisoner, I asked our driver about it and was informed that our studio was a little more than a three hour drive to Port Marion, where the "village" from the series still attracted fans of the show every year. That put a whole new spin on things as far as I was concerned.

After a long drive through the lovely English landscape, with its hedgerow-lined roads and fields of sheep, we finally crossed over into Wales. No big difference there, just more hedgerows and sheep, but still indescribably beautiful. When we drove over the tiny bridge into Monmouth, our driver told us we were close to our destination. He pointed out several pubs as we slid through the ancient village, pubs we'd certainly frequent during our stay. Pubs that had likely served pints to the likes of Robert Plant and Jimmy Page and would do so for a couple of Spoons and perhaps a Gallagher brother or two in the not so distant future.

SPOONFED

Rockfield Studios was on the outskirts of town, nestled in Welsh farmland at the bottom of a gently sloping hill and the crumbled remains of some ancient tower. We would come to think of it as our castle. The studio was a musician's dream, especially one raised on old British progressive rock music. Housed in the old Rolls Royce estate, a very long driveway took us to a gated entranceway into a huge open courtyard. We were immediately in a scene right out of an old English novel. Everything was perfectly preserved and locked in the 1800s, but behind the walls was another story. To our right were the control rooms and studios, the middle section housed seven self contained, two-story apartments and a dining hall, and on our left, where several horses were being saddled up, were stables which once served as reverb chambers. Led Zeppelin, we were told, had used these to great effect.

John greeted us on arrival. Seeing we needed a short rest, he gave us time to move into our new homes before giving us a quick tour of the grounds. Once in our apartments, I was once again struck by the familiar smell of cooking gas. I'd almost forgotten about it since our stay in London. Here it was again, confirming we were on British soil once more. Each apartment had a small sitting area, bedroom upstairs and a tiny kitchen, which would never see use once we experiencing the in-house chef's cooking. Unpacking could wait. We were eager to look around.

First destination: the studio. John was excited to show us the brand new Neve mixing console that had just been installed. We'd be the first to use it. There, looking back, was some poetic justice in that, which of course eluded us at the time. We'd been the last band to record on the old, well-used Neve board at Air Studios when we finished the *Arias & Symphonies* album in London. In a way, we were catching the end of an era by retiring the old machine. Here we were, about to embark on the last Spoons studio album for some time on a brand new board, which would go on to be used by countless

John Punter protecting the shiny new Neve board.

other bands. Those Neve faders would, in a way, serve as bookends to our recording careers.

Dinnertime was fast approaching and John led us to the main dining room. The studio apparently came with a Cordon Bleu trained chef. I half expected a Frenchman with a tiny mustache and chef's hat to arrive when Miss Marple appeared, right out of an Agatha Christie novel carrying large trays of steaming food. And so we met our cook and saviour Mrs. Gutteridge. She would make our stay feel like a holiday at a five star resort. No bangers and mash or squishy peas for these musicians. She'd treat our palettes like royalty for the duration of our stay.

Wine flowed like the streams that ran through the Welsh countryside. We were, after all, staying at an all-inclusive. How other, less disciplined bands endured, I have no idea. We were just finishing our first meal with glasses of port, when a strange little man burst into the room, jumped onto the dining table, downed a glass of wine, did a jig and then disappeared just as quickly. I had a fleeting image of wild eyes, disheveled hair and an old ruffled sweater covered in burrs. This surely had to be some country bumpkin who slept in the woods, who'd been drawn to us by the smell of liquor. No, quite the contrary, this was Kingsley Ward, the owner of the studio, the slightly eccentric host of this fine establishment. Such a regal name for such a peculiar man. This would be the first of many such contradictions during our stay in Monmouth, Wales.

And what an unforgettable stay it would be; one that could inspire notebooks full of words and music. Fortunately so because, very unlike me, I hadn't completed all the song lyrics by the time we arrived at Rockfield. Things became a bit tense as I scrambled to get something on paper when vocal tracks needed to be done. But, as I'd hoped, our fairytale surroundings crept into the words and mood of the album and saved the day.

The songs *Waterline* and *When Time Turns Around* are great examples. I listen to them now and can almost picture the Welsh hills and fields of sheep. Just like *Arias & Symphonies* and *TalkBack* had been, albums become little time capsules filled with all sorts of memories and feelings that go way beyond the literal meaning of the lyrics. Each song comes with its own cast of emotional castaways. What they conjure up will vary from person to person, for the writer even more so.

Lyrically, *Waterline* was really just an extension of *Old Emotions*, which had come from *Red Light* before it. I was still intrigued by the whole locked up emotions and "private library" idea. In *Waterline*, repressed feelings come floating to the surface in someone's life, someone who's had to deal with some very difficult things. "The submarines keep surfacing." Old emotions, good or bad, can't be kept down, hidden forever.

The song *When Time Turns Around* pretty well expressed how I felt at that time in my life. Working with John again, being back in the British Isles to record, returning to the grand, lush sound we had created with the *Arias* album; it really did feel like we'd come full circle and were being given the chance to do it all over again. Time would only tell if the old chemistry was still intact.

What was intended as a six-week stay in Wales would stretch into three months. That's a quarter of a year, at a very posh and very expensive studio. Totally outrageous, of course, when I think about it now. John just kept asking for more time and the gang at Anthem kept saying yes. We stayed so long, in fact, that at one point we started daydreaming about buying homes in Wales and living there. But who wouldn't, treated like kings and spoiled by Mrs. Gutteridge's cooking?

We quickly settled into a comfortable and leisurely work routine that was rarely deviated from. It went roughly like this:

1. Wake up. Usually with difficulty. Have a very big breakfast.
2. Consume lots of coffee. Try to recover from the night before.
3. Spend most of the day recording with a small lunch break.
4. High point of the day: One of Mrs. Gutteridge's outrageous dinner feasts.
5. An attempt at after-dinner recording. Usually unsuccessful.
6. Off to one of the local pubs. Reward for a good day's work, we tell ourselves.
7. Back to Rockfield. Social time in the common room. Billiards. Movies. More drinks... Off to bed.
8. The cycle repeats. See above.

Before long, understandably, Rockfield felt like an adult play-land. A combination of studio, all-inclusive resort and living, breathing museum of rock, it was the ultimate home away from home. As long as work was being done, Anthem wasn't too concerned. Apart from one visit from Pegi from the Toronto office to check in on us, we were pretty well left to our own devices. So much trust can be a dangerous thing.

One pub, the Vine Tree, became our regular hangout. After one night of merriment, a series of events transpired which would make us the talk of the town and get us into the local newspaper.

We had a small yellow car at our disposal to run to town in, to take us to the video shop or chemists. Whoever was brave enough to attempt driving on the left side of the road could do so. On one particular post-recording evening, we piled into Kingley's van and our little yellow Mr. Bean mobile and headed to Monmouth for a few pints. The in-between bits are a little vague, but we all returned to the studio later that night with Kingsley while Steve Kendry stayed behind at the pub with some newfound friends. Everyone went off to bed in their apartments as they always did. No one gave a second thought as to where our drummer might be.

Next morning, Steve arrived looking like he hadn't slept all night, which he hadn't. It seems things went a little awry after we left. He'd stayed late into the night drinking at the pub with his new buddies. What followed could have ended up with a much more serious conclusion. Instead, it sounded more like a scene from a Monty Python or Fawlty Towers episode.

When the pub closed, Steve jumped into the little yellow studio car, put the keys into the ignition and drove it slowly down the, fortunately, deserted main street of Monmouth. There were just one or two problems. He forgot to turn the headlights on. He forgot he was in the British Isles and lapsed back into driving on the right side of the street. He neglected to see the parked police cruiser, which he of course hit. Not a very good scenario all around. Surprisingly, Steve spent just the one night in the company of the local constabulary. There was some talk about him losing his license in Wales for a year. Devastating. Mostly, it just became a joke among the local townspeople. A lot of ribbing about Canadians not being able to handle stiff Welsh ale.

We would take anything they could throw at us for Steve's sake. If he was going to get off that easily, we considered ourselves lucky. Him being dragged off to Scotland Yard was one adventure we'd gladly avoid.

There was one other little detail, one that might have had something to do with the expediency and casual way things played out. The newfound friends Steve was drinking with at the pub that fateful night; the ones, in fact, who'd been buying him pint after pint, were none other than respectable members of Monmouth's fine police department. One day I should look up the word for "Oops!" in the Welsh dictionary.

There was an air force base somewhere in the vicinity of the studio and we decided it might be fun to capture a recording of one of the Harrier jets that zipped by from time to time. We hoped to use it like we had used the lightning crash in the opening *Trade Winds* on the *Arias* album. This proved to be more difficult than we thought. John left a microphone set up in the studio courtyard so he could push record the moment one flew by. The problem was, there was so little warning and the jets passed by so quickly that the best we could get was the tail end of the incredible whoosh they made going by. In the end, we settled for the much slower moving army helicopter that was apparently sent to check up on us periodically. Its whirring sounds are what you hear at the beginning of *Sooner Or Later*.

One day while we were recording, things took a turn for the more serious. Like a scene out of a Euro crime-flick, a dozen police cars and unmarked vehicles sped into the studio courtyard. Skidding to a stop on gravel, the doors flew open and all sorts of official looking men jumped out and immediately proceeded to lock down the whole complex. We were in the middle of recording the title track *Vertigo Tango* when several special services officers burst in and shut us down. Had we broken some antiquated bylaw that took illegal recording of government aircraft very seriously? We weren't altogether sure. The officers that made sure we didn't leave the studio weren't talking.

One, who appeared to be some sort of senior official, actually proclaimed, "It'll all come out in the wash." A line you'd expect right out of a classic Sherlock Holmes story. Another officer watched over Steve and stood beside him in the drum room, with his hands over his ears and straight faced like a Buckingham Palace guard, as Steve bashed out the tracks for *Vertigo*. We would have laughed if things weren't so serious.

Kingsley, the owner of the studio, finally appeared a few hours later, apparently having been interrogated and looking the part. Without explanation, the officials packed up, got back in their vehicles and sped off. Kingsley sat down with us and tried to make some sense of a very strange day: It seemed that Rockfield Studios had been one point on a route used to smuggle drugs in recording tape boxes throughout Europe. In an attempt to muddy the trail, the seemingly innocent looking boxes were sent from one studio to the next and never opened until the final destination. A young intern, who no longer worked there, had been part of the elaborate scheme. Kingsley was devastated. There'd be no jigs on the dining room table that night.

Periodically, we arranged for a few days off to sightsee a little during our stay. We managed day trips to beautiful Hereford, the closest large city, and to see the ancient Roman baths in Bath. A lot of quaint shops, endless stretches of cobblestone and the usual assortment of panhandlers who, invariably, were accompanied by the most rare and extreme results of canine crossbreeding. Spotting the strangest dog we could find soon became a pastime.

One excursion took us to Windsor, back in merry old England, just outside London. This required some travel by rail and, knowing my fondness for trains, became a little adventure all on it's own. Train travel in North America is one thing, but train travel in Europe is a whole other experience. It's the stuff of old movies and Agatha Christie murder mysteries. I would enjoy every moment.

Carol's father Jack happened to be an eminent judge for equine competition and friend of Prince Philip and was judging at the Royal Windsor Horse Show that week. He and the prince had written the competition rulebook together. Arriving in the picturesque town of Windsor we poked around a bit and then, after some enjoyable dead ends, finally caught up with him between judging classes. He took us to watch side-rink for a while as he completed his duties and then lead us behind the bleachers to where the stables and horses were kept. We were whisked through security as if we were taking a casual stroll in a public park. This, you see, was very unusual, considering that Her Royal Highness the Queen of England was also backstage.

There were a few secret service types milling about, a lot of black Range Rovers, but not much else to imply any kind of high security. Apparently when it came to horses, Her Highness's second most loved thing in the world after her corgis, all caution was thrown to the wind. I stood in amazement as I watched her get into the back of a black limousine and proceed to drive by, maybe ten feet from me. Like it was the most natural thing in the world. I, of course, snapped away on my camera to capture this unprecedented moment. I'd never be this close to the Queen again. It wasn't until many weeks later, when I went to have my rolls of film developed back in Canada, that I suspected something beyond my field of perception had transpired on that sunny day in Windsor. Of all the rolls of film I'd shot during our three-month stay in Wales, the roll from that day was blank. As if some giant magnetic device had blocked or erased my photos of the Queen, like some high tech gizmo from Q Branch. This was the stuff conspiracy theories were made of. To this day, it remains one of my life's great mysteries.

During our ever-lengthening stay at Rockfield, we took in visitors quite regularly. Sandy's boyfriend Jim moved in for a while, as did my brother Gary and our long time friend and photographer Andrew MacNaughtan. Andrew came equipped and took great advantage of the Welsh countryside and its many castles. One of Kingsley's daughters drove us out to a few picturesque locations, including Raglan Castle, which she claimed had been used in the Monty Python And The Holy Grail movie. Fortunately that day there were no French soldiers to taunt us from the parapets.

Exploring castles with our friend Andrew MacNaughtan.

SPOONFED

A few years ago I found one of the rare photos I took of Andrew: the subject capturing the photographer. It shows him walking by one of the castles we visited, trench coat blowing in the wind, his camera slung over is shoulder. He's looking back at me with that familiar Andrew grin, probably about to say something like, "Move it, we need to get to the next location before the we lose the light."

Always the gentle perfectionist, I remember Andrew most as my friend in that one picture. Little did we know it then, but that would be our last photo shoot with him until many years later; until 2011 in fact, when we needed new band photos for our *Static In Transmission* release. Change, it seemed, was on the horizon once more as the 80s were winding down.

One incredible shot that Andrew took of us against a red sunset in Wales became the photo for the *Waterline* single cover. Looking at it now, I'm struck by how grown up we suddenly looked. We weren't those innocent kids posing with our instruments on the inside sleeve of the *Stick Figure* album anymore, nor the young adults trying to find their identity, shot awkwardly against rosebushes and gazebos.

We'd come a long way since our ill-fated Aldershot High School premiere. Ironically, that photograph of a very mature and confident Spoons was captured at what would be the end of our careers.

Not the final end of course, since a lot has transpired since then. But it was our last hurrah in a decade of excess and flamboyance. The world, as we knew it, was about to change. All of a sudden, our time in Wales was coming to a close. Our stay reminded me again what an amazing world there is out there to discover. It had undeniably left its mark on all of us.

In Wales, the '80s about to wind down.

Just taking a walk down a sidewalk or hiking up a hillside was like exploring a new planet. Every blade of grass, every stone, every insect was different from what I'd grown up with in Canada. Even the giant Harry Potter sized slugs that came out in herds when it rained seemed alien to me. It was like living in some enchanted wonderland. We'd started to believe that we could stay forever, so bewitched we were. But, like most things, time undoes even the strongest spells.

By the third month of recording at Rockfield, we'd had enough and couldn't wait to get home. Goodbye Wales, goodbye Rockfield, goodbye castles and sheep. It was time to return to the real world and face the music.

28 Struck By Vertigo

After the quaint charms of Wales, coming back to Canada felt like a return in a time machine from more ancient and simple times. We'd been comfortably cocooned in our own little fantasyland for three months, oblivious to the rest of the world. I missed our little castle and the bleating of sheep, even the scent of cooking gas in the morning. I soon started to experience Mrs. Gutteridge withdrawal symptoms. The twenty-first century was cruel and harsh.

The mood around the Anthem Records offices, we found, was a tad chilly as well. We'd been so wrapped up in making our epic album that we'd forgotten to ask how much it was all costing. When we saw the close to a quarter-million dollar price tag on our little adventure, reality came surging back like the blood in Sandy's tiara-bound head. Even I was outraged. How were we ever going to pay this back? Ray and Pegi, I'm sure, were thinking the same thing.

When we released the Vertigo Tango album, initial reaction from our fans and the press was good. We'd finally returned to the grandiose feel of the *Arias* days, thanks to John Punter and the influence of the fairytale setting of the studio. For a long time we'd come up with any excuse we could to justify the cost of our little extravagance. Surprisingly, when it came time, Anthem gave us more money to make more videos. In for a shilling, in for a pound, I suppose.

We shot the *When Time Turns Around* footage in the clock tower of old Toronto City Hall at Bay and Queen streets. The rickety wooden winding stairs that took us to the top were straight out of Alfred Hitchcock's film Vertigo, a perfect location, considering the title of the album. Going up was no picnic, but we knew going back down would be much worse.

We spent the whole day filming behind the face of the giant clock at the very top of the tower, all the while dreading wrap time. When it finally came, it was pure mental torture. It probably took us twice as long to get down than it did to climb up, one hand on the wall and the other clutching the pigeon splattered railing. Hadn't we learned from the CN Tower escapade? We decided, no more photo or video shoots in high places. No good could ever come of that.

The *Waterline* video was more sensible and shot at various locations around a private girls school in Toronto. In one reoccurring scene, I slowly row a small boat across a misty lake. That lake was in fact the school's indoor swimming pool, done up with shadowy lighting and a smoke-machine. A young female model was hired to play a ghostly character in the video and her underwater scenes were also filmed there. I figured that our record company still had high hopes for us if they were willing to go to the expense of hiring an under-water cameraman in scuba gear. Maybe so, but it would ultimately turn out be the last big cheque they'd be writing on our behalf.

When Time Turns Around and *Waterline* were released as singles and did quite well. *Waterline* crossed over into radio formats we'd not touched on before, including, of all things, country radio. The songs went over very well in our live shows. But the album wasn't selling close to what we'd hoped; certainly not in quantities we needed to recoup the six-figure cost of making it. It was becoming ever more uncomfortable to visit the Anthem/SRO offices. But was there really anyone to blame for what was happening or, to be more precise, not happening? We'd made a very good album with some great songs with a superb producer. Maybe something else was working against us, something beyond our control.

Looking back now, it's quite obvious what was going on. The '80s, with all its quirks and idiosyncrasies, was winding down. We'd made an album that we probably should have

200

made years earlier, instead of prancing off to the US with *Bridges Over Borders* under our arms. Tastes were changing. Musical roots were being rediscovered. Glam was out and grunge was in. Spandex was being replaced with plaid shirts. The old pretense was being replaced by a new one. We hadn't seen it coming and we couldn't do a thing about it.

And so our last video, due to Anthem's understandable unwillingness to put more money into a sinking ship, was done on a non-existent budget. Luckily Andrew MacNaughtan stepped in and created a sparse black and white video for *Sooner Or Later* inspired by similar releases by Depeche Mode. All grainy and art school, it was shot in and around my in-law's horse farm near Halton Hills.

Knowing my affinity for The Prisoner TV show, Andrew snuck in a few key images from the show that really had nothing to do with the song, but made me happy. The giant white balloon patrolling the grounds and the man in black holding an umbrella in a field are straight out of the series. Ironically, despite the trend toward more raw and less produced videos, MuchMusic only played the video a few times and decided it was too "indie" looking. Really!? We thought indie and raw and real was the new standard. If we weren't confused enough already, we certainly were now.

This would be the final blow to level the Spoons house of cards. It was the one and only time I ever received a nasty phone call from our record company. It was at the end of a national tour we were doing with Larry Gowan, before he became Lawrence.

I still remember listening on the phone, hardly saying a word and finally putting it down, feeling like the world had just been pulled from under my feet. The rest of the band just stared at me, fearing the worst. I downplayed it, of course, but knew deep inside that it was pretty well over.

I didn't see it then, but our label was probably feeling the same frustration we were. The musical landscape as we knew it was changing and it was futile to fight against it. As we had caught the beginnings of a new wave when we first set out as the Spoons, we were seeing the start of the next one. And now we were the old guard. We were history, in every conceivable sense of the word.

And so, as fate would have it, the album title *Vertigo Tango* would finally make sense in the grand scheme of things after all. We were literally dancing on the edge of something frightening and unknown. Even the lyrics from the opening song *Sooner Or Later* seemed to know what was coming.

> *"Sooner or later, you will remember*
> *Sooner or later, the world will wind down"*

And it did. We continued to perform here and there and Anthem wouldn't officially call it quits until a year or so later, but it was over. The long and mostly glorious run we'd had, had run its course.

We really couldn't complain. We were all in good health, financially stable and hadn't burned too many music business bridges along the way. But it was still incredibly hard to take. We'd had so many years of carefree touring and album-making that we thought it would never end. New bands, I told myself over and over again, were lucky to get label and fan support for more than an album or two. We'd been very fortunate. Ten years wasn't something to take lightly.

Still, the end is something that no one wants to accept or come to terms with, no matter how much we try to justify it. It would be a long time before I finally did.

29 A Short Intermission

Of course the end is never really the end. I continued to write and aimed a little outside of what the Spoons had done. Part of me, I have to admit, kind of liked what was coming out of the grungy west coast. I was, after all, a guitar player through and through and more guitar was never a bad thing. I decided that I'd had enough of drum machines and synthesizers. When I made demo recordings of my new songs, I went out of my way to make them as raw and simple as possible. I found new influences in the songwriting and recording approach of artists like Matthew Sweet, The Red Hot Chili Peppers and Lenny Kravitz. I hid away my chorus and delay pedals and swore I'd never use them again. There was no reason to believe the '80s were anything but dead and gone.

The first solo band I assembled after the Spoons was Punch House, named after one of the pubs we frequented in Monmouth, Wales. We played originals and obscure British pop songs. I will never forget one show at a bar on the old Ontario Place grounds overlooking the lake. I think people were a bit confused about my new direction. I learned very quickly that you can only take your old fans so far off the beaten track before losing them. Throwing in a Spoons song ever so often was not only a good idea, it was a safety net for me as I balanced on a very unforgiving wire. That was a fact of life, no matter how excited I was about my new songs.

I saw very quickly that starting from the ground up again wasn't going to be easy. All my '80s credentials didn't add up to a hill of beans to booking agents and bar owners. When I mentioned to someone in the industry that I might have some new demos to send to record labels, they suggested I not even mention the Spoons. Had the '80s really become such cause for embarrassment? Is this how the old '70s bands had been treated when the new wave hit in the early '80s, when hotshot new bands like the Spoons came waltzing in? Was this the ultimate poetic justice? It sure felt that way.

Playing at that little bar at Ontario Place, just steps from the Forum where the Spoons had packed them in night after night, was a bitter pill to swallow. I felt very alone and uncertain of my future. I had no reason to believe that what the Spoons and I had accomplished would mean anything to anyone ever again. How could it? The rocket that was time was shooting forward and its tail was trailing off and leaving us, the children of the '80s, behind to quickly fade away.

I decided I had to adapt as best I could or meet certain doom. I was thirty years old, but felt like a teenager. There was no way I was giving up. Not that easily. I embraced new bands like Oasis and Stone Temple Pilots. I came to love them as I'd loved my progressive idols and British synth-pop bands. I was thankful to be a guitar player and not a keyboard player. If I thought I had it rough, those poor souls were hitting rock bottom lower than I ever would.

I found my stride again writing songs and, thank God, found another studio sanctuary like Soundpath had been to the Spoons in the '80s. Nestled away in a North York neighbourhood, Harlow Sound became my new safe haven. Run by a slightly eccentric schoolteacher named Dave Harlow, we hit it off immediately. We had a similar slightly off-keel appreciation for art and music. Eclectic pieces of modern sculpture he'd created were scattered around his property like a Dali landscape. Just going to the studio was like stepping into another world.

I recently came across old reels of tape from those Harlow Sound sessions; songs with titles like *Happy House, Mona Lisa* and a dark, haunting tune called *The Easiest Summer*, full of Verve angst. I was never going to let go of my moody

inclinations, no matter what kind of music I submersed myself
in. The soul of a prog-rocker, as you can guess by now, never
really dies. It became easy to create again, almost effortless, the
way it should be. The future didn't look so bleak anymore.
Above all, it kept the hope in me alive that my days weren't
numbered. Not yet anyway. I still had things to accomplish.

Then, in 1992, my first daughter Madison was born and
the world changed forever. By then, I'd bought my first house
in Etobicoke in Toronto, and now there was a family to fill it.
Just like that. Overnight. It's funny how life's profound turning
points just creep up on you, even with nine months warning.

A first child comes with countless memories attached to
them, but one will stay with me forever. Still an infant, I would
sometimes set up Madison's jolly-jumper beside me in the
music room where I rehearsed at home. I didn't think she was
paying much attention and let her play as I worked on my
music. Then, one day, as I sang one of my songs, her big,
brown eyes suddenly welled up and tears started running down
her cheeks. She just stared at me, without making a sound, her
face full of emotion. Even at her tender age, it had stirred up
something deep inside. Either that, or she'd mistaken my
singing for cries of pain and was worried about her dad. I
quickly hugged her and reassured her that everything was okay.
But it was too late. Her course in life was set.

Madison recently completed her university degree as a
flute major. After years of piano lessons, she discovered the
flute in the high school band and never looked back. I, of
course, understood completely when the band became her life.
It's a game-changer. For three summers now she's performed
with the prestigious Ceremonial Guard on Parliament Hill in
our nation's capital, dressed in the famous red uniform and tall
bearskin hat; a position that required her to submit to two
months rigorous basic training at a military base. I'm always
amazed by the unexpected turns music can take you down.

SPOONFED

One summer Madison was given the honour of keeping the keys to the iconic bell tower at the Parliament Buildings and coordinated the chimes during special performances on the hill. You can't imagine how proud I was of her, seeing how far she'd come. Whether it began with her jolly-jumper introduction to music or the sanctuary of her high school band, I can't wait to see where life takes her next.

Looking back now, it seems like my little break from the Spoons was perfectly timed so I could direct my attentions to other, more important things, like raising a family. I wanted to see Madison grow up and being home, not on the road, made that possible. But that didn't stop me from performing locally.

When my band Punch House disbanded, I quickly recruited Colin Cripp's brother Curtis on bass and fellow Hamiltonian Jim Scotland on drums and played shows around Toronto. I showcased my new songs in small Queen Street bars like Ultrasound and the Rivoli. At least I didn't feel like I was standing still. There were times I actually started thinking the indie band life wasn't going to be so bad. That is, until the lack of payment for performance factor set in. That only goes so far.

For a while, like a lot of musicians who procured their actor's union memberships doing videos and TV commercials in the '80s, I dabbled in screen work to help pay the bills; a few bit parts, some stand-in work on major films. I found the movie industry to be comfortably similar to the music business. The same cast of characters, just with different titles.

One day I bumped into Tom Lewis, an old acquaintance and fellow survivor of the '80s. He'd been on bass duties with the band Eye Eye the last time I saw him, when they opened for us at the Ontario Place Forum. I remember passing each other in the tunnel that led from the change rooms to the stage, as they were coming off and we were going on. I'd always liked his playing and, when we jammed, found it very easy to work together. He soon joined me in the studio for recording sessions and came to appreciate the fine wine and Asian cuisine of the Harlow household as much as I did.

But when it came to winning over new fans, I was about to get a hard lesson. I won't soon forget a show in the early '90s opening for Gowan at the Diamond Club in Toronto, the same fateful venue where I once bumped into Devine. All the press was going to be there, as well as the old Anthem/SRO crowd. If there ever was a chance to get noticed again, this was it.

I was eager to show off my bold, new direction and we started the set with *Happy House*. And right then and there I learned an important fact of life. I would forever be linked to my musical past, no matter what I did. Anyone who liked the Spoons would feel let down if my new songs were too unlike my '80s roots and anyone into the alternative, grunge scene would never accept me. It was musical purgatory, stuck between the past and the future. People would clap politely, but they wouldn't really mean it. Not really.

Incredibly, that didn't stop me. Tom and I, along with new drummer Terry Martel, formed Beyond 7, named after a Japanese brand of condoms. We liked the slightly psychedelic ring to it. The real meaning behind the name became our little twisted secret. Somehow we convinced John Punter to come on board and mix some songs we'd written. He'd relocated to Burlington by that time. Imagine that, our brilliant producer and friend from England deciding to settle down in the hometown of the band he'd come to produce there in the '80s. I love life's little plot twists.

Over a few weeks John helped us complete *Revelations Per Minute*, a play on words from the abbreviation RPM. He'd kept the tone section from the same old Neve mixing board at Air Studios in London we'd finished *Arias* on, the same one I'd snagged a few fader knobs from, and brought it along. It was

207

the secret weapon to his sound and he guarded it with his life. It seemed we were both still toting around tokens from our past.

One song off the album called *Miss America* actually got airplay across the country. Maybe people were starting to relax a bit about my '80s infamy. I will never forget when one afternoon I received a phone call from the president of a major US label, telling me how much he liked the song *Better Believe* off my CD. He was interested and asked if I had more songs like it to send him. For a little while, I was over the moon. It was like getting an early release from a long prison sentence. Perhaps this purgatory thing wasn't forever after all.

In 1994, during this time of reinvention and small hopes, my second daughter Nicole came into the world. Thank God for real, tangible wonders, in the middle of a sea of doubts. My sister-in-law Ellen, a midwife, just happened to be there when Nicole's head started to crown in the hospital room, with no doctor in sight. To the astonishment of the attending nurses, she calmly took over and delivered her right there.

Nicole would go on to be the only non-musical child in the family, excelling at gymnastics and anything athletic, including a stint in cheerleading. Not everyone, I was relieved to see, would choose to go down dad's path in life. One cheerleading competition found me sitting in the seats at Canada's Wonderland, watching her compete on the same stage the Spoons performed on several times in the '80s, when it was still known as Kingswood Theater. Those poignant moments, believe me, don't go unnoticed. Nicole is now in her third year at university and plans to become a schoolteacher. She has the perfect personality for it: strong, sweet and a natural leader.

Like her sister, she's never been overly impressed by her dad's musical past. She's also painfully honest. I remember a fan coming up to me at a fairground and wanting my autograph one summer. Nicole was maybe ten years old then. She just stared, a confused look on her face, and then asked me afterwards, "Are you famous or something?"

In a way, I'm glad that my children were never spoiled by my successes. They stayed normal, good kids whose dad's job just happened to be a little different than other dads' jobs. It didn't seem strange or special to them in the least. Having guitars and amplifiers around the house was just a regular part of life. To be honest, their casual attitude about my career was probably a good thing for everyone concerned, humility wise that is. Their stunned reaction to my hair and clothes on seeing the old Spoons videos for the first time, was quite the wake-up call. Nothing like family to bring you down to earth again.

Not expecting very much to happen with the Spoons ever again, I continued to write and perform with one band after another, sometimes several at a time. For a while I became a member of the already established 3MDM, Three Men And A Drum Machine. Drum machines were obviously fine by me and the two other members, Danny Scott and Carl Cooper, shared my love for the new British music. We performed some pretty large shows, most notably at the Danforth Music Hall in Toronto with a full Scottish pipe band joining us for the finale. Three songs that I'd written for myself ended up on an album 3MDM released independently, the first time I let someone else sing my songs. Carl was the front man and I didn't mind in the least taking a back seat for a while. It was nice to have the pressure off. It gave me time to regroup.

Then, one day in 1994, out of the blue, the call came in from Ready Records. Angus at our old label thought it might be worth putting a Spoons "best of" compilation CD together. At first it didn't seem like a particularly brilliant idea, since the '80s were still quite fresh in everyone's minds. Wasn't it too early to be making such a nostalgic move? Would anybody even care? When Universal Music came on board as distributor we started taking the whole thing a little more seriously. I set to work selecting the songs for the compilation and writing liner notes for the CD package. And when I began putting my memories to paper, I realized for the first time that there was a real story worth telling. I honestly hadn't thought about it in that way until that very moment. We'd had a pretty amazing adventure together over the years. One that other people might want to read about it. The great response I received from those liner notes when the album came out was totally unexpected and probably the spark that set the whole idea of writing a book one day in motion.

To keep things simple, the CD would only embrace the early Spoons years, the years with all the original members intact. It would have become too complicated business-wise if Ready involved Anthem Records. I wasn't so sure if Ray and Pegi had yet forgotten the hefty *Vertigo Tango* price tag, so I secretly felt relieved not having to go down that road. We stayed with songs from *Stick Figure Neighbourhood, Arias & Symphonies, TalkBack* and the *Tell No Lies* EP; plenty of good material to choose from. In most people's minds, I believe, the songs from the best years.

John Punter was brought in to remaster. Whenever John was involved, I felt more at peace with the world. Andrew MacNaughtan toyed with some album cover ideas. One involved a stack of cutlery. Mercifully that idea was short-lived. We'd been running with the idea of *Collectible Spoons* as the album title and this seemed as good an idea as any. It was, of course, way too literal an image for a collection of our songs. Angus at Ready eventually suggested reviving the old CN Tower shots from the *Nova Heart* extended-play record and we all, I think, let out a sigh of relief.

Little did I know then, but my little intermission from the Spoons was about to come to an end.

30 Collectible Cutlery

With the release of *Collectible Spoons*, we decided to give one more Canadian tour a shot. We'd laid low long enough. Hopefully the public was starting to soften their anti-'80s stance. And what did we have to lose? We'd see the country once more, which I always loved to do, sell some CDs and then go home again. The old fans would be glad to see us one more time, we'd be happy to relive the past and that would be it. As far as I was concerned, it would probably be our last tour. However short, we'd enjoy the time we had.

We'd been rehearsing regularly at our friend Scott Carmichael's warehouse residence in Oakville. It was so vast, he eventually erected a huge stage in the main room and proceeded to put on parties unlike any other, often featuring local groups like Teenage Head, Harem Scarem and, of course, our little band. We even worked out a few new song ideas there that would never see the light of day. I vaguely remember titles like *Monday Morning* and *The Ghosts Of September*. When it came time to hit the road, he agreed to join us on our little adventure as tour manager.

And then, sadly, Scott Macdonald announced he was leaving the Spoons to pursue a proper career as a schoolteacher, in the Philippines of all places. Not only was he leaving the band, he was leaving the continent. This was serious. He'd married a young lady, also a teacher, with family ties there and saw it as a great opportunity, which of course it was. I couldn't really blame him, but still, it was very hard letting him go.

Scott was one of the most talented and even-tempered people I've ever worked with. I never saw him lose his temper once, a rare thing in this business and probably the reason he makes a good teacher. He said the over-seas job would last three years. Thirteen years later, he's still there. I asked him on one of his annual visits back to Canada what he missed most about his homeland. Hockey and chocolate milk, he replied without hesitation. Oh yes, and playing on stage with his old friends.

We quickly brought in Sue Bennett to take on keyboard duties. She'd performed with a Genesis cover band called Over The Garden Wall. Enough said. I was sold. I also thought it would be interesting to have two females and two males on stage; a completely different dynamic for a band going out into the great unknown one last time. Because, to be honest, we had no idea what we were heading into.

No one could have predicted what was looming just around the corner. We'd been oblivious to what was bubbling just below the surface, about to burst through the cracks like lava from an old volcano that we'd all thought was long dead. We would go out with one mindset and return with a completely different view of the world. That little meaningless tour would end up being one of the best we'd ever had.

Maybe, because we expected nothing, we were overwhelmed by what happened next. We weren't prepared for the appreciation and passion of audiences who'd suppressed their love of '80s music for too long. The old fans weren't so embarrassed about the music they grew up with anymore and new fans were willing to admit it was worth a second listen. A young band from Toronto called Anyhowtown toured with us as openers and proclaimed right from the start how much they'd liked us growing up. Everywhere we went, we were accepted with open arms, by fans and other bands alike. How did that happen? It was much too good to be true.

But it was still very early on – the retro '80s phenomenon wouldn't show its full bloom for some time yet. There was no reason to believe that our happy little comeback was anything more than a temporary freak of musical nature. My future with the Spoons was still a huge grey area. Thinking we'd probably just done our last tour, I realized that for the first time in my life I'd better consider other avenues of income. I'd still play the odd Spoons show now and then and perform weekend gigs with my other bands, but I needed to start thinking seriously about the dreaded "real job."

I'd always had an affinity for drafting class in high school. I even had ideas about becoming an architect for a short while, when I wasn't daydreaming in my bedroom about becoming a big-time superstar musician. I left my drafting table and architectural designs behind, but the thought obviously stuck and appeared years later in the opening line of a certain song.

I was quite good at drawing and design, a talent I inherited from my father. Perhaps something in the genes that had lingered since his extended stay in a Russian prison camp, where art literally kept him alive. Some innate survival instinct he passed on. When I first met Patrick Boshell at a small pub in Streetsville, Ontario, it was through our shared love of music. But it would be my long forgotten drawing skills that would lead to me down an unexpected and very different path in life.

Patrick played bass, we hit it off right away and, as often happens when the musically minded become friends, we formed a band. Between gigs, Patrick introduced me to the world of fiber optics and the future of telecommunications. I found it quite interesting, as far as non-musical endeavors went. When the company he was working for needed a computer draftsman, he was surprised to hear of my hidden drawing talents The fact that the last time I'd used them was in high school, before the advent of computers and design software, didn't concern him at all. We were friends and played in a band together. Everything else was minor details. I had the job if I wanted it.

I quickly learned the basics of several computer design programs and soon found myself working for a major fiber optics company in downtown Toronto, with my own private office overlooking the atrium and a college education worthy salary. When the president of the company came by my office periodically to see my designs and put his hand on my shoulder to say "Nice work," any guilt about skipping the career queue was quickly dispelled. It didn't matter how the work was getting done. It was getting done and done well, pretty much on instinct and a bit of imagination.

So, while Patrick and I played in our little band by night and helped build the telecom cities of the future by day, the retro '80s movement was slowly but surely growing stronger. I couldn't in a million years have imagined what was waiting just around the corner for the Spoons. No one could have. One of those great, completely unexpected surprises had been unfolding, the kind I've learned to never rule out again.

Then, in 1998, if the future wasn't looking bright enough already, my son Matthew was born. This time, at the insistence of my midwife sister-in-law, we had a home birth. Good thing too, because the ice storm of the century had made the world outside a slippery obstacle course. While Madison and Nicole waited nervously in their room, Matthew came peacefully into the world. Now there were five of us. Perhaps the possibility of a Partridge Family band wasn't that crazy an idea after all.

Matthew would go on to be one of the most naturally gifted musicians I've ever heard. As young as seven, he plunked away at the piano and soon imitated anything he heard, from movie themes and radio hits to Spoons songs. He did it effortlessly, sometimes with one eye on his Game Boy. Any attempts at music lessons hit a wall. But that was all right by me. I was almost afraid to mess with his natural abilities. Soon he started to compose his own songs, some verging on Philip Glass abstraction, others full of incredible emotion, but always contradicting his young age and lack of training. I wonder if Rob Preuss had been like him as a child. I now know what the expression "child prodigy" means. Lately, Matthew's world revolves more around BMX biking. But after a day of grinding and 360 tail-whips, he still sits down at the piano and fills the house with indescribable music. I tape him secretly sometimes, building up a library of song ideas, in case I might need them some day. As I watch him grow up, I cherish the years we had together sharing our love for Disney theme parks, James Bond and Emma Peel. It's bitter sweet seeing him turn into a young man and go out into the world on his own. Some days now, I've come to realize, I feel more like a boy than him.

All of a sudden, while I'd been busy raising a family and drafting away at my computer, the '90s were winding down. The era of uncertainty was mercifully coming to an end. And, miraculously, the Spoons and I had weathered the storm. More and more people, it seemed, were rediscovering music that wasn't even a decade old. The old wave was somehow new again. What had started slowly at first had steadily built into something real and unstoppable. The '80s were back.

I'm sure there were many that rolled their eyes when it began, but the general masses were accepting. Radio stations started having regular all-'80s music segments. One band after another from that era came out of the woodwork to tour again. Even '80s inspired hairstyles and clothing reared their ugly heads on runways and in mainstream fashion again. I, like many others, had suspected it would be a short-lived phenomenon. I'd give it a couple of years, say thank you very much and then watch it slip into the shadows once more. I couldn't have been more wrong.

Since our little tour for *Collectible Spoons* in 1995, it has grown into a real living, breathing thing. I now believe, seeing retro '80s' longevity, it has become another legitimate genre of music, like R&B or progressive rock. It may have begun its life as nostalgia, but it remains to this day a viable entity unto itself. When new bands like Interpol and the Killers came out with blatant '80s inclinations, the stage was set. The old drum machines and synthesizers were dusted off and pressed back into service. We were excited and, to be honest, more than a little relieved. The party was back on and this time we were one of the expected guests.

We would happily go along for the ride, wherever it might take us. More and more requests for festival appearances came in as our songs got regular airplay on the radio again, Our beloved CFNY placed *Nova Heart* at number 46 on their century countdown.

The Chart Magazine named *Arias & Symphonies* as one of the most influential albums of the 80s. You have no idea of much that meant to us. The unthinkable was happening and we were totally and utterly blindsided by it. The Spoons would have a second life.

Two Spoons and a Monkee, backstage at the Capitol Theatre.

31 Unexpected Guests

Then, in the summer of 2004, my father passed away. It was a slow, drawn-out decline that ended with brain cancer and finally took one of the toughest people I've ever known. He'd crawled under barbed wire fences from East to West Germany as a kid and survived three years in a Russian prison camp. He'd travelled the world several times and escaped more than one ambush in the off-the-beaten-track locales that he preferred to the usual tourist traps, not to mention the local cuisine that would have downed the less hearty. He was an adventurer like no other and instilled in me a hunger for the exotic and alternate to what the mainstream had to offer. His eccentric philosophy on life, his on-the-edge-of-the-wilderness cottage where we rehearsed, his eclectic library that set my mind reeling; they were all parts of shaping who I am.

It was almost a relief when my father took his last breath, the illness having stolen everything from him that he once was. One of the last things he told us before he lost the ability to communicate completely was that an old, childhood friend from Germany, one who'd died when they were young boys, had come to visit him in the hospital the night before. He was so happy to see him again after all these years and it seemed to lighten his heart. My father didn't say so, but I'm sure he believed his friend was coming to take him into the great unknown. Maybe his eccentric views on life, things that he tried to instill in me, weren't so eccentric after all. He always said not to fear death, but to see it as another chapter in our existence. Maybe, to him, it wasn't a great unknown that he was going into at all.

They say that the sense of hearing is the last thing to go. After breathing his last breath and his heart stopped beating, I held my dad close and whispered into his ear one of the most wonderful childhood memories I have. Of a hot summer afternoon when I was about ten years old, with him and my brother Gary, hunting for frogs and crayfish in a reedy marsh in our favourite park. One of those lazy, simple days that stays with you a lifetime. I told him that we would all meet there again one day; that we'd share that wonderful and perfect time again. I'm sure my father would have been glad to see that some of his beliefs had rubbed off on me. There are times now when I miss him more than I ever thought I would. I know instinctually what he'd say at moments of doubt or indecision. He would have understood the workings of the spiral of time more than most. Sometimes, when I least expect it, he seems very close by.

It's not the planned-on things that I've learned to count on in life. As my father also believed, it's the hidden, unexpected ones that make the world go around. One day, digging through my basement, I came across a dusty, old box of studio tapes from the murky past. Somewhere behind the ski boots and half-full paint cans. Like finding long lost treasure, my eyes bulged when I saw the forgotten song titles. Here, before me, were dozens of demos of unreleased recordings from between the *TalkBack* and *Bridges* years.

There was *Love Drum* and *Ciao* and the original *In The Hands Of Money* that *Bridges Over Borders* had borrowed from. I couldn't wait to play them and, when I did, was amazed at how well they'd stood the test of time. Working at Soundpath had paid off once again. It suddenly occurred to me that we just might have enough material for an album. An album of lost songs.

I decided early on that *Unexpected Guest At A Cancelled Party* would be perfect title for this compilation. The actual

218

song had been used as a B-side for a single off the *TalkBack* album, so we couldn't rightfully include it here, but the name fit perfectly. Finding and releasing these songs was completely unexpected, and the '80s, in a way, was a party we'd thought was over a long time ago. Apparently, it hadn't run its course quite yet and these late arrivals were worth letting in the door.

The songs showed us in some of our most playful early years, between 1982 and '83. We'd performed *Show & Tell* in a dance club scene in the film Head Office, starring Eddie Albert of Green Acres and Judge Reinhold. Derrick was off on his honeymoon at the time and we had one of his triplet brothers sit in for him on drums. I knew they'd come in handy one day. Not being a drummer, he just bashed away along with the backing track, nowhere in time to the music. If the scene, filmed at the old Copa Club in Toronto, hadn't been cut from the movie, you would have seen him hitting the snare on one and three, instead of the two and four. But nobody noticed. The takes with General Public performing were used instead. But it remains a perfect example of what we were up to musically at the time.

The songs *Unpremeditated Love* and *In The Hands Of Money* would later be stripped bare and reassembled to become *Bridges Over Borders*. Here you can hear their humble origins. A favourite moment for me is the dark reggae instrumental breakdown in *Spaces*. It borrows a little from *Girl In Two Pieces*, a direction we didn't delve into very often. The epic *2,000 Years* is in many ways *Nova Heart* part two, lyrically and conceptually, and probably the most *Arias*-like song on the CD. It's the one track off the album that we would perform live; a snapshot of the Spoons from another, almost forgotten time.

Unexpected Guest was released and we played bigger shows than we had in a long time. My passion for music was reignited and I kept myself busy with as many projects as humanly possible. I formed a side band called the LostBoys with Chris Chimonides on drums and Paul Brown on bass. We recorded an album's worth of songs under the pseudonym Thread, but never released it. *Alien Skin* and *Story Of My Life* are probably some of the best pop-rock songs I've ever written. As the LostBoys, we still perform those songs today and people wonder why we haven't exploited them more. Never say never.

And I didn't stop there. I recorded and put out an album under the name Five Star Fall. Hopefully this title wouldn't be a harbinger of things to come, like my previous Spoons albums had been. Long time collaborator Tom Lewis played bass and fellow Burlingtonian Mike Shottan drummed and recorded the album *Automatic Ordinary* in his basement studio. It would be a huge step back to the Spoons sound and the music I was best at making. Although I didn't see it yet, things were moving in the right direction. Five Star Fall sounded a lot like the new wave of bands influenced by the sounds of the 80s. In this case, ironically, directly influenced by my own musical past. One song off the album called *Mercurial Girl* was even added to the Spoons live set list. It fit in that seamlessly. Obviously, what I was doing independently was starting to line up more with the Spoons again.

Five Star Fall never played one live show. As a performing band, we never really existed. But, looking back now, I can see how significant it was in bridging the gap back to the Spoons. It was full of the grandiose sound and production I'd tried so hard to escape from in my early independent days. As all things tend to do in life, my writing and taste in music had come back around full circle. And it was a fortunate thing that it did. Other people's tastes in music, it seemed, had also come around full circle again.

Incredibly, it would be another four years until the Spoons released an album of new songs. We'd have to go through more upheaval and personnel changes before that happened. The ever-winding road of a band never lets up. For a short while Mike Shotton of Five Star Fall filled in for Steve on the drums.

FED

Somewhere along the line Sue left and was replaced by Janine White of the goth band Johnny Hollow. Keyboard players, it seemed, were coming and going like Spinal Tap drummers.

Years later, Johnny Hollow would record their own haunting version of Nova Heart. With its industrial beat and dark, echoed cello melodies weaving throughout, it was perfect as the background music in that year's season finale of the vampire TV series Lost Girl.

But, for some strange reason that defies logic, I still didn't feel it was time for a new Spoons album. When we performed, it seemed what people really wanted to hear was the old songs they grew up on. When we had the chance to play our hits with a symphony orchestra, we were surprised ourselves by the power of the music that everyone had come to know us for. We learned not to take for granted what a lot of young, new bands were working hard to build up. We had a pretty good collection of songs that meant something in people's lives. It was a safe place to be. But safe isn't always fun.

When Duran Duran made a come-back with their song *Sunrise*, a little tickled started to grow in the back of my mind, wondering if we couldn't do the same thing. More and more new bands were bringing the '80s sound back and making the original '80s acts valid again in the process. There was a time when I joked that we'd probably do better if we came out as a Spoons clone band, seeing the popularity of tribute acts. Now doing it on our terms seemed a real possibility again. We even stumbled on a Spoons fan site that was so well done, we simply asked the administrator, Darrin Cappe, to keep it running for us. But contemplating a full-length album was a whole other matter. I'd need a little more convincing for that to happen.

I met Steve Sweeney through my friend Tom Lewis and, when Janine moved on to plunge head first into Johnny Hollow, he slipped easily into place. Raised on progressive rock as Sandy and I were, we had plenty of common ground to start from. And he, after all, had been residing at Putney Bridge in London as we completed our *Arias & Symphonies* album at Air Studios way back in the infant '80s. Fate meant for us to meet one day and we finally did.

With yet another new keyboard player in place, we continued to perform regularly as our songs got increasingly more airplay on the radio. This retro thing wasn't letting up any time soon. We played huge outdoor festivals and theatres and started integrated video footage into our live shows again. We made good use of Steve Sweeney's filmmaking background to achieve the show I'd always hoped for. We'd come a long way since our old shoestring laser beams and exploding glow sticks.

When we made it into Bob Mercier's 2010 book the Top 100 Canadian Singles, I think that tickle in the back of my mind grew into a full-blown ache. Being listed alongside the likes of the Guess Who and Rush gave me that final jolt to the brain that I needed. The self-doubter was finally slipping into the shadows and self-confident Gord was emerging once more. State of mind can bring about incredible changes. Not just in music, but in all things in life. The simple act of lifting a mental cloud can release all the happy endorphins required to achieve what before felt unachievable. But, of course, it's not as easy as it sounds. Lifting clouds takes time and care. Sometimes it can take years. Clouds are heavier than they look.

I remember clearly the day I brought the basic idea for *Imperfekt* to a Spoons rehearsal. Our new home was Melodyman Studios in Burlington, where we could practice in privacy in the luxury of a recording studio. Regular rehearsal factories had never worked out for us. Imagine us running through *Waterline* as a thrash metal band pounded away next door and a reggae group tried to fight against it on the other side. That just wouldn't do.

The vaguely punk origins of *Imperfekt* had been kicking around in my head for at least fifteen years; my anti-perfection, pro real-thing anthem. I'd never intended it for the Spoons, but when I showed everyone the idea, they instinctually jumped in and it sounded more natural than I'd ever imagined it would. I think the song had a message we all could relate to. It was the first time in a long time that I felt that communal excitement in the room that can ignite great things. That one little song idea opened up another huge door, one that had been waiting, closed for way too long. We had the beginnings of a new album.

Sandy and her husband Jeff Carter had a little studio in their garage in Guelph and they suggested we demo the song there. Some very unexpected things happened. Sandy and I began recording *Imperfekt*, and writing a second track called *Breaking In* during lunch breaks, using drum machines and playing all the instruments ourselves. Anything I couldn't handle on keyboards, Jeff would step in and take care of. Before we knew it, the songs were done and we hadn't even brought in the rest of the band to record. Suddenly we had two really good songs that sounded more like the old Spoons than anything we'd done in years. We'd unexpectedly hit a sweet spot, where adding anything else would ruin what we had.

We decided to release the songs as is and the rest of the guys were very good about it. I did feel a bit guilty, leaving them out of the recording process, but even they had to agree, the raw, honest sound of the new songs was undeniable. When Jeff Carter showed us his cover art concept with the mannequin head on it, I knew the stars in the musical universe were aligning once again. I always wondered when our trusty, old friend would reappear. Well, there she was, in all her glory, looking better than ever and ready to grace the cover of our first new release in over two decades. We were finally, after so many years, on the right track again. When I thought we'd surely used up all the track there was to use. More and more ideas started filling my head, like a valve had been opened, and

223

the dormant song-writing machine was set back into motion. Before long, the floodgates wouldn't just open up, they would come crashing down. I was in full-fledged writing mode again and it couldn't have come at a better time. The album that I never thought would be made, was writing itself.

Back on track again: Imperfekt and real.

32 Words Smash Walls

The fact that thirty years had gone by for us as a band was a strange and incredible thing to wrap my head around. There was no way that that many years had come and gone. Impossible. Time can be cruel, but it can also be mercifully deceiving when it wants to be. Suddenly it was 2010 and high time for a proper celebration.

When Rob Preuss caught wind of our thirtieth anniversary concert, he jumped right on board. But it wouldn't be so easy with Derrick. We'd have to wait a few more years to talk him into a full-fledged reunion. I recall going to his house in the late '80s and seeing his last set of drumsticks from his last concert with us in 1985 mounted on a plaque on the wall. I didn't realize he'd hung them up for good and never intended to play again. That made me a little sad. It would take a lot more convincing to get him behind the drums again.

The thirtieth anniversary party, held at the Tattoo Rock Parlour in Toronto, was a magical night. Fans signed a giant happy anniversary card as they filled in and the festivities got under way as our old friend David Marsden officially opened the night with some touching words about his kids from Burlington. From judging us as Impulse at a battle of the bands in a dusty field, to introducing our first song on the radio, to seeing us off on our first big US tour at LaSalle Park, he'd been there all along. It only made sense that he kicked off the night.

Rob joined us for half the show as we played the old songs. We also premiered *Imperfekt* that evening, and an early version of *Numb*, a song that would also end up on the album yet to be made. I could feel the reaction to the new material spread through the room like it had at that first Spoons rehearsal. Exactly what I needed. I wonder sometimes if the audience hadn't been behind us as much as it was that night, if *Static In Transmission* would ever have been made. It was a definitive turning point for me. More than even the band knew.

We would go on to record our new album at Sandy and Jeff's studio in Guelph over a leisurely three months in the warm middle of 2010. Originally I had ideas of working at a downtown Toronto studio and bringing in a big name producer. When I saw how easy it was to work with Jeff, driving to Guelph every day seemed a much more pleasant alternative to fighting traffic and dealing with big city distractions. In a way, this would be a like going to Monmouth, Wales instead of New York City. Very low pressure. Very good for the soul and getting things done.

Fortunately the creative flow was non-stop by then and the *Static In Transmission* album pretty well made itself. In fact, the songs were recorded in the order that they'd on the final album. This was something we'd never experienced before. It just happened all by itself. There was one slot, just near the end, where I felt something was missing, and that was filled by *End Of Story*, the last song I wrote. I was hoping for something with a bit of *Nova Heart* magic to it and somehow it came together. We even ended up hiding the *Nova Heart* keyboard melody in the track. That late arrival is now my favorite song on the album.

Lyrics always come last for me, a task I often dread. Now they just fell onto the page, all by themselves, like automatic writing. The rare times that happens, I put everything else in life on hold until it runs its course. Those moments of free, unbridled expression are worth their weight in gold. And because of it, a common thread started to emerge throughout the *Static* album, even though I didn't intend it to. Whether on a personal level in *Breaking In* or on a more global scale, as in the song *Words Will Smash Walls*, the album explores communication between people. Sometimes difficult, usually distorted, often hard to read, always complicated. A subject I knew all too well. The lyrics from the song *End Of Story* pretty well say it all:

"You slipped into my life and stuck around a while
And then you reconnected all the broken wires.
You send and I receive and all the messages are clear
You know that's all I ever really wanted."

I meant the people close to me in my life. But I also meant the listener, the audience that'd been there all those years and followed me through all the ups and downs and twists and turns. As simple and cliché as it sounds, all I really wanted was to be understood. And, obviously, like everyone else, to be appreciated and liked for what I've tried to do. I just happen to be a guy who writes songs and expresses himself in words and melody. I bet most people have similar ideas ringing around inside their heads; something hidden they wished everyone could see and appreciate.

There was a depth in *Static In transmission* I hadn't felt since the *Arias* album. Finally, after things drifting apart for so many years, I felt they'd finally come back together again. If this would be our last album, I'd be happy to have it as our swan song, a perfect bookend to our career. It's funny how and when the creative muses decide to visit again. I welcomed them back, my forgotten little friends, and hoped they'd stick around a while. Because no one knows for sure how long things will hold together. I'd enjoy every minute of it like it was my last.

Sandy and I realized it was time to bring in some new band members. Though they were incredibly good about it, not involving Steve Kendry and Steven Sweeney in the recordings had created a gap between us. I don't think that Steve was too pleased about our renewed interest in the drum machine either.

SPOONFED

I brought in Chris McNeill to audition one day and he and Sandy hit it off right away. He'd played with me in a few side-project bands and had no objections to playing along with machines. We had our new drummer. When we told Steve, he took it like a gentleman, wished us well and went on to pursue his love for jazz. I was relieved. Breakups can be ugly.

When it came to keyboard players, things became a bit trickier. We found that there were plenty of good pianists and organ players around, but few and far between when it came to those who understood the ways of vintage analog synthesizers. At one point we contemplated having Rob Preuss back on board and met with him to discuss it. By this time he was well established in the New York theatre scene, as keyboardist and assistant conductor for *Mama Mia*. We reminisced about the good old days, but I knew deep inside that juggling the Spoons with his theatre commitments would be a problem. If only we could find someone with his youthful attack on the keyboard and appreciation of all things wonderfully analog.

After a few discouraging auditions in Sandy's Guelph studio, I made one last attempt and called local music stores to see if any keyboard teachers fit the bill. Almost as quickly as Rob's original reply to our want ad in the Burlington paper three decades earlier, a nineteen-year-old named Casey MQ phoned me. Being patient would pay off. We talked, we met, we played and he was in. He had exactly the sounds and style the Spoons needed. We had found our new Rob. That he had an uncanny resemblance to our very first synth player Bret Wickens made the whole thing even more profound. The pieces were falling into place.

And so, with the new line-up, we performed in front of a hometown crowd of almost 20,000 on Canada Day 2011 at Spencer Smith Park in Burlington. The park where my father sat at a bench having lunch almost forty-five years earlier, on an unexpected stop between Toronto and Niagara Falls. The day he had the idea that it might be a good place to raise a young family. I hope he was watching on proudly as we broke into *Nova Heart* and the crowd erupted. His brilliant idea that afternoon long ago had undoubtedly played a part in getting me on that stage. I will be forever thankful.

We released *Static In Transmission* and it seemed our fans were as happy about it as we were. After so many years, my world and the listener's had finally synced up. Steven Sweeney produced a video for the song *You Light Up*, featuring Toronto much like the *Romantic Traffic* video did. We hadn't toured the country in a long time, not since 1995 for *Collectible Spoons*, before retro '80s was even an idea. There were many places I missed visiting. High on the list was Halifax, the land of Russian circuses and submarines in the fog. But I would never have guessed why we'd be returning so many years later.

Geri Hall, the wife of a friend in Oakville, had recommended us for a special episode of a TV show she acted in. That show, This Hour Has 22 Minutes, was planning a special '80s episode that coincided with Halloween. I wouldn't take that personally. Alongside appearances by fellow Canadians Alan Thicke, David Suzuki and Ben Mulroney, we would be the special musical guests at the end of the program. When I learned that the CBC show was taped in Halifax, there was no way I could say no.

There was obviously going to be a lot of '80s bashing on the episode, given the satirical nature of the show, but the director ensured us that we wouldn't be the brunt of any jokes. We would simply close the show with our song *Nova Heart*, nothing more. I almost believed him, until we were sent to the hair and makeup department to find an assortment of frightening mullet wigs waiting for us. I had to be polite, but firm. There would be no wig wearing by this band. The makeup ladies looked genuinely dejected by this lost opportunity. Back to the wig vault went the mullets.

The show really was one of the funniest they'd ever done. The 80s, after all, were prime for the picking. Wig-free, we performed in front of a studio audience, many of them dressed in costume. But the best would be saved for last, after the show was over. That evening, in what will be one of my favourite new road memories, we wandered the streets of Halifax with some of the cast and crew of 22 Minutes, on Halloween night, many of them still in full '80s attire. Shaun Majumder hadn't escaped the clutches of the wig ladies and, in mullet and bad suit, became our impromptu tour-guide of the old city. A better return to one of my favourite places in the country couldn't have been planned if we tried.

The timing of our appearance on the show couldn't have been better either. The week before, one of the reoccurring characters, the Princess Warrior played by Mary Walsh, had confronted Toronto's major Rob Ford in his driveway. Things became a little heated and accusations flew. The media had a field day with it. Our little '80s episode the week later would be one of their most viewed shows ever.

Looking back now, I wonder if the universe was giving me this happy, little diversion before the world would turn dark for a while. A few months later my musical life slipped into the background as my mother battled heart problems and eventually open-heart surgery. Five replaced arteries and two valves later, I saw the woman who brought me into the world as a baby reduced to a small, helpless child herself. I visited her in her Hamilton hospital almost every day for six weeks as complications prolonged her stay. It was incredibly hard to watch. It was my turn to care for her. I had gone from being an adult, to feeling like a boy again with my son, to now being the parent watching over my mother, in a matter of years.

I realized all of a sudden exactly where I was in life. In our younger years we build up everything that we are, to the point where we seem to find our place in the world. Then we coast for a while, enjoying who we've become and what we've achieved. We think that part will never end. But, of course, it does. Then life starts to ramp down, to disassemble all we've built. It seems as if more is taken away than is given to us. As difficult as it was to accept, I knew that was where I was now.

Miraculously, my mother made a full recovery. Despite a few lingering effects of heart surgery, she enjoys life and still cares more about her sons than herself. Since the day I bought my black Les Paul as a kid and she helped me keep it a secret from my father, my mother has supported me like no one else. Even as a shy teenager, writing love songs behind closed doors, she encouraged me and made me feel comfortable about my dreams and myself. Of course I needed my father's more practical and left-brain influences to balance things out, but she was and remains my biggest fan. It took me a long time, but I now understand what unconditional love is.

Sometimes it takes life's ordeals to make you realize a few things. Not the least of which is the understanding and appreciation of what we have, what we've achieved and the people who have surrounded and helped and loved us along the way. Our parents, our children, our closest friends; the band mates you've shared a thousand stages with.

It was 2012 and suddenly we were faced with the thirtieth anniversary of *Nova Heart* and the *Arias* album, the music that put us on the map. This time, by hook or by crook, we were going to get Derrick on stage and reunite the complete original line-up. I put off asking him for a long time, afraid to face the fact that he'd probably say no again. But when I finally did, I was surprised to hear that he'd actually consider it. By that time pressure from fans had been building on-line and he probably saw it was inevitable. Thirty years wasn't something you could argue with forever.

A few weeks before the show Derrick confirmed that, yes, he was in, but only for a song or two on the timbales, like he used to do for percussion breaks at our old live shows. I remembered the sad, little plaque on his wall and assumed he hadn't sat behind a drum kit for a very long time and this was all he could handle. We'd set up some percussion so he could be up front with Rob, Sandy and I while Chris McNeill stayed on stage and played the drums. I thought this would put less pressure on Derrick and he could make his guest appearance, say thank you very much and leave. I was wrong again.

We'd scheduled two rehearsals at Melodyman Studios in Burlington, one with Rob and one with Derrick. When Derrick arrived I could tell right away he had something brewing in the back of his mind. He immediately made it clear that he would play several songs on the drum kit, as well as joining us for a few other tunes on percussion, or he'd do nothing at all. And he wanted to play *Nova Heart*. He was pretty adamant about that.

He'd done a complete about-face from not being sure about showing up at all. Chris graciously handed him the drumsticks at rehearsal and, when we started into *Nova Heart*, it was like coming home again. It felt like no time had passed at all. This was going to be one hell of a reunion concert.

We'd decided to book the Revival Club once more. It had served us well before. But no one could have predicted the groundswell of excitement around this particular night, especially when word of a full band reunion got out. Adding our friends Images In Vogue to the bill only fueled the fire. By the time it was too late to relocate to a bigger venue, it was clear that the night would be sold out. Probably more than that.

Initially, I had all sorts of dramatic ideas for the evening. One involved placing an electric cellist in the balcony opposite the stage to play a haunting intro to *Arias & Symphonies* before the lights came on and the full band kicked in. She would also join us for other sections in the *Arias* portion of the show, adding to the orchestral feel of the album. But, when we realized we needed every bit of space available for the audience that night, the idea was quickly discarded.

Usually pre-show time is very relaxed and intimate, kind of the calm before the storm. This night was another story. Extra staging and speakers had to be brought in and sorted out to accommodate all the equipment that two bands required. One small problem; all the extra gear was going to eat up more audience space. Adjustments had to be made. We feared the show, by now, was definitely oversold.

Members of Images In Vogue started trickling in. Some had flown in from the west coast to be there. It had been a long time since we'd played together. Someone reminded us about the infamous bowling match between our two bands, televised on MuchMusic in the '80s. To some, the Spoons and Images In Vogue had always represented a sort of east versus west rivalry. Tonight, we were just two bands caught up in the excitement like everyone else.

For me, of course, the best part was seeing Rob and Derrick on stage again. The way it had been so long ago, when we were just kids, with so much ahead of us. Even the simple act of doing sound check together before the show felt surreal. I knew it would all be over much too quickly, so I absorbed every detail of it, hoping to keep in my private library forever.

Rob brought along his original Roland Jupiter IV synth for the night and set up alongside Casey's keyboards. On the opposite side of the stage we set up the timbales for Derrick's appearance partway into the show. By the time Images got their equipment up, wedged between ours, there wasn't an unused square inch of space on that stage. This was going to be a big show, on a Ringling Brothers three-ring circus scale.

Images In Vogue played a masterful set and kicked off the night in perfect '80s form. They remain one of my favourite Canadian bands of all time and sounded as good as they did when we first played together in Vancouver in 1981.

And then it was our turn. The *Arias* crest, with its regal Lipizzan stallion, towered above the stage, reminding everyone why they were there. Our friend Maie Pauts from Boom FM, the radio station presenting the show, introduced us that night. We'd been using a newly recorded intro for our shows since *Static In Transmission* was released, but that evening we returned to our trusty, old *Trade Winds* to set the mood. The lights went down and time stood still.

The club was packed to the bursting point and a crazy electricity filled the air I hadn't felt in a long time. I heard from a few fans later that they had to leave for fear of being crushed. Fortunately, a snowstorm had kept a good chunk of our west end fans away or things might have been worse. There was a lineup outside waiting to get in, hoping to take the places of anyone too faint of heart to endure the crowd. As we walked onto the stage during the intro, it felt like the rise to the top of a giant rollercoaster drop. When the lights came on and we started into *Arias & Symphonies*, our little car fell into the abyss. For the next hour and a half, we were weightless.

Rob began the night with us and when Derrick finally joined in, after so many years of failed reunions, we were complete once more. It was the first time we'd been on stage together for twenty-six years. An impossibly long time. But it made the sweetness of the moment so much greater. We performed most of the *Arias* album that evening and the looks on the faces in the crowd pretty well reflected how I felt. This was something we'd all been waiting for. Something we'd almost given up on ever happening. Four kids from Burlington were back together again. We may have grown up and gone our separate ways, but that night we were a band again, the way most people remembered us. We were the Spoons. Casey and Chris joined us for the second half. At this point, it really didn't matter what we played. By the end of the night, it was a full-blown jam. We brought everyone back on stage for the closer *Walk The Plank*; Rob, Derrick, even Jian Gohmeshi, who was in the crowd that night sharing the moment with everyone else. I'm sure our old friends Andrew MacNaughtan and Reg Quindinho were also there in spirit; big smiles on their faces.

If we ever got the chance to relive one small '80s moment, this would be it, one to hold onto for a very long time. It may as well have been the Spectrum in Montreal or the Ontario Place Forum. Once in a while, if you're lucky, the spiral of time comes back around again, close enough to let you have a little taste of something you thought was lost forever. It might not be the real thing, but even its shadow is more powerful than anything you could imagine. As temporary as it was, that night we all shared a wonderful and fleeting moment.

Reunited: Casey, me, Chris, Jian, Rob, Derrick and Sandy.

235

33 Static Sent, Message Received

When we released *Static In Transmission*, I was pretty well reserved to the fact it would be our last album. The very idea that we'd made it at all still amazed me. But, if it was going to be our last recording, I wanted it to say something about how I felt after all these years, after our little adventure with it's unpredictable ups and downs and twists and turns.

In the way that *Trade Winds* had opened *Arias & Symphonies* and the first significant chapter of our musical lives, I felt the last song on *Static In Transmission* should in some way be the other bookend to our amazing career, a fitting farewell after a most wonderful journey. The lyrics for *Closing Credits* are simple, uncomplicated and clear, just as they should be when saying something so important to me.

"And as the credits roll
And all the crowds go home
The house lights come on
And everything we made's undone

No more make-believe
No more starring scenes
Was it all a dream?
Or someone else's words instead?

'Cause in the end
When all is said
Can we still pretend?
That everything we did
And every single word we said
We meant?

...We did."

2014: In front of 20,000 fans in Burlington, where it all began.

Yes, we did.

Like everyone else on this crazy, little planet rushing through the universe, I hoped that all the Spoons and I set out to do and say in life would come through in the end. I hoped that the static in the transmission would finally clear enough to let me connect with the people around me, on a real human level.

I've spent a lifetime feeling like an outsider, an observer looking in, a kid raised on a Twilight Zone skewed view of the world. Despite all our successes and times in the spotlight, I never felt like I really fit in or that we truly achieved everything we could as a band. But I believe that's probably a good thing for any artist, or anyone for that matter. That way we never stop aiming higher.

And then, I realize, most people probably share my view of the world. How many of us feel like passengers on a train speeding along toward some uncertain destination, catching fleeting images of the world around us as they fly by?

We make stops here and there along the way, but the final destination stays illusive. The future is one of life's wonderfully frightening mysteries.

Maybe what we strive for is just a dream that we cling onto hopelessly and stubbornly. Perhaps it doesn't really exist. Maybe it's not what we really want at all. Given enough time, we can talk ourselves into believing almost anything. Even our own deceptions. Maybe, in the end, it doesn't really matter. Just as long as we have fun on that train trip and enjoy fully the unplanned stops along the way. I certainly have.

I decided a long time ago to appreciate the unexpected little things; in music, in love, in life in general. I count on them to make it all worthwhile. The unforeseen surprises are where the real magic happens – a lot like unexpected guests at a cancelled party.

All I know is, my train hasn't reached its final destination quite yet. I don't think I really know what that destination even is anymore. Maybe it's better that way.

My train is still chugging merrily along through the countryside, perhaps somewhere between Lübeck and London or Burlington and New York City. It doesn't really matter. Just as long as the train keeps moving.

I can't wait to see where the next unexpected stop will be.

About the author

As singer, guitar player and songwriter for the Canadian new wave band the Spoons, Gord Deppe has been in the music business for over thirty years.

Born in Vancouver, B.C., his family moved back and forth between Canada and Germany several times before finally settling in Burlington, Ontario. There, in 1980, fresh out of high school, Gord, Sandy Horne, Rob Preuss and Derrick Ross would go on to make Spoons a different kind of household word.

The young band would also catch the wave of a brand new video-driven phenomenon that was about to hit TV screens nationwide. The video for their hit *Nova Heart* would be aired on the very first broadcast of MuchMusic. *Romantic Traffic*, shot in the subways of Toronto, remains as one of the most iconic Canadian music videos of all time.

Gord and the Spoons have stayed active to this day, continuing to record new music and perform across the country. This is Gord's first published book.

Chris McNeill, me, Casey MQ and Sandy.

The adventure continues…

Manor House
905-648-2193

240